The Surprise Princess

The Wedding Series
Prelude to a Wedding
Wedding Party
Grady's Wedding
The Runaway Bride
The Christmas Princess
Hoops (prequel to The Surprise Princess)
The Surprise Princess
Not a Family Man (prequel to The Forgotten Prince)
The Forgotten Prince

More romance by Patricia McLinn

Marry Me Series
Wedding of the Century
The Unexpected Wedding Guest
A Most Unlikely Wedding
Baby Blues and Wedding Bells

Seasons in a Small Town
What Are Friends For? (Spring)
The Right Brother (Summer)
Falling for Her (Autumn)
Warm Front (Winter)

Wyoming Wildflowers Series
Wyoming Wildflowers: The Beginning (prequel)
Almost a Bride
Match Made in Wyoming
My Heart Remembers
A New World (prequel to Jack's Heart)
Jack's Heart
Rodeo Nights (prequel to Where Love Lives)
Where Love Lives
A Cowboy Wedding

A Place Called Home series
Lost and Found Groom
At the Heart's Command
Hidden in a Heartbeat

THE SURPRISE PRINCESS

The Wedding Series
Book 6

Patricia McLinn

PROLOGUE

Ashton, Wisconsin

Katie Davis stared into the old suitcase that her father had never known her mother kept hidden in this attic niche.

Her mother had spanked her for trying to open it. She had never tried again. At first for fear of another spanking from the woman who never before had raised a hand to her. Later because Katie had recognized her mother's reaction as deep fear.

At times she'd wondered why Anna didn't throw out the suitcase if it frightened her so much. But there had never been that kind of communication between them.

Her mother was gone now, eight years ago when Katie was in college. Her father had died when she was a child.

And here she sat in the attic, looking into the suitcase. Driven by a magazine article about a young woman who looked so much like her, right down to having a left little finger as long as her ring finger. The Bariavak Hand, the article called it.

The magazine said the king of Bariavak had been struck by the resemblance of this young woman to his daughter at the same age. They had formed a bond and shared the holidays. The king was going to walk the commoner down the aisle when she married.

But then the article-writer added a final paragraph:

King Jozef still searches for his lost granddaughter. And somewhere out there could be a young woman who doesn't know she has a grandfather and a kingdom.

Why that had driven her to the attic Katie was not prepared to examine.

Better, far better, to explore the suitcase's contents.

At first she saw only yellowed, tattered paper. But as she lifted the paper out she saw it had been protecting other items.

She found a piece of embroidered fabric first. Her heart raced as she examined it, but it gave no answers, only raised more questions.

She set it aside to draw out documents.

And realized that what Anna Davis had feared from the past had just become what Katie Davis needed to fear in the future.

CHAPTER ONE

"Katie!"

She stopped at the familiar voice behind her, but didn't turn. Looking at Brad Spencer was a luxury not to be indulged too frequently. Like with a rich dessert, limit the portions or pay the consequences.

She heard him jogging up the path from Ashton University's main campus to the Sports Center, which sat astride a small ridge. The sun had melted most of the snow deposited earlier by a brief, spirited squall. But that was a small victory considering snow piles edged the paths in lumps and ice held Lake Ashton tight.

"I was looking for you." Brad was not the least bit winded.

To save time, she said, "Your expense report's been submitted."

As executive assistant to Ashton's head basketball coach, Katie wasn't expected to submit expense reports for the assistant coaches and she didn't for the other assistants. But if she didn't for Brad, he'd never get them in, the budget would always be out of sync, and she'd take the heat from the financial people. That's what she told herself.

"That's not why I was looking for you. Though, thanks." She didn't need to look at him to know he was grinning. "Got a couple trips to Chicago coming up and I won't mind the money."

"You won't have it for at least two weeks."

"That's okay." Brad put a hand on her arm. She stuttered a step. He didn't notice. Thank heavens. "Reason I came after you is there's a guy waiting in the office. Wants to talk to you and C.J."

His explanation made a heck of a lot less sense than coming after her to ask if his expense report was done.

There were always guys waiting for her in the office. Or on the phone. Or sending emails or texts. Well, not really *for* her. They wanted the information or help or problem-solving she provided. Not *her*.

Besides, she was walking *toward* the office, so why had Brad come from the direction of main campus?

"Thanks. But, why?"

"I thought you should have some warning before you went in there." Before she could repeat, "why?" he continued, "I guessed wrong about which path you'd take. I've been trying to catch up ever since. Boy, you've been on the move."

"Needed final authorizations for the contract with the company handling arrangements for the trip this summer."

From the moment approval came through for the men's basketball team to play in Europe in July she'd been caught in a whirlwind of activity. Hiring this company would knock a thousand details off her to-do list.

"Make sure they line up fun stuff for us," Brad said. "By the way, you didn't stop at the travel office. They said to remind you they still need your passport number."

Perhaps because she was looking for a distraction, motion caught her gaze. Brad was clapping his hands against well-muscled arms in an apparent effort to warm up.

"You're not wearing a coat."

He agreed with her brilliant assessment with his usual cheer. "Nope. Good thing I had to run to catch up with you or I'd be frozen."

"You're already frozen. Your lips are turning blue." Which made his eyes look even bluer. How did he *do* that?

"C'mon, then. Let's get inside." He slung an arm around her shoulders with ease. By basketball-playing standards he was short, which meant he was mere inches over six-foot instead of a foot or two. He had enough advantage over her five-eight to huddle her close and hurry her toward the doors.

Katie enjoyed that Ashton had preserved the original Physical Education Building's classic facade when the expansive Sports Center was built around it several years ago. But at the moment she simply wanted to be inside so she could escape his hold.

Too much closeness. Too much movement. Too much … "Brad."

"Keep going," he urged, holding on when she would have slipped loose. "Before I turn into an icicle. You not only have a coat on, you're wearing the infamous Katie sweater."

"Quit making fun of my sweater."

"Quit wearing it and I will."

"It's warm and practical and has—"

"Pockets. I know. You've said that before. They sag you know. From all the stuff you put in them."

"Which proves I need them to carry things."

"To carry things or to disappear? That thing's like a gray shroud. Blends right in to your desk and that tweedy stuff on the chairs. Gray on gray on gray."

"It would serve you right to turn into an icicle." She tried to shrug off his arm. "You—oh!" Her right boot heel caught a patch of ice, taking the express route forward.

His arm tightened around her shoulder, the other arm clasped around her waist, turning her motion into an almost graceful pirouette. "Got you."

Despite herself, she looked up into his smiling face, into those dangerous blue eyes. Oh, yeah, he had her, all right. If only he—No. She wasn't going down that road.

They were friendly colleagues. That was enough.

Just like one spoonful of a decadent dessert was enough. It was.

Inside the men's basketball offices, she slid off her coat and shook it.

"Hey!" Brad protested. "You sprayed me with ice water."

"If you'd worn a jacket like a normal person, you wouldn't have felt it."

"Sure I would," he said, "because I'd have taken mine off the same time you took yours off and I'd still have gotten the ice shower."

"That's—" Katie bit off her rejoinder because she'd spotted the man waiting for her. He was attractive, conservatively dressed, and—despite a small grin—more serious-looking than most people who came in the office.

No, not serious, that wasn't quite right. Players or others often came in with matters that weighed heavily on them. Yet she had the sense that this man's *serious* was weightier.

She was certain she hadn't met him before, yet he looked familiar. She smiled as she extended a hand.

"Hi, I'm Katie Davis. I understand you want to see Coach Draper?"

"Yes. Coach Draper and you, Ms. Davis. My name is Pierce."

"I'm sorry, Mr. Pierce—" She left a pause to let him correct her if Pierce was his first name. Instead he gave a slight nod. "—Coach Draper is in a meeting. You'll have to be satisfied with me for now in discussing…"

He ignored the opportunity to fill that in. Most visitors would have jumped on it to introduce their objective—selling something, angling for tickets, or—

"I'm sorry, Mr. Pierce, I should have said, if this is about an interview, the media office—"

"No. Not an interview. Perhaps Coach Draper can join us later. Or you can relay to him what you think he needs to know. If we could find a private space, Ms. Davis?"

"Of course. We can—"

"No."

She and the man turned toward Brad, who stepped up from behind her, looking at Mr. Pierce.

"She doesn't talk to you alone," he said. "Something's going on, and you're not talking to Katie without somebody else being there to back her up."

She shook off her surprise. "Of course I can talk to him until C.J. comes. I do it all the time." She turned to the stranger. "Unless … Brad is an assistant coach. Perhaps he would be better—"

"No. I want to talk to you. Coach Draper, too, if he were available.

But since he's not…"

"Since he's not, you can wait to talk to them together." What had gotten into Brad?

"I can wait," the other man said mildly, but with steel behind it, like he'd wait until hell froze over.

"There's no need for that. We can talk now—"

Brad cut her off, looking at her for the first time. "I know you don't want me, Katie. But if I can't get Coach out of his meeting, I'll get Carolyn over here. You—" Back to the other man. "—are not talking to her alone."

"That's—" she started.

"This is between Ms. Davis and—"

"No," Brad repeated. It was a tone she'd heard him use with players, though not frequently. He wasn't budging.

"C.J.'s in a meeting at the president's office. So there's no—"

"Fine." Brad hit a speed dial number on his phone. "Carolyn? Brad. There's a man here who wants to talk to Katie and Coach. Together. He won't say about what, except it doesn't seem to be basketball, and there's something weird. … No, he's in a meeting with the president. She needs you to come be with her. … Right now. The basketball office. … Yeah. Conference room. … I won't." That sounded grim. "Okay."

"Brad, you shouldn't have bothered Carolyn," Katie started.

"She'll be right here."

The man named Pierce ignored Brad. "Ms. Davis. If you don't want this professor or anyone else—" That held an edge. "—in this discussion, we can set up an appointment in private."

"Oh, I don't mind Carolyn—I just didn't want to bother her." Which was moot now. She released a breath. Okay, to be honest, she'd be glad to have Carolyn. This whole thing was feeling … well, *weird*, as Brad had said. It was almost as if this had become about her, instead of the man wanting to see C.J.

Considering the man's stone face and Brad's uncharacteristic unfriendliness, it was up to her to smooth the way. She fell into the familiar routine of welcoming someone to the office. "Let's go into the conference room and I'll get coffee. Or would you prefer tea? Something else?"

Mr. Pierce said he'd appreciate black coffee.

When she turned in pursuit of coffee, she ran right into Brad. Her hands came up reflexively, pushing off to regain space. She felt the power beneath the softness of his sweatshirt. His hands rose, too, but she'd already removed hers, so he didn't need to fend her off.

"Sorry," she said automatically. "Brad, you don't need to—"

"He's not talking to you until Carolyn's here."

"Oh, for heaven's sake. Fine, you two stay here—" Staring at each other like junk yard dogs, she thought, but didn't say. "—while I get the coffee."

She had deposited a tray holding a carafe of coffee, cups, and various additives on the table between the two men, and returned to the main office for a basket of snacks when Carolyn swept in.

"Katie, what's going on? What does this man want?"

Katie recognized a subtle easing in her muscles. Carolyn, cool and competent, was a good person to have in your corner. "I have no idea beyond what Brad said on the phone. I could have handled this, but Brad got weird about it."

"Brad did?" Carolyn removed a teal scarf that set off her taupe coat. Katie didn't look that polished with only herself to take care of, while Carolyn had two kids, a dog, a house, and a career … not to mention C.J.

Katie almost smiled at that thought. C.J. wasn't helpless by any means, but he didn't let much interfere with his priorities—Carolyn and the kids, then basketball and the family dog. As far as he was concerned all the rest were distracting details.

Carolyn was good at details. Noticing them, then handling them.

Like the day she'd called Katie, then a senior, into her office after an Eighteenth Century British Literature class and demanded to know what was wrong.

Katie's mother had died four months earlier, leaving no insurance.

Anna Davis hadn't been able to contribute much from her pay at a dry cleaner's, yet without it, the loans, scholarships, and two campus jobs Katie had cobbled together were falling short of keeping her in school.

Carolyn got all that and more out of Katie. She'd suggested C.J. hire Katie as part-time administrative assistant at a rate that let her drop the other two jobs.

That was October. In January, C.J. asked Katie to work full-time. Carolyn declared there would be no full-time position until Katie graduated. The week after receiving her degree, Katie's status became permanent full-time. Three years later, C.J. had made her executive assistant, with a healthy raise.

"So where is this sinister stranger?" Carolyn asked now.

"He's not sinister. He's perfectly nice. Even though he's attractive."

"Even though—? Never mind. Brad doesn't think he's perfectly nice, and he's not prone to histrionics. Though he can be protective of those he cares about."

Katie ignored that. "Mr. Pierce is in the conference room. They both are."

"Then let's see what this is all about." Carolyn stepped ahead of her to hold the door.

Inside, Katie set the basket in front of the visitor, who rose as she made the introductions.

Something flickered across Carolyn's face as she extended her hand. "I'm also Katie's long-time friend."

"Mentor," Katie said.

Brad shot her a look, but allowed no time for interpretation as he stood. "Now that Carolyn's here, I'll go. But I'll be out in the office if you need anything. I'll send C.J. in when he gets here."

"He won't be back for quite a while," Katie objected.

Brad said grimly, "He will be when I let him know about this."

"There is absolutely no need to inter—"

"Yes, please do, Brad," Carolyn said.

He gave Katie a hard look, then closed the door behind him.

Carolyn draped her coat over a chair and gestured for Mr. Pierce to resume his seat and for Katie to take the chair at right angles to him. Carolyn sat beside Katie.

"Ms. Davis, as I said, my name is Pierce. Hunter Pierce." He extracted a holder from his jacket pocket and showed an ID with the ease of practice. "I am a special agent with the Department of State's Security Division. Perhaps you have an idea why I am here?"

"No." She shook her head for emphasis. It had started spinning and the shake didn't help. *Department of State? Hunter Pierce?* "Some business with Coach Draper, of course, but—"

"No. My business is with you, Ms. Davis. I asked for Coach Draper in an effort to protect your privacy."

Her breath wouldn't come out. "M-my…?"

"Let's cover the formalities first. That might eliminate any need to … extend the conversation."

Breath whooshed out audibly. "Yes. I'm sure we can clear this up and all get back to work." She tried to smile.

It must not have been her best effort, because he looked even more solemn. But all he said was, "Your parents were Bob and Anna Davis. Your full name is Katharine Mary Davis."

"Yes, but—"

"Where were you born?"

"Portland, Oregon. I have my birth certificate. It's all in order." Why had she said *that?* A memory flashed, standing at a counter as a child, looking up, her mother handing over a paper to someone unseen. Her mother's hands shaking as she said, *Here is our Katie's birth certificate. It is in order.*

And then a more recent memory. In the attic. No … no. She'd decided. There was too much at stake.

"Your family moved here to Ashton when you were two?"

"Yes. How did you kn—?"

"And both your parents are now deceased."

"Yes. But—"

He held up a hand, stopping her words. He looked from her to

Carolyn and back. "Before we go any further, I must ask you each to sign a non-disclosure agreement."

He took out crisp documents from his pocket, spread one open in front of each of them and placed a pen on the table.

Katie skimmed the language once and was going back over it. "This is—This is serious."

To her surprise, Hunter Pierce's eyes lightened and she could swear he almost grinned. "Yes, Ms. Davis, it is."

"I will not pledge not to tell my husband," Carolyn said. "Not if Katie's interests are involved."

"If he will also sign a copy, I think we can accommodate that, since both of you appear to serve in the capacity of advisers to Ms. Davis."

Carolyn added a phrase to the document then signed. Hunter Pierce didn't look pleased about Carolyn's insertion, but said nothing as he folded the paper and waited for her.

Katie had a notion of saying she wouldn't sign. But now that Carolyn had signed, what reason could she give other than a voice in her head shouting *Run, run, run away and hide?*

She signed.

The man from the Department of State folded her sheet and slid both into his pocket.

"Now, what is this about?" Carolyn asked calmly.

"With all the coverage in recent months about King Jozef and his long-missing granddaughter reports to our offices and other interested parties have flooded in. Reports we've received about a young woman in Ashton, Wisconsin have particularly interested us. Not only because of a match with certain descriptors, but also because this young woman had stayed almost entirely under the radar. Remarkably so."

He looked at her as if expecting a response. She was also aware of Carolyn's eyes on her. She licked her lips. "Reports? I have no idea what you're talking about."

"Don't you?" he asked mildly. Then his face and tone became completely serious. "Tell me, Ms. Davis, have you ever had reason to think you might be Princess Josephine-Augusta of Bariavak?"

CHAPTER TWO

"No. Absolutely not."

She wanted to say more, to produce words that would end this now and forevermore, but her throat spasmed closed. Words jammed up against the block like stampeders at a locked door.

"What makes you think Katie might be Princess Josephine-Augusta?" Carolyn asked, as if this were a rational conversation.

"We're not saying she is, you understand. It would require an investigation to confirm."

"Yes, we understand all those cautions. But you wouldn't be here, the State Department wouldn't be interested in Katie, if you didn't have some basis for thinking it is possible."

"Carolyn, you know this is impossible." Katie produced a credible chuckle. She raised both palms to Hunter Pierce in bemusement. "Impossible."

"There are physical similarities as well as—"

The door opened and Coach C.J. Draper strode in. "What's going on here?" He moved like a much younger man, despite the mangled left knee that had pushed him out of the pros and into coaching. Gray lightly streaked his mop of hair, but that didn't age him much either.

Carolyn reached out a hand toward him. "C.J., close the door, please." He did. "This is Hunter Pierce, an agent with the Department of State's Security Service. Hunter, this is my husband, C.J. Draper."

The other man stood to shake hands. "Coach Draper. It's a pleasure to meet you, sir. I've followed your career and teams for a long time."

"Thanks, but you're not here for basketball, are you?"

"No, sir. Ms. Davis—"

"C.J.," Carolyn interrupted, "they think Katie might be a princess."

"Princess? She's an empress. But that doesn't mean you get a mid-year raise," he added to her, squeezing her shoulder before backing up to sit beside Carolyn. "No princess renegotiations. In fact, since princess is a demotion from empress, you should give some of this year's raise back."

"C.J.," Carolyn said as only she could say it. "This is serious. Hunter was about to tell us why he—why the Department of State—thinks she might be this missing princess."

"What missing princess?"

Carolyn spurted a little puff. "The granddaughter of King Jozef of Bariavak, who was kidnapped as an infant during an uprising about thirty years ago, an uprising that earlier had killed his son-in-law. His daughter—the baby's mother—died shortly after the kidnapping. The baby has never been found. It was generally assumed she was killed by the fleeing rebels who kidnapped her. But speculation about her started again late last year when the king was at Washington, D.C., events with a young woman who bears a strong resemblance to Bariavak's royal family. That young—"

"Wait a minute. How do you know so much about this, Carolyn?"

"Because our daughter has been talking of almost nothing else since the story broke."

"What story? All she's been talking about is—*Oh*. This happened around the first of the year?"

"Yes."

"That explains it. Heading into the meat of the conference schedule. I wasn't paying attention to any news."

Katie wanted to fling her arms around C.J.'s neck. Amid all this talk about a princess, he remained the same.

He continued, "I remember Steph talking about Washington. I thought it was weird she was so interested in politics. A princess makes a lot more sense. Especially a missing princess. But I thought she said they found this missing princess. Lose her again?" He shot at Hunter.

"No. She wasn't—isn't—"

Carolyn stepped in. "The young woman some people speculated was the king's long-lost granddaughter had befriended the king and kept him company during the holidays. She became so close to the king, in fact, that he is going to give her away when she marries Hunter."

Of *course.* That's why he'd looked familiar. How had Katie not remembered after the hours she'd stared at those pictures? The pictures of the king of Bariavak with April Gareaux, some including the man she was going to marry—Hunter Pierce.

"Have I got that right?" Carolyn asked Hunter.

He grinned, revealing an entirely different man beyond the serious agent. "You hit the high points, ma'am."

Carolyn smiled back at him. "The high points of the official story, but is it the whole story? Or the real story?"

"Ma'am," he said, making it clear he wasn't going to divulge anything beyond that official story.

She nodded her understanding. "Congratulations to you and April Gareaux. We hope you'll be very happy."

"Thank you." He looked confident that they would be.

C.J. spoke up. "Okay, but what makes you think our Katie's this missing princess?"

"I'm *not.*" None of them paid attention.

"That's what Hunter was about to tell us when you came in, dear," Carolyn said.

"I can tell you that similarities have been noted. Similarities of looks with the Bariavak royal family, for instance."

"She and your April do look very much alike," Carolyn said.

"We don't." This time everyone turned to Katie. Perhaps she'd been too emphatic. "She's lovely and polished and sophisticated. I don't look anything like her."

"Surface." Carolyn dismissed the surface as only someone naturally lovely and polished and sophisticated herself could do. "Bone structure, coloring, and features are strikingly similar."

Katie tried a dry laugh. "I don't think April Gareaux would appreciate hearing that."

"April agrees with the professor. She's seen your picture." A twitch eased the neutrality of Hunter's mouth. "She'd also tell you the polish came lately. In addition—" His face went neutral again. "—there's the Bariavak Hand. It's a strong trait in the royal family."

Automatically, Katie covered her left hand with her right. But C.J. and Carolyn had been seeing that hand for years, and clearly Hunter Pierce knew about it before he arrived. So what sense was there in reverting to that childhood habit? None. She deliberately removed her right hand.

"It shows up in the general population," she said.

"April Gareaux has the trait, doesn't she?" Carolyn asked.

"Yes. It runs in her family. Did Bob or Anna Davis have the trait?" Hunter didn't wait for Katie to answer. "No. Neither of them."

"It's a recessive gene." She had done a school research project, curious about the peculiarity of her left little finger being as long as her ring finger.

"We would go back another generation or two to check if the gene runs in the Davis family—" The way he said Davis spread unease over her. "—but we can't because there is barely any record of your parents until they arrived in Ashton with you as a child."

"That's not right. There are records from Portland. Before that, they immigrated. Though there was a lot of confusion in the country they came from because there'd been—" She broke off abruptly.

"A failed rebellion?" Hunter supplied.

"They never talked about it. Where they came from or the past. They said I was an American and that's what counted. I agree."

"They never told you where they came from?" C.J. asked.

"No." She tried to sound matter-of-fact, but she heard defensiveness in her voice.

"You must have wondered."

Her parents had not encouraged wondering. "There clearly were very bad memories for them. I didn't want to make them unhappy."

Hunter Pierce cleared his throat. "There are no records in Portland until two years before they moved here. Not of Bob Davis or of Anna Davis. No family, no records of immigration to the United States. There are discrepancies in other records, such as the Social Security numbers they used."

"Maybe they were in witness protection. You know, they'd been in the mob but turned state's evidence."

"C.J., this is not funny." Carolyn spoke to him but was looking at her.

"It's a little funny to think of our on-the-straight-and-narrow Katie being born into the mob."

"It makes as much sense as me being a princess," Katie said.

"There are questions that need to be answered, Ms. Davis." Hunter Pierce looked at her steadily.

"Okay, you have discrepancies in records that *might* indicate Katie's parents were not Mr. and Mrs. Davis from Portland, but what do you have—beside a trait you acknowledge pops up in the general population—that makes you think Katie might be this princess?"

"Good question, Carolyn," C.J. said.

Hunter inclined his head slightly, acknowledging her point. "Mostly circumstantial indications."

"For instance?"

"For instance, the Davises showing up in the United States not long after the rebellion collapsed. For instance, a cell of Bariavakian rebels had safe houses and support in Portland. For instance, medical records show the blood types reported for Mr. and Mrs. Davis could not have produced a child with Katie's blood type—a blood type that is the same as Princess Josephine-Augusta's."

"Did you know that? About your parents' blood types and yours?" Carolyn asked her.

She could only shake her head. "How do you know their blood types?" she demanded of Hunter.

"Took some digging. Apparently neither believed in doctors. But we finally found them on employment records. That was also where we finally found photographs of Bob and Anna Davis, who apparently also didn't believe in photographers."

He said it with a hint of wryness, but it was true.

One Christmas she had begged for a camera. After she'd gone to bed, she had heard them arguing about it in their odd language. She could tell from their tones that her mother was pleading that she be allowed a camera. Her father had refused. It ended with the sound of a blow. The next morning the side of her mother's face was swollen and bruised. Katie never again mentioned a camera to them.

She became aware of the others watching her. She cleared her throat. "They didn't care for photographs. Or doctors. But that's no reason to—"

"There's more. In Bariavak there was a man named Davogner Bordanic and his girlfriend, Annika. The names are interesting— Davogner Bordanic becomes Bob Davis. Annika becomes Anna Davis. No, you're right, Ms. Davis," he said before she could even produce words, so he must have read her objection from her expression, "that's not proof, either. But the coincidences are beginning to add up."

He drew another paper from his pocket, unfolded it, then put it face down on the table.

She couldn't look away.

"Here's another coincidence. Davogner and Annika disappeared. They were definitely not among the rebels arrested or imprisoned. They were not among those who died in the rebellion. They were last heard of in Bariavak five months before Bob and Anna Davis first appear in any record of any kind in Portland. That last sighting in Bariavak was immediately before the kidnapping. Only after the rebels' defeat did anyone know of Bordanic's involvement with them. That's significant for two reasons. It turns out he was fairly high up in their hierarchy yet he could have slipped across the border, unlike the known leaders. It also turns out that his girlfriend Annika worked in the royal palace. When King Jozef's daughter Sofia gave birth to Princess Josephine-Augusta, Annika was assigned to the nursery staff."

Carolyn made a small sound beside her.

"Which brings us to another coincidence of names. Princess Josephine-Augusta's full name is Josephine-Augusta Katrina Mariana Sofia. Katrina Mariana. Katherine Mary. It was customary for the nursery staff to call her Katrina."

Katie's chest burned. But still she could not take her eyes from that paper.

"Then there is this." He flipped it over. "This is one of only two photographs of Davogner Bordanic we have." He tapped the photo on the left, pointing out the grainy face of one man in a crowd. "Eight years later, this is a photograph of Bob Davis from the files of his employer here in Ashton."

C.J. whistled softly.

She insisted, "You can't determine anything from old photos like those. You can barely see the face."

"They're certainly suggestive," Hunter said calmly. "Granted, the best way to determine the truth is with a DNA test. Unfortunately, we don't have certifiable DNA from Princess Josephine-Augusta. Nor of Princess Sofia, or even her mother. Testing a maternal grandfather isn't ideal, but—"

"No."

"It's not an invasive test—"

She pushed back her chair.

"Katie—"

Carolyn reached for her, but the chair blocked her. C.J.'s knee slowed him. Hunter was on the far side of the table. She was out of the door before anyone could stop her.

Brad was there, just outside. She tried to sidestep him, but he stepped the same way and she bumped into him. His arms came around her. Those wonderful, strong arms. For a moment, she let herself sink into him, let herself take in his scent, his warmth.

"Katie." His hand smoothed her hair. The way she'd seen him do with C.J. and Carolyn's kids after they skinned a knee.

The way he'd soothe a child.

She pushed away, using the momentum to get past. "Tell C.J. I'm taking the rest of the day off."

The walk to her front door seemed longer than usual.

Probably because she'd spent hours wandering.

Walking the campus had been her refuge since childhood. First, tentative forays from her neighborhood to the edges of Ashton University, then deeper and deeper. She'd found her way to the Meadow, the campus' heart. Its soul was Lake Ashton. Where the Meadow met Lake Ashton was her favorite refuge.

Today, though, the spot hadn't brought its usual peace. She'd been blindsided, thinking danger came only from the items in the attic.

Planning how to handle this, she'd walked and walked and walked, even when snow began to fall.

Maybe tired legs explained why she didn't dodge fast enough when she heard wind stir the huge Norway spruces that marched alongside the front walk, protecting the small frame house from view from the street. Snow that had dusted the trees into Christmas card scenes showered icy pellets on her head.

That was fitting.

A noise jolted Katie's heartbeat.

It took only an instant to recognize it as her phone, but she'd already jerked in reaction, knocking the suitcase lid closed.

It rang again. Slightly muffled. She looked around, but saw only the attic's detritus. Automatically, she patted at her hips. In her pocket.

The display announced Brad as the caller. She drew in a breath and let it out slowly before answering.

"Hello."

"Katie. Are you okay? Did I wake you?"

"No—I mean, yes, I'm okay. No, you didn't wake me."

There was a pause. "You're at home? I rang the bell. There was no answer. With your car here, I thought maybe something ... but of course you could be out with someone."

Could be, but so rarely was. "You're *here*? At my house?"

"Yes. At your front door. And it's damned cold out here."

"I'll be right down."

Swinging the front door wide, she asked, "Is anything wrong?"

Without waiting for an invitation, Brad stepped in, carrying a large bag. "That's my line. Here's dinner. I know you didn't cook."

"Dinner? How could you know I didn't cook? Why would it be your line?" She knew she'd jumbled the responses but that fit her scrambled brain.

Brad Spencer walking in her front door like he'd done it a million times. In fact, he'd done it precisely once. When he and a couple players had moved in furniture she'd bought at a university sale. That was not long after her mother died, so it must be eight years ago.

"Whoa, you've done a lot with the place."

"You remember?" she asked stupidly. He must have or he wouldn't have noticed changes.

"Sure. It looks great. I like the floors."

She'd pulled up the old carpeting herself, finding hardwood floors. She'd saved up to have them refinished and now kept them gleaming beneath simple area rugs.

"Thanks, but—"

"Like the paint job, too. And the artwork."

The walls were off-white, which brightened the small rooms. The artwork she bought from student shows.

"Thank you, but—"

"How about showing me the kitchen before this gets cold." He hefted the bag. "You like Chinese?"

"Yes, but—"

"Glad to see you don't wear that gray shroud here. Though those are some interesting accessories. I'll serve. I don't want the extra fiber you might add to our dinner."

She glanced down and saw dust and cobwebs festooned across her front. "Oh. I didn't—"

"You go wash up. I'll find plates and stuff. Kitchen's through here, right?" He was already moving past her, unerringly heading for the kitchen.

She'd worked with him long enough to know that rousting a determined Brad Spencer was no easy task. Besides, she realized, she was hungry. Why not eat the food he'd brought.

She ducked into the bathroom, wiped at her clothes, removing evidence of her time in the attic, and washed her hands.

He'd found the plates and silverware, had glasses of water poured and was setting out the food when she returned.

"Made a lot of changes in here, too, huh?" he said.

That started conversation about what she'd done to the house since it became hers. He made it easy and she was proud of the work she'd done on a stingy budget, making the little house's spare interior bright, open, comfortable.

"When are you going to start on the outside?"

"I'm not. I like the outside."

He raised his eyebrows as he handed her a fortune cookie, but didn't argue. "Okay. Then I'll ask the other question—what are you going to do about this princess stuff?"

CHAPTER THREE

She dropped the cookie. "You eavesdropped! I can't believe—"

"Nope. But apparently you *could* believe it or you wouldn't have said it."

"I won't believe Carolyn or C.J. told—"

"They didn't. Not your friend Hunter Pierce, either."

"But…"

He picked up the fortune cookie and put it back in her hand. "If these things are accurate, it should say something about 'Tall Man isn't as stupid as you think.' "

"I have never thought you were stupid. In fact, you don't give yourself enough credit…"

She felt heat rising up from her chest over her throat, into her cheeks.

He made no attempt to disguise that he was watching what had to be an accompanying surge of color. "I don't give myself enough credit for what?"

Defiantly, she unwrapped the cookie with the maximum amount of plastic crinkling. "For your ability as a coach. You should be a head coach somewhere."

"Oh, God, not you, too. I hear enough of that from C.J. I'd far rather talk about this princess stuff."

"Well, I wouldn't." She cracked the cookie in half and chomped down on one piece.

He reached across and pulled the fortune from the other side. "Before you add some paper fiber to your diet," he said, letting it drift gently to her plate. "If you don't want to talk about it, I guess you don't want to know how I knew about the princess issue."

Damn him.

But she'd never been one to bite off her nose to spite her face. "Fine. Yes, I want to know."

"Steph."

"What? Stephanie Draper? Carolyn and C.J.'s daughter?"

He nodded. "She said at New Year's how much you look like the princess in Washington. So when the story was all over the news before and after the king's surgery, I paid attention. Not to mention the interns in all the athletic offices were saying you're a dead ringer for the woman everybody thought was the lost princess."

"I'm not," she said quickly.

He looked down to pick up his fortune cookie and started to open it. "That Hunter Pierce from the State Department seems to think—"

"How do you know he's State—?"

"Katie, Katie. We already went through this. The news, the magazines. He wasn't front and center, but he was in enough pictures not to miss him."

"I don't want to talk about this," she said abruptly.

"Okay. You want to wash and I'll dry?"

"No need. Dishwasher." She stopped chewing on the edge of her thumbnail. "I'll clean up. You don't need to stay to do that."

"In other words I don't need to stay," he said wryly. "You don't think you're any good at having friends do you?"

Thoughts fought for precedence. *She'd never had friends. She didn't want him to be a friend.* She closed her mouth.

"When Carolyn described herself as your friend you changed it to mentor." Brad snagged his jacket from the back of a chair. "Not the first time I've heard you do that."

She hadn't even taken his coat. Not that she had much practice at those sorts of hostess gestures.

"I didn't mean—"

"That's okay. Carolyn's your friend whether you call her that or not. As for me," he said with exaggerated martyrdom as he headed for the front door, "I can take a hint."

She trailed after him once again. "Thank you for dinner."

With one hand on the doorknob, he grinned at her. Her insides felt like their elevator dropped a dozen floors in a second. His other hand came up and for a fraction of a second, she thought—.

He touched his fingertip to her forehead, then traced it down the bridge of her nose and on to the tip, where he gave it an extra tap. "You're welcome, Squirt."

He hadn't called her that since she'd gone full-time in the office and told him she expected to be treated with respect and being called "Squirt" didn't qualify. So why did she feel now as if her knees had turned to goo?

He was about to step off the small, square of concrete that counted as the house's front porch, when she pushed past the gooey knees to say, "Brad?"

He turned back, the dim light managing to glint highlights in his blond hair. "Yeah?"

"How did you know I hadn't cooked dinner?"

"I was outside watching. Light never went on in the kitchen. No light anywhere except a faint one up there." He gestured toward the gable at the end of the house, where a small window provided ventilation. "So I ordered Chinese and had it delivered to my car. Goodnight, Katie."

Before she could absorb the idea of Brad Spencer sitting outside her house waiting for a light to go on, he was out the door, sliding down the snow-slicked walk, and muttering a curse when the Norway spruces dumped on him.

Brad's fortune said, "Truth surfaces in the end."

Thank heavens he got that one. Unless the same one was in both cookies? No. Hers said, "What cannot be undone must be considered many times."

The doorbell rang as she gave the counter a final wipe.

Her heartbeat thundered. For absolutely no good reason.

She flipped on the light and jerked open the front door with unnecessary force, then stopped dead. "Carolyn."

"I hope it's not too late, especially to drop by unannounced."

"Of course not, come in."

"We had a homework crisis. Finally got the kids settled." Carolyn's explanations continued as Katie took her coat and hung it in the closet. Something she hadn't done for Brad. Both unexpected visitors, but then he had brought her dinner, so by rights she should have—. Carolyn's next words stopped that mental meandering. "C.J. and I are both concerned about you, Katie. He would have come, too, but with the kids … He lost the coin toss."

Carolyn took the new overstuffed chair Katie indicated. She took the old, lumpy couch, which was the next item on her list to replace.

"There's no reason for you to be concerned, Carolyn. I'm fine."

"You reacted quite strongly to what that Hunter Pierce said."

"Wouldn't you? I'm not even a very good Katie Davis," she said with a dry laugh, "so the idea of being a princess … It's ridiculous."

Carolyn looked even more solemn. "You shouldn't say you aren't a good Katie Davis, even in jest."

She hadn't been jesting. She kept her eyes down, because if Carolyn saw that answer in her face…

"I realized that even knowing you all these years I know nothing about your parents, except your mom's death. Will you tell me about them?" her visitor asked.

"They worked hard. Kept to themselves. They weren't terribly social. I take after them, so that should show how insane this idea is."

With Carolyn silent, she gathered steam. "Without my mother's financial help I wouldn't have been able start at Ashton. Without her support I wouldn't have had the grades to qualify for Ashton. She truly did look out for me. Personal things like my hand…"

Only after it was out did she think that bringing up the so called Bariavak Hand might not bolster her argument that Hunter Pierce's position was laughable.

"What about your hand?"

"Oh, it's silly. Childhood stuff. I used to hide my hand all the time. I'd been teased as a child as long as I can remember—*before* I can remember—about it being strange to have such a long little finger. She always tried to protect me."

Carolyn looked thoughtful, but said only, "They must have been very proud of you."

Proud of her? She'd never considered that. They'd been mostly concerned that she not draw attention, not cause trouble, not rock the boat.

"They worked so hard, there wasn't time for pride."

"You said your mother looked after you. What about your father?"

"My father died when I was ten. I don't believe he left her anything but this house. She was so worried we'd lose the house. She worked two jobs and, as soon as I could work, I helped out. If I hadn't gotten the scholarships…" She looked up. "And if you hadn't stepped in after my mother died, I would have had to leave school. I'm so grateful to you and C.J."

"You've more than thanked us over the years, especially with all you've done for C.J." She sounded almost absent-minded, then her tone became crisp. "Katie, I'm going to say something … I was struck a bit ago when you said you'd been teased about your hand from before you could remember. So how could you have known?"

"Oh, my mother said—" She bit it off.

Carolyn nodded and went on in her calm voice. "If it happened before you remembered, the only way you *could* know is if someone told you that you'd been teased about your hand. That would have been an effective way to encourage a child to keep a betraying characteristic out of sight."

Carolyn went on as if this were a common conversation. "When you started my class, you would keep your sweater sleeve pulled down over that hand. After your mother died you slowly stopped. I wondered at the time if it was because you weren't being reminded to cover your hand."

Was that true? Had her mother urged her to hide her hand? She honestly couldn't remember.

"She was good to me," she said.

Carolyn nodded, but it was more as if she were acknowledging that Katie had said the words than that she believed them. "There's something else, Katie. Your reaction to what Hunter Pierce said was so out of character. Not at all like you."

She tried to laugh. "You mean all the other times you've seen me react to a crazy story about me not being who I am?"

Carolyn remained serious.

Katie pushed her hair back. "I needed time to process what he'd said. Wouldn't you if someone said crazy things like that?"

Carolyn frowned. "I'd certainly be shocked. But maybe that's part of it. I had the feeling you didn't want to hear what he was saying but you weren't as shocked as you tried to make us think."

"Of course I was. How could I not be?"

She gave a small shrug. "I don't know. But what matters is where you go from here. What are you going to do, Katie?"

This she felt confident answering.

"I'm going to get up and go to the office in the morning. I'm going to work on organizing the trip to Europe this summer along with all the usual tasks for the end of the season, recruiting, and summer camps. That's what I'm going to do."

Just the way she had since a magazine article had sent her up to search the attic.

CHAPTER FOUR

She got to the office early, which allowed her to be deep into the routine of handling whatever came up … which so seldom followed a routine.

C.J., Carolyn, and Brad came in together. Had they been talking about yesterday? About her? No. She wasn't going to indulge in paranoia.

She offered a breezy hello, but kept her focus on the computer screen, which meant she only felt all of them looking at her then exchanging concerned looks, instead of actually seeing it, so it could have been her imagination.

"Heard anything from that Hunter Pierce today?" C.J. asked.

"Not a word." Her cheer felt forced. "I don't expect to. It'll all blow over."

"Didn't get the feeling he's a man to let something blow over," Carolyn said mildly.

C.J. leaned on her desk. "Katie, maybe you should consider—"

"Don't push her around, C.J." Brad's sharpness made Katie blink, which is why it took an extra moment for her to realize C.J. and Carolyn were also staring at Brad. His next words were closer to his usual easy style. "She's so used to taking orders from you, she'd do what you said automatically. You wouldn't want that, Coach. That's not your style."

"Didn't know I had a style," the older man drawled. "But I'm still trying to get over you saying Katie's used to taking orders from me. She runs this place, and we all know it."

Carolyn said peaceably, "That's true. She'll have you all sailing through Europe like clockwork this summer."

"Not me." Katie practically wanted to sing with relief that the subject had changed. "The company we've hired to handle all the arrangements will do that. The final papers are in the system with printouts in the folder at the top right of your desk." C.J. still liked to read some papers at home.

"Of course they are." Carolyn smiled. "What a great trip that's going to be."

"You and the kids could still come," C.J. said.

"You're going to be so busy bouncing around the continent having fun with your boys and Katie, you'd never have time for us."

Katie needed to deliver the news that she wasn't going on the trip, but this was not the time.

"We're going to have an educational trip. We'll study culture, politics, and history, as well as play basketball," Brad said primly.

"See, I knew I'd get through to you eventually, Spence. Couldn't have said it better myself. You'd think there was a reporter lurking around," C.J. said.

"Or somebody from the administration or the NCAA," Brad said.

C.J. nodded. "Suppose you'll get some of those questions when you go to Chicago tomorrow. Isn't that red-headed TV reporter still chasing you? Not that I have to worry about you putting your foot in your mouth. In fact, you're so good at it, your talent is wasted as a mere assistant coach. It's time you have your own program."

As Brad had indicated last night, they had this conversation frequently. She knew it was because C.J. wanted the best for Brad, wanted him to succeed in his career. He was a great coach. Technically, yes, but even more in his handling of players, both those on the team and the prospects.

Still, she didn't look forward to Brad leaving. After all, he was an integral part of the program.

"No way. I don't want those headaches. The hassles. The media. You keep being the front man and I'll sit at the master's feet."

C.J. frowned. It was a mock frown, yet Katie saw concern. "Am I going to have to use one of these big feet to kick you out of the nest?"

Brad grinned. "I'd cling to the edge and climb back in. So we might as well go hit the court to see if you can use those big—and slow—feet to block out that play I was telling you about, Coach."

C.J. cuffed his shoulder. "These big, slow feet can still get around you. Don't think they can't."

As they bantered their way toward the court, Katie let her breath out in slow, small increments.

Not slow enough, not small enough.

The second she looked around and found Carolyn watching her, she realized that.

Carolyn said slowly, "I worry about Brad sometimes."

"About *Brad?*"

"You know those four who were C.J.'s first recruits—Brad, Ellis, Frank, and Thomas—had quite the ride during their playing careers. The media, the fans, the girls. I suppose I should say women, though emotionally..." She shook her head. "You would not believe the way some of them went after those guys. Ellis was too smart, Frank was too shy, and Thomas was sure anyone who chased him simply realized how wonderful he was. But Brad ... Brad was optimistic enough to keep hoping one would turn out to be genuine, but too smart not to recognize when he was wrong. Until ... Well, I shouldn't keep you from your work and I suppose I should head for my office. Though if you'd like to talk..."

Talk? No.

Hear what came after that "until"? Oh, yes.

But if she asked wouldn't Carolyn guess what Katie had kept hidden for so long?

No notice. Draw no notice.

The warning sounded in her head in her mother's voice.

Were the words from a specific instance? A distillation of an attitude? Or her imagination?

But they were good advice. Especially now.

"No, no. I need to get to my work, too, Carolyn. Have a good day.”

What could the other woman say after that?

Brad came out of a high school gym set into a hill in a suburb west of Chicago and headed for his car. A tall figure leaned against it. When he recognized the man he muttered a curse under his breath.

“You didn’t think I was going to go away, did you?” Hunter Pierce asked.

“Why not? You got your answer.”

Pierce looked at him steadily. “Because it’s not that simple. I think you know that.”

“I’m not the one to be talking to. It’s Katie’s business. Has nothing to do with me.”

“Oh, I don’t know about that. When the direct route doesn’t work, indirect is the way to go.”

“It’s Carolyn and C.J. you should talk to, then,” Brad said.

“I have. After you and I talk, you should talk to them, too.”

Brad wasn’t sure he was up for that.

C.J. had a way of looking at you that made you feel like you’d been pinned to a wall. So you stood as straight as you could and met his look square because if you didn’t, you’d be the scum of the earth. It was that look that had made him consider not taking the scholarship C.J. had offered … and it was that look that had made him grateful many times over that he had taken it.

And in some ways he was easier than Carolyn.

“Let’s go get a drink,” Hunter Pierce said.

“I don’t—”

“If you care about her, you’ll come.”

They closed the bar, though each nursed a single drink for the entire time.

The next day, Brad had brunch at an Evanston home, just north of

Chicago, with Pierce and a half dozen people he'd never met before, including April Gareaux.

Her similarity to Katie was uncanny. Was that why he'd liked her immediately? Was that why he'd listened to her with a more open mind than he had to Hunter Pierce?

By the time he was driving back to Ashton, he knew he'd talk to C.J. and Carolyn. Maybe he even knew he'd do more.

As much of an impact as April had on him, it was something Pierce had said, while he'd looked at the woman he was going to marry. "If you don't help us with this, Katie will never know. If you do nothing, she will never know. Take it from me, she'll always wonder unless someone shows her it's the only way you can move ahead."

"Coach Spencer's back," student intern Maura announced the moment Katie returned from lunch.

"Good. So he wasn't abducted by aliens? No ransom demands from desperate kidnappers? He isn't languishing in prison, the victim of tragic mistaken identity?"

Maura giggled.

"If he were abducted by aliens," Trevor said, "they could have done their experiments and returned him by now." He was serious. Maura's fellow student intern was always serious. Especially about things like alien abductions. On the upside, Trevor was great with graphics and other techy skills. "We wouldn't know until he started exhibiting strange behavior."

"So we'd never know," Katie deadpanned.

"*Katie*," Maura said, half giggling, half horrified. Well, if she was half giggling maybe the girl was finally getting over her mega crush on Brad.

Not that Katie could blame her, considering she'd gone into a mega crush on him the day she'd started in the office. As much as she wished otherwise, her recovery was still in doubt.

"Coach Spencer's in the office with Coach," Trevor announced.

C.J. was always Coach—*The* Coach.

"With the door closed," Maura added with heavy significance. "Coach would have to be royally pissed to close the door."

Maura and Trevor led the interns who helped keep the office gears grinding. They had their drawbacks—Maura's flair for drama, Trevor's penchant for literalness—but who didn't? They were smart and dependable.

"Perhaps," she said gently, "the door was closed so they could talk without being drowned out by the roar of all the work getting done out here."

Without looking up, Trevor said, "Yeah, I told that guy from IT two computers need new fans."

Maura rolled her eyes, but grinned. And got back to work.

Katie shot one look at C.J.'s closed door—a rarity—and got to work herself.

It was nearly an hour before the door opened. She happened to be facing that way, as she looked over Trevor's shoulder to discuss positioning the Aces logo on a new page for the website, so she saw both men looking serious … until they saw her and simultaneously produced big smiles.

That made her uneasy.

Granted, it took much less than usual to make her uneasy since Hunter Pierce's visit. Not hearing more from him somehow made it worse. Even with Brad gone and Carolyn and C.J. accepting her statement that it was too outlandish to discuss, uneasiness dogged her.

They came toward her, C.J. saying they wanted to go over a few things.

She went back to her desk, ready to take notes.

No notes were necessary, because they took turns telling her things she already knew about the upcoming schedule for recruiting, campus visits, and Alum Night, when former players returned for the season's second-to-last home game. That event always included several of Brad's teammates from the first season C.J. coached.

"…plus, I'll be going back to Chicago," Brad said.

"Got that, Katie?" C.J. asked.

She raised one eyebrow at him. He was sitting on the edge of the empty desk beside hers. "I saw it on the master schedule," she said.

"Yeah, but it's been changed. Something, uh, came up—opportunity to see a great prospect. He goes tomorrow."

"Tomorrow? That's a fast turnaround." She tapped in her first note. "Okay. I'll change the arrangements. And your expense reports are up to date. If you need an advance…?"

"Nope. I'm fine."

She had the feeling the conversation had ended, yet neither man moved. C.J. was looking at Brad. Brad was frowning at a corner of her desk. She checked—there was nothing on that corner but space. Now her single raised eyebrow was raised at him. "Something wrong, Brad?"

"No, nothing's wrong. Just thought—why don't you come with me?"

"What?"

"Great idea," C.J. said.

She repeated her unclever syllable. "What?"

"To Chicago," Brad said. He met her eyes for an instant, then looked away. "I'll be catching a couple high school players, then the team comes in for the game Saturday."

She knew all that. But—"I don't go to out-of-town games."

"Why not?" Brad asked. Now he did look at her. She looked away.

"About time you did," C.J. added. "It can only help you to see what Brad and the others do when they're out of town."

"Help me how?"

"Background," C.J. said with a broad gesture.

"But—"

C.J. stood and started toward his office, clapping Brad on the shoulder as he passed. "Good idea. Real good idea, Brad. Glad you're going, Katie."

"I didn't—"

But her boss was already in his office with the door closed—a second instance of that rare occurrence in one afternoon.

"Cool," said Maura. "You'll have so much fun."

"Yeah. It'll be fun," Brad said. He didn't sound entirely convinced. Then he added with his usual certainty, "I'm driving. No way are we trusting your collection of rust and bolts to get to Chicago, much less back. And do not bring that sweater."

CHAPTER FIVE

Katie came out of her front door as Brad reached the porch.

She pulled the door closed and locked it. When she reached for her bag, it was gone.

With his long legs he was already depositing it in the trunk of his car when she reached him.

"Thank you, but—"

"You're welcome. C'mon, get in. I want to get on the road."

Why? It was the same question she'd had when he'd set their departure time so early. But then, as now, the realization that he must have something to do in Chicago ahead of this evening's tipoff stopped her from commenting. She didn't want to know what his plans were for Chicago.

He held the passenger door open. She got in without saying anything.

But when he took the driver's seat and started the car, he immediately said, "What's that look for, Squirt?"

"Do not—".

"Sorry, but you know that single raised eyebrow gets me. You do it because you know I can't."

"I had no idea you couldn't raise only one eyebrow."

"Hah. Okay, put that aside. What was the look for?"

"This isn't what I expected."

"The car? It's just a sedan."

"I know."

"Few repairs. Gets me where I need to go. Good mileage. What's not to like? It's reliable and practical."

That was what she hadn't expected. A sports car, a convertible, a luxury model. Any of those wouldn't have surprised her.

Before she came up with a way to say that, he was continuing. "Besides, we're even. This—" He gestured toward the house as he backed into the street. "—wasn't what I expected either. The inside sure isn't what I'd expect from this outside. Looks like a house I would've skipped going to on Halloween as a kid and—"

"That's ridicu—"

"—would've TP'd or egged in my wilder years."

"—lous. Egged? You better not have."

"Why not? Wicked witch's house—that's what it looks like with those spooky evergreens looming over everything."

"They're an excellent wind-break."

"Yeah, if your house was all by itself on the frozen tundra." He gestured at the neighborhood they were leaving. "You've got neighbors, in case you couldn't tell from inside that forest."

"The trees provide privacy."

"From what? Aliens spying from outer space? They're twice as tall as the house and take up most of the yard. Getting to your front door's like hacking through a rain forest."

"I doubt Norway spruce grow in the rain forest."

"Is that what those things are?" Fat rain drops spattered the windshield. He flipped on the wipers. "Maybe they have room for them in Norway, but your house looks like it's their captive—the little anybody can see of it."

"I like them."

Stopped for a red light, he dropped his hands from the wheel to his thighs, calling her attention to the worn denim of his jeans. It looked like it would be soft. She jerked her gaze up, and found him looking at her, apparently waiting for their eyes to meet, because he immediately said, "No you don't."

"What makes you think you know—"

"If you liked them, you would have said that first, instead you talked about wind-break and privacy."

"I haven't considered them." That was as much as she was willing to concede. "I've been busy with the inside."

"You pay the interns to work on your yard, don't you?"

"How do you know—?"

His chuckle stopped her. "Like everybody doesn't know everything anybody in the basketball office does. Anyway, you should get someone who knows something about landscaping. Ever hear of curb appeal? Yours is curb repel."

"I'm not planning on selling," she said stiffly.

"Ever?"

"How should I know?"

"Well, if you think you're ever going to you should get rid of those behemoths and think about curb appeal. I could give you pointers. I worked for a landscaping company summers all through school."

"No, thank you."

"Suit yourself. So, why don't you want to check out if you're a princess?"

She glared at him. But since he was watching the highway, it had no effect. "You tried that before, remember?"

"Tried what?" he asked, all innocence.

"Criticizing my house then—"

"Just the outside."

"—segueing to that ridiculous—"

"Not according to the State Department."

"—speculation. It's so clearly not true. It's laughable."

He glanced at her. "Then check it out and put it behind you."

She crossed her arms. "I'm not going to discuss this with you."

"Okay. Though any normal person would want to know, so you trying to ignore it is really strange."

"There's your answer—I'm not normal and I am strange."

He grinned. "Way to turn it around on me, Katie. Okay, if you're not going to talk about what I want to hear about, you can listen to what I want to talk about."

"Which is?" she asked warily.

"How this recruiting class is shaping up. Get my tablet. I want you to check some stats for me. The benefit of having a passenger."

Clouds piled up behind them, but as they crossed the Chicago city line, the sky ahead was bright.

"Do you mind if we make a stop on the way in to downtown?" Brad asked.

"No."

"Thanks. It might take a while, but we've got plenty of time."

He must have counted on her saying yes because he was already exiting the Interstate and heading into neighborhood streets.

The snowpiles here were higher and grungier. But lines of small neat houses sat on small neat plots, mostly bungalows in red brick, beige brick or white frame. He drove with a confidence, even anticipation—slowing for a school zone before they reached it—that made her think he knew the area.

Could this side-trip be why he'd wanted to leave so early? She'd thought he probably had plans to meet someone. A female someone. The hotel had seemed more likely than this neighborhood—especially since he was bringing her along.

Still, this gave her the opportunity to say something she needed to say.

She licked her lips. "Brad, I want you to know, I don't expect you to entertain me. I can meet you at the games." He looked over at her and she quickly added, "We don't have to sit together, of course. I appreciate the ride, but I can find my own way—"

"Two of us going to the same place, but going separately? That doesn't make sense. Think of the budget."

She almost smiled. Instead, she looked down the side streets as they passed, seeing more rows of neat houses, some with snowmen standing guard. "Still, if you have plans. Things you want to do while you're in Chicago…" Women you want to see. "I'm perfectly happy to entertain myself and make my own way."

"I do have a few things I want to do in addition to work, but I was counting on you doing them with me." The side of his mouth she could see lifted. "Nothing wicked."*Darn it.* That thought, even in the privacy of her own mind, brought heat into her cheeks she knew from experience was accompanied by color.

He glanced at her, curiosity in his eyes, but he didn't ask. So she didn't have to lie.

"Besides," he said, "this side trip means we won't have time to do anything before the game except check in and get something to eat. So anything else will wait until tomorrow."

He turned left, cruised almost to the end of a long block and parallel parked with practiced precision.

With a hand under her elbow he guided her onto the porch of a neat frame house painted white.

He rang the doorbell. A head bobbed into view through the lowest of three rectangular windows high on the door and disappeared.

As the main door swung open, a mildly scolding voice came, "You said you were going to call."

"I was afraid you'd scoot out on me if you knew I was coming."

A robust laugh erupted from a short gray-haired woman no one would ever think to call a little old lady.

"Andy, this is Katie Davis, she's C.J.'s executive assistant and she runs the basketball office. Katie, this is my grandmother, Andrea Colecchi Spencer."

Brad's hand at the small of her back urged Katie forward at the same time the woman gripped her hand in something between a shake and a tug, drawing her inside.

"Ah, Katie," she said as if she'd had a suspicion confirmed. "Come in, come in before all the cold air in Chicago rushes in."

"Let me take your coat," Brad said. His attempt to follow through had them bumping and brushing in the small entry. "Andy, back up. You've got us hemmed in here and your grand entry hall would make most elevators seem spacious."

"Oh, dear, I am sorry. I had no intention…"

As she twisted out of her coat, Katie caught Brad regarding his grandmother with an arrested—and slightly wary—expression.

The older woman stepped back, the coats were removed and hung up and they stepped into a small living room. A mantel over a decorative fireplace glittered with a closely-packed assemblage of trophies, framed photos, and plaques.

"A few of Brad's awards," Andrea Spencer said with a would-be casual gesture.

"The shrine," Brad muttered behind her.

"Most are packed away, of course, since there's no room for even a significant portion of them."

He groaned.

"These come from his playing days at Ashton, just as he predicted. So he was right about going there. I was wrong. There. I said it. I was wrong."

"Once, according to you," he said with a grin, then added quickly, "How about some of your cake, Andy? I'm starving."

"If you came here only to eat me out of house and home, you can turn around and leave." The fond smile lighting her face belied the words. "You did enough of that as a teenager."

"Of course I did. Why else would I come?"

"Ignore him, Katie." The woman led them through a compact dining room to a pentagon-shaped space with open doors revealing a bedroom, a smaller room that appeared to be another shrine to Brad, an old-fashioned bathroom, and, finally, a kitchen to their right. "I do, however, happen to have a ring cake—"

"Vanilla with almonds and lots of icing?"

"—and I can offer you some tea."

"Milk," Brad said, opening the fridge. "As cold as you can make it."

"That sounds wonderful, Mrs. Spencer," Katie said.

"Please, call me Andy. All of Brad's friends do. Come through to the porch. There's still some sun. Can't miss any opportunity for sun during our winters."

She settled them at a small table centered on windows at the end of the addition. She and Katie sat beside the windows facing each other, with Brad pulling up a chair at right angles. His grandmother poured Brad's milk into a tall white pitcher and the tea steeped in a deep blue pot. The cake had pride of place on a raised dish in the center of the table.

Talk ranged from Andy's garden waiting for spring under the snow to Brad's youthful weeding assignments to the delicious cake to Brad's teenage appetite to the current season to Brad's playing days to the future prospects of this year's players to the accomplishments of Brad's teammates. Brad introduced the topics about current affairs, his grandmother segued to his past, then he would switch to a new discussion.

With a second wedge of cake on his plate, Brad reached for the milk pitcher. Under the table, Katie felt his leg shift. She'd kept her legs tucked back, but her caution did no good now as the side of his leg brushed against her knees.

"Sorry, Katie." With his right hand around the pitcher, he reached his left under the table and spanned her leg above her knee, holding it in place when she would have retracted it. "You have position. Call that foul on me."

"Foul?" His grandmother asked.

"Basketball talk," he said easily.

At some level Katie noted the older woman had known—she'd shown a thorough familiarity with basketball. But that level was way, way, way back. Most of her was occupied with sparks along her nerves *whooshing* to wildfire status under his touch.

"No, uh, no problem."

"There." He leaned back, pitcher in hand. His leg moved away. More slowly, he removed his hand. "All set."

"Have another slice," Andy urged her as Brad dug into his.

"It's delicious, but no thank you."

"Katie's got to save her appetite for the swank restaurant we're going to," he said.

His grandmother cocked her head. "The concession stand?"

"No." His mock indignation was perfect. "A burger joint near the school. Best burgers in the Chicago metro area."

"Bradford—" His grandmother's grin undermined her remonstration.

Katie said, "To know if it's the best, I'd have to test all the other burgers."

Apparently delighted, he said, "That's my plan. Got to admit it's good for the budget."

"But not the arteries."

As their chuckles faded, Andy said, "Brad, I need you to do something for me."

"Sure. What do you need?"

"Shoveling."

His eyes narrowed. "The service did the walk and it looked fine."

"They don't do the back."

"That's because you said you didn't need the back shoveled, refused to let me pay for it, and insisted it be removed from the contract."

"No need for it in the contract. But the walk to the garage needs to be shoveled today. You go on now. I'm going to pour Katie more tea and we're going to talk."

"You don't have anything in the garage. Not since you rented it to Ferdy down the street."

"Nevertheless, the walk needs to be shoveled."

The standoff lasted another fifteen seconds. "Fine. I'll shovel the walk." He retrieved his jacket, opened the back door a sliver, then turned to her. "Do not believe a word this woman says, Katie."

"Bradford, that is no way to talk about your grandmother. In addition, you are letting all the cold air in. Go."

He went.

CHAPTER SIX

Andy was smiling as she got up for the teapot. She poured, fussed a bit, then sat back down across from Katie.

"He's a good boy. He was going to shovel as soon as I asked him, but he has to have something to say. Does it the same with the garden come summer. Stakes the tomatoes, puts the mulch down so there's not much weeding. I raised a good boy. C.J. Draper coached a good man."

Katie blinked. She'd met Brad's mother and stepfather several times when they came by the office. So why did Brad's grandmother say *she* had raised a good boy?

"Brad was an unsteady student in high school, with excellent test scores but erratic grades."

"That's—"

She debated if her next words should be "none of my business" or the more neutral, yet dampening "interesting." Andrea Spencer talked right past her hesitation.

"His basketball performance was the same. He'd play brilliantly in close games or against superior teams. In easy games he was ... unpredictable. Still, colleges recruited him, hoping for the brilliance. He had decided to accept an offer from a large state school. I had concerns that such a large program might leave him too much to his own devices. But Brad was determined. Only as a favor to me did he postpone making the commitment.

"Then Coach Draper came to see me. Do you know about that first group of young men Coach Draper signed to scholarships at Ashton University?"

She did. It was basketball lore, especially at Ashton. A well-known coach had been hired to guide the team's move up to Division I. Then a bigger program hired him away. With no coach, no recruits, and a Division I schedule ahead, the school had gambled and hired untested C.J. Draper. He had recruited four unlikely players—three freshmen and a junior college transfer. They became the core of the team that reached the NCAA tournament's Elite Eight that first season, and even better in later seasons.

Brad's grandmother didn't wait for her response, however.

"Coach Draper had quite the uphill battle that first season. The top prospects had long signed with other schools. He needed to find players who had been overlooked. A friend of his knew Brad's high school coach. Coach Draper came to see him play. He talked with Brad, his coaches, his teachers, and then he came to see me. Other coaches who had recruited Brad had heaped praise on him. Coach Draper said Brad was a project he was willing to take on if I would commit to—as he put it—holding his feet to the fire on the home front. I was more than willing."

Andrea Spencer smiled, and her quirk of deviltry was so like Brad that Katie smiled back.

"Brad, however, was not."

Katie blinked. "He wasn't? He didn't want to go to Ashton?" She couldn't imagine Ashton without Brad.

"Not at all. He was set on that large school with a reputation as a party school."

"Then how...?" Andrea's smile was satisfied and wise without losing any of the deviltry. "I preyed on my grandson's overriding weakness for underdogs."

"Weakness for underdogs?"

"Oh, yes. From the time he was a toddler, he'd stand up for anybody being picked on, even if he didn't like them. If he brought home a puppy, it was the runt. Why do you think he kept Spencer as his last name? His mother was the underdog after the divorce. She'd returned to her maiden name, so he did, too. When she remarried and Phillip would have adopted Brad, he wouldn't hear of it, because the Spencer name was still the underdog. Not always tactful, our Brad. That was part of the trouble that led to his living here. Wasn't until Brad's sisters—half-sisters—started growing up and he saw what they put their father through that he connected with Phillip."

She leaned forward and said confidingly, "Sometimes the poor boy gets confused and thinks *I'm* an underdog he needs to champion." She sat back, satisfaction strong in her face. "Why do you think he's out shoveling a walk he knows I won't use. Yes, sometimes I use his weakness for underdogs—but only for his own good. Like about Ashton."

"What did you do?" Katie asked, mesmerized by the image of Brad being manipulated by his tiny grandmother. She probably should stop her from sharing personal details of Brad's life ... but she was only human.

"I told him Ashton and Coach Draper didn't have a chance. They'd be chewed up and spit out by Division I basketball. Any players who signed with the Aces were destined for abject failure. There was a moment there when I thought I'd laid it on too thick. But, no. Two days later, Brad announced—with great defiance—he was signing with Ashton. As you heard, I've let him go on thinking he was right and I was wrong." Andy cocked her head. "You don't approve?"

"Me? It's not my place to approve or disapprove, Mrs. Spencer."

"Ah, gave yourself away there, dear, calling me Mrs. But I don't regret it. Not for a minute. Coach Draper sat in that chair you occupy now and promised Brad would receive an education, in and out of the classroom, and he kept his promise. You know Brad was held out of four games his sophomore year because his grades were too low?" The woman sounded oddly proud. "That was the action of an honorable man, keeping his word, and that is when Brad truly began to become a man."

Katie happened to know Carolyn, then the team's academic advisor, had a share in that suspension, but no sense pointing that out. No time, either, because Andrea Spencer was going on.

"If my husband had lived longer, Brad would have learned that here at home. I did my best, but … Well, as I said, Brad got into some trouble. Caused tension at home, what with his mom and Phillip starting a second family. Brad was a champion of throwing gasoline on every fire. Sometimes he reminds me so much of his grandfather…"

Andy tapped the edge of her teacup decisively. "First time I met Ted Spencer, I tingled. Felt that way more often than not through our married life and that's saying something for fifty-six years together." She looked out the window. "Not that they can't make you crazy mad in a heartbeat. I suppose you know that about Brad."

"Oh, no. You misunderstood. We're colleagues, *professional* colleagues."

"Pretty girl like you shouldn't tell fibs." The older woman clicked her tongue, then sighed. "Professional. That's my one disappointment. Not that I don't respect a man like Coach Draper … But I had hoped Brad might become a lawyer, like his friend Ellis. Or a teacher like Frank—such a sweet boy. Or, even, like Thomas Abbott, a businessman."

"He does all those things as a coach," Katie said. "And he does them extremely well."

Andrea Spencer looked at her. "Does he?"

"Absolutely. He has to know the laws and rules to protect his players and the school. Coaches are advocates for their players, too. And then they have to turn around and be good businessmen, keeping an eye on the budget. Not to mention knowing business to deal with supporters and alumni. And of course they're teaching all the time. About the game, but also like you said about C.J., about being adults and living in the world."

"C.J. said you were a very sharp young lady."

"C.J.?"

"That recruiting trip was not the last time he sat in that chair. He often stops by when he's in Chicago. He speaks highly of you. Now I've met you, I see what he means. I have high hopes for you. Very high hopes."

There was something about the way Brad's grandmother said those words that unsettled her. The door opening left no time to consider it, however.

"The walk is shoveled, and I'm guessing the dirt's been dished, so give me another piece of that cake fast. We have a game to get to."

They registered, dropped their things at the hotel, stopped for burgers as promised, and were climbing the bleachers, looking for seats, as starting lineups were announced.

As they climbed over a gray-haired man who'd staked out the aisle seat and wasn't giving it up, two men about Brad's age greeted him by name from two rows up. Both looked at her curiously.

They were assistant coaches from two rival teams, and she'd met them when their teams played at Ashton. Clearly they didn't recognize her.

Brad had told her he was primarily here to connect with a senior forward who'd already committed to Ashton—a courtesy call. But it was also an opportunity to watch a hot young guard named Eric Bridge.

There'd be no contact with Bridge, since he was a sophomore. But it was good to let him see Ashton's interest, preparing for when they could communicate with him this summer.

Brad was making notes at halftime when Katie noticed the man on the aisle, who'd stood to stretch, look longingly toward the concession stand.

"We'll be happy to save your seat, sir," she offered, leaning around Brad. He accepted with thanks.

Almost before he'd vacated the seat, the two rival assistant coaches showed up.

"Spencer," said good-looking Heath Taub. "Not hard to guess why you're here."

Brad grinned. "Wouldn't think it would be hard for even you to guess, since I'm here to see our freshman-to-be, who also happens to be the player you most wanted to sign last go-around."

"Hah. On to greener pastures, now, Spencer. Don't try to tell me you're not drooling after Eric Bridge."

"Hi, Katie," said the other man, pleasant and solid. "Sorry I didn't recognize you right off. Guess it was seeing you out of context."

"Hi, Walt. Good to see you. How's your family?"

Heath snapped his fingers, "Katie—Coach Draper's Katie. I didn't recognize you. You look great, Katie." His voice dropped on the last sentence, as if it were private and sexy.

She stifled a chuckle. "Hi, Heath."

He reached past Brad to cup her shoulder and rub. People sitting beyond her didn't leave enough room for her to avoid the caress. Brad resolved the issue by batting away the arm stretched in front of him.

"I'll be sure to tell C.J. you were drooling over her," he said coldly.

The other man straightened, alarm in his face. Walt laughed. "Not even Taub's willing to risk the wrath of Coach Draper. And my family's fine, thanks for asking, Katie."

"Good. Your daughter's all over that flu?"

"Don't encourage him. Take pity on me, Katie. I've already heard all that family stuff." Heath Taub pretended to shudder. "What matters is you and me. How'd you like to go for a drink with me tonight?"

"No. Thank you."

"She's not going anywhere with you, Taub."

"Don't tell me I'm intruding on a budding relationship here." He said it with mock dismay, but avid eyes.

"No," Brad said. At the same time she said, "Not at all."

"Because I'd hate for you to have your heart broken, Katie. You know Spencer has quite the reputation. Yes, I see you do know. So come out with me after the game and I'll make sure you're armored with all the facts. And, who knows, we might find time for a few other things."

Brad made a sound low in his throat.

Heath smiled. "Talk only, of course. Unless…"

"It's moot," she said briskly, "since I already declined."

"You could change your—"

"She said no, Taub."

"Why're you sticking your oar in, Spencer? It's none of your business."

"I'm making it my business. I'm responsible for—"

She interrupted. "You are not. I'm responsible for myself. Thank you for the offer, Heath, but no thank you."

"Teams're coming back," Walt announced. His eyes met Katie's and glinted with laughter as he murmured, "Great halftime show."

As they headed to their seats, Heath's voice carried back to them, "Can you believe how much better she looks out of that ratty old sweater?" and Walt said drily, "You're thinking about getting her out of all her clothes."

"Damned right."

Her eyes met Brad's for an instant. He said, "He's right about the sweater, but I should still knock his block off. The worm."

"A good-looking worm," she said matter-of-factly.

His head snapped around. "You haven't fallen for his bull, have you? You're not taken in by his slick line of—"

"I can spot bull and slick lines." She acknowledged the return of the older man on the aisle with a smile and a small wave. She dropped her voice. "Though, in fairness, we weren't meant to hear."

"You never know with Taub," Brad said darkly. "He's got a reputation about women."

"So do you."

"I've dated some, sure. But—."

She chuckled, and it sounded good. "Some? How about the entire alphabet, from Audrey to Zaria."

"Not true. And I have never—I don't—This is serious, Katie, you've got to know, he's got a bad record with nice, innocent girls."

"Brad. For heaven's sake." Her half chuckle didn't mask her annoyance. "I'm a grown-up. I hope I'm nice, but *innocent girl?*"

"You might think you—"

The crowd roared around them, coming to their feet.

Brad cursed under his breath. "Totally missed it."

"You'll see on the film that Eric Bridge drove the lane, looked like he was going for the shot, no-look passed to the center, who put it in easy."

He kept his eyes on her for several breaths. "Thanks." Then turned his attention to the court.

CHAPTER SEVEN

At the end of the game, Brad went to talk to the home team's coach.

Katie stood by the bleachers, watching the warmth of the men's exchange.

"Excuse me, you're with Coach Spencer from Ashton, aren't you?"

She turned to see a dark-skinned woman dressed in the home team's colors of green and white. "Yes, I work in the basketball office with Coach Spencer. I'm Katie Davis." She extended her hand.

The other woman met it. "I'm Gwen Stasek, Coach Stasek's wife."

"Oh." Katie released her hand. "I don't know if we can talk—"

"It's fine," Heath Taub said, sliding in with a broad smile. "Even if she were Eric Bridge's mother, you could exchange a civil greeting."

The woman nodded in reassuring confirmation. "You're fine with coaches, it's the prospective recruits and their parents you have to be careful about."

"I'm mostly in the office, so I'm not as familiar with off-site rules. I don't want to make any mistakes."

"That does you credit for—"

"Speaking of Eric Bridge's parents," Heath interrupted, "they got a chance to see their son have quite a game tonight. Love to see parents' proud faces after a game like that. They were here, right, Gwen?"

"I'm not pointing them out to you, Heath."

Katie chuckled at the woman's bluntness and Heath's deflation. She assumed her most innocent voice, "I'd point them out to you, Heath, but I don't want you to be tempted to arrange a way to introduce yourself and get in trouble."

"You know the fam—You mean you've met—." His mouth was

having trouble completing sentences while his brain processed the implications. High schoolers were allowed to visit college campuses at their own expense, and could have contact with the coaching staff and other personnel then. So Katie could have met the Bridges that way—which would mean Eric Bridge was very interested in Ashton. Heath's face fell.

Katie patted his arm, "We'll talk about something else, since this seems to be upsetting you."

"No, no, not at all." His smile was broad, and fooled no one. "But I better go say hello to Coach S now."

Brad had left Coach Stasek only to be stopped by a coach from the opposing team. Katie saw Brad give Heath an assessing look as he passed, then his gaze came to her.

She turned back to the coach's wife, chatting about the team's season and prospects.

When Brad arrived, he gave the other woman a quick hug. "Gwen." Then he frowned at her. "Was Taub bothering you?"

"Bothering me? Not at all."

If he took that to mean she didn't find the man's attentions bothersome, it served him right. He was treating her like a naïve nitwit.

"If anyone was bothered it was Heath." Gwen chuckled. "Katie led him around by the nose. Especially since I happen to know Eric Bridge and his parents haven't visited Ashton—yet. So, tell me, *would* you recognize Eric's parents, Katie?"

"Oh, yes. I do pre-scouting background for C.J. That was Eric's maternal grandfather sitting on the aisle, the man we climbed over."

Gwen laughed. "Surprised, aren't you, Brad? She was way ahead of you there."

"She often is. We better get going. See you later, Gwen."

Brad guided Katie through the thinning crowd with a hand at her back.

A polite gesture. That's all.

"Your conversation must have gone well," Katie said when they reached the parking lot. She expanded the distance between them. Not drastically. Just enough that his hand dropped from her back.

"Why?"

"You're in a better mood."

He cut her a look, but no, even in the raw outdoor lighting it was clear she really thought that was why his mood had improved since halftime. "It went well. Good to see Brent—the forward—"

"I know."

"—and always like to catch up with Coach Stasek. But not all the game-playing's on the court. From what Gwen said, you did well with Taub."

She made a dismissive sound—saying the other coach wasn't much to handle, so little credit came with handling him. He felt a little tick at the back of his head, as if someone had flicked their fingers there the way an early teacher had when he wasn't paying attention.

But then Katie started talking, and he shifted focus.

"Sometimes I forget how good you are until I see other coaches in action." She quickly added, "I mean all of you, all of C.J.'s assistants."

"On behalf of all of us, I say thank you." He let her precede him between two parked cars, heading for his in the next aisle.

"Of course, you're a natural at this. Probably planned to coach from the time you could walk."

"Me? No way. I planned to be a rock star. Can't sing. Can't play an instrument. Think drugs are stupid. But other than that it was the perfect job for me. Did you know there's no major in being a rock star at Ashton? So I needed a fall-back career. But I was a real dark horse for becoming a coach. C.J. always thought Ellis should be the coach," he said of one of his teammates. "Not me."

"No." For a second he thought she'd stopped short with shock. Nope. They'd reached the car, but she *was* surprised. "Well, he has to know better now."

He beeped the car door open then held it. "Does he? Ellis Manfred would have been an amazing coach. He'd be an amazing whatever he wanted to be. Me? I had only one thing. Only one thing I could do."

"Only one thing you wanted to do."

"Maybe…. Probably."

"And that's why it's the one thing you should do."

"Now you sound like Andy." He tried to make it sound irked, but she clearly heard the solid base of amusement.

Yet she frowned. "Your grandmother didn't object to your coaching?"

"Object? She was all for it."

"But…"

"But what?"

"Nothing."

He closed her door and went to the driver's side. "Going to tell me about that but?"

"Does your grandmother get confused sometimes?"

"Confused?" He laughed. "No way. Devious, yes. Why? Did she say something—"

She interrupted. "Your grandmother is sweet. How can you call her devious?"

He narrowed his eyes at her. "You didn't catch it?"

"Catch what?"

"All of it. Starting from when we walked in." He joined the stream of departing vehicles.

"When we walked in? She welcomed me and told you to take my coat."

"And blocked us so we were jammed into the corner."

She chuckled, then glanced at him and stopped. "Why would she?"

"To see how we reacted. Like two bugs pinned under her microscope," he said. "Doesn't stop me from loving her. But loving her doesn't stop me from seeing it, either. She definitely wanted to see how we reacted."

"To what?"

"To each other." He had to look her direction as they turned into the busy street. That was convenient.

"Oh. But…" She swallowed, then resumed, "Of course she's curious how you get along with coworkers."

"Yeah, right. Like Heath and Walt were interested in coworking with you."

"Not Walt. He's married."

He snapped his head around. "Aha! So you did know Heath was coming on to you."

"No."

"No you didn't know? Or no he wasn't coming on to you?"

"Both?" Although she clearly tried to suppress it, a small smile tugged at her mouth.

He looked over at her. Longer than he probably should have in this traffic.

He turned back to the road. "I've got somewhere to stop right after the game Sunday if you don't mind. Could delay us getting back to Ashton. Hope you don't mind."

He'd told C.J. and Carolyn he wouldn't commit to the idea until Sunday. But now he had. "No, I don't mind. Getting back later's not a problem." She said it lightly, trusting.

This might be the last time she trusted him.

CHAPTER EIGHT

Saturday was basketball from waking to sleeping.

She and Brad left the hotel early to catch the first game in a high school tournament north of the city then drove back to connect with the team. They reached the hotel as the team was finishing the late lunch/early dinner that served as their pre-game meal.

C.J. gestured for them to sit next to him, but Brad immediately got called over by three players.

"Did you see the salad servers in the gift shop, Katie? They're the right color, but I don't know if Carolyn would like them." C.J. frequently bought his wife odd items, all in the same color brown.

"Haven't been in the gift shop. Did you get my email this morning about the Europe trip?" Katie asked her boss as she sat.

"Yeah. Didn't you get my answer?"

"An answer of 'okay' doesn't tell me if you caught all the nuances."

He grinned. "Is that why you CC'd Maura? So she'd ask me about it while the team was loading up?"

"Precisely."

"And she emailed you before the bus left the parking lot in Ashton, so you already know everything you need to know, which is why I emailed 'okay.' "

"Sometimes I think we're enabling your bad habits."

"That's what staff is for," he said triumphantly. "Which reminds me, the travel department sent me something about not having a passport."

"I'll take care of it."

"Is this something I need to worry about?"

"No."

"Okay. So, how's the trip been so far?"

"Very interesting."

"Details."

"This from the man who doesn't have time for anything but basketball, especially on game day?"

"It's you and Brad. You telling me it's not about basketball?"

After that, it seemed smarter to give him the requested rundown, though she skimmed over certain elements and emphasized basketball.

And what was the first thing he said after she finished? "So Brad took you to meet Andy."

She'd said absolutely nothing about that side trip. If C.J. Draper weren't such a good boss, he'd be downright annoying. "He stopped to see his grandmother on the way and I happened to be in the car with him."

"You know she and her husband took him in when he was in middle school?"

"I, uh, gathered there was something. But since it's none of my business—"

"You've seen how he gets along with his mom and step-dad, so it's okay now. But it was pretty rocky when he was younger. *He* was pretty rocky. His dad was out of the scene early. Then his mom remarried when Brad was a kid. And they started having babies.

"His step-dad's a nice guy, but kids don't always appreciate nice. Especially not at that age. When Brad hit the age to rebel, there was his stepfather, along with half-siblings ready-made as a magnet for his discontent. He was heading down a bad road. His grandparents agreed to take him on. That was the first step."

"Andy credits you for the rest."

"Me? No way. That was Coach Brezyinski. His high school coach. Tough old Marine who took Brad by the scruff of the neck after his grandfather died, shook him good, then set him back down on his feet." He shook his head. "Coach B scared the bejeebers out of me. He told me I was going to offer Brad a scholarship, and that was that."

"That's not what Andy said."

"She's got her story and I've got mine. Besides, Carolyn was the force to be reckoned with for Brad when he got to Ashton. She always said he could do whatever he wanted when he set his mind to it, and she decided he was going to set his mind to a lot."

"Even if he had to be suspended a few games."

He grinned lopsidedly. "Yep. And wasn't that some kind of fun? Wouldn't want to go through those weeks again. But it did him a world of good."

They sat in silence a moment—as silent as a room could get with the team no longer occupied with eating. She was too absorbed in considering what he'd told her to wonder what he was thinking ... until he turned to face her.

"So, with all this talk of Brad's history I forgot what I started out wanting to know. How're you doing, Katie? What with getting out of the office, out of your comfort zone. You tend to resist that."

Why did she have the uneasy feeling he was shifting the context from this trip to something broader. "I'm capable of expanding my comfort zone. For something I want to pursue."

"As long as nobody sees you doing it," Brad murmured from behind her.

She jumped, shot C.J. a look, wondering if he knew how long Brad had been there.

"It's like you're allergic to being noticed," Brad added as he took his chair.

Her mother's hand tugging her back, keeping to shadows. No notice. Draw no notice.

"I don't want to be noticed." She regretted the words immediately.

"Why?" C.J. demanded.

"Doesn't mean you shouldn't be," Brad said before she could answer C.J. without truly answering

"Not everyone's like—" She stopped, waving her hand, wiping away the words.

Instead of accepting her implicit request that her words be ignored,

Brad said, "Not everyone's like me?"

"I didn't mean—"

"Sure you did. But that's okay. Sometimes not being noticed back-fires."

"Because I won't get promotions?" she said dryly. "I've had offers. I'm happy with things the way they are."

"Are you?" His voice sounded peculiar.

Before she could examine that, C.J. muttered, "You're a fine one to talk, Spencer."

"Not the same thing at all. I'm talking about someone who hides out as Cinderella, then suddenly shows up in all her glory for the ball and doesn't realize it can give the wrong kind of guys the wrong kind of ideas."

"Now, that sounds interesting," C.J. said.

"There was nothing—"

"I'll tell you about it later, Coach, when she can't claim she was blind to a bunch of hounds drooling over her."

"It wasn't a bunch—"

"Hah! So you admit there was drooling going on."

"I don't admit anything. You're being—Where are you going, C.J.?"

"Gotta call Carolyn. Got a question to ask her."

He asked about the kids first, as always. They were fine.

"How'd you like a set of wooden salad servers from the gift shop, Carolyn?"

"You didn't call to ask about wooden salad servers. Why are you distracted, C.J.?"

"I'm not distracted."

"You're calling me *before* a game."

He conceded the point by dropping it. "I, uh, I had the strangest notion today."

"Oh?"

"Yeah. Sitting with Katie talking. And Brad came up."

"Yes."

"Yes, what? Yes, as in yes you heard me and want to know what comes next? Or yes as in confirming what I was thinking but hadn't said yet so you had to be reading my mind again?"

"The latter." Only then did she chuckle a little.

"That's a hell of a complication, isn't it? I mean if she is, you know, what Hunter Pierce thinks she is, what the hell happens then?"

"I suppose that's up to them."

They ate Sunday breakfast with the team—happy after last night's last-second victory in a game they hadn't been expected to win. The team boarded the bus for the return to Ashton, while Katie and Brad headed to the early matinee game of a junior college tournament.

She read stats to Brad as he drove.

"That's the last one," she concluded.

"There's no reason you shouldn't want to be noticed more, Katie."

She should have made up players to keep him from switching to this topic. "Not again—"

But she was too late. He was already going on. "Want to know the first time I noticed you?"

"No."

"I mean really noticed you. Of course I'd noticed you the way any man notices the new girl in his environment the day you started, but—"

"I was not a girl. I was "

"Girl." His firmness overrode any argument. "With that sweater you always wore."

"It gets cold in the office."

"The gray shroud. You might as well add some fruit or birds and it'd be what a grandmother—"

"*Grandmother?*" Though to tell the truth, she'd heard that before.

"—would wear. Not *my* grandmother. But some grandmothers. Though Andy might be hurt to hear your tone of outrage at being likened to her."

She glared. He returned it with an expression of blue-eyed, guile-less innocence. Lying with a look. The man was a bald-faced look-liar.

"Anyway," he said evenly, "what we were discussing before you derailed my train of thought was when I first noticed you."

Dignified silence might be her best option.

"It was a couple months after you started in the basketball office. You'd smoothed out that mess with the travel office, and we already knew we couldn't function without you. And—"

He made a turn, and she hoped they were getting close to the tournament site.

"—I saw you out walking on campus. On the paths."

"I'm on campus a lot. Especially then, since I was taking classes."

Another turn, this time into a crowded parking lot.

He nodded, cruising aisles for a spot. "So now you're wondering what about you being on the campus paths made you so noticeable, right? Has you worried, huh? Well, I won't keep you in suspense. It was how much you didn't want to be noticed. Stood out like a neon sign in the middle of a park. There were all these other students and staff and faculty streaming along, each one perfectly willing to be noticed and some of them doing their damnedest to grab attention." He pulled into a space. "And then there was Katie Davis, working so hard to not be noticed that she barely let herself even be *on* the paths. I think if you could have melted into the grass you would have."

She felt the strangest urge to laugh. *Don't draw attention.* Her parents had drilled that into her … And perversely it drew the attention of Brad Spencer.

She closed her purse, unhooked her seat belt. "Fine. I'm an oddity. I thought we'd settled that the other day."

He turned off the car and shifted toward her. "Not an oddity, Katie. A mystery."

She looked up. Into the lose-your-soul-and-your-mind blue of his eyes.

"I'm not a mystery."

"You are to me."

CHAPTER NINE

His concentration on basketball gave her a break during the game, but she braced for a renewed—what? Assault? Attack? Inquisition?

Instead, he was silent and frowning as they walked to the car while most people remained in the gym for the next game.

As they reached the main road, he sounded stiff when he said, "I've got that other stop to make now. Sorry."

"I remember. It's no problem."

"You'll like these people." But he didn't sound happy about it.

And he didn't look happy as they walked up to the front door of a handsome, inviting house in Evanston, the first suburb north of Chicago. He rang the bell.

Voices—children's and adults'—and a dog's bark preceded the door swinging wide to show a man smiling broadly. "Come in, come in. Quick, before the hordes get you." He waved them in as the other arm extended back as if to hold off two kids and a fuzzy dog of indeterminate parentage. The kids and dog ducked under the restraining arm with ease, staring up at them with friendly interest.

"Good to see you again, Brad. And you must be Katie. I'm Paul Monroe. And these two bandits—" He scooped up a child in each arm, setting off waves of giggles. "—are all my fault. Nick and Cassie," he added, hitching first one then the other higher by way of introduction. "Say hello to Katie and Brad."

They did, as the man instructed Brad to hang his own and Katie's coats on a line of pegs by the door.

As they reached a stairway, Paul Monroe set the two kids down on the second step and said, "Upstairs now, and no pestering Anne

Elizabeth, the both of you."

"But Da-ad—" Tried the girl, the younger one.

"We talked about this. Now go."

The boy said glumly, "We might as well go, he'll get Mom if we don't."

They trudged upstairs.

"As you can see, I'm a fearsome disciplinarian," Paul said deadpan. "C'mon back and meet everybody, Katie. This is my wife, Bette."

A woman with the same dark hair and blue eyes as the little girl met them where the hallway opened to a large room. Even before entering, Katie saw a fireplace, comfortable groupings of seating with a number of chairs perfect for curling up in. "Welcome, Katie. We're so glad you could come. These are our good friends, Leslie and Grady Roberts. And Tris and Michael Dickinson over there putting toys away."

Both couples had smiles as warm as the Monroes', though Katie felt a layer of discomfort edged in. Was she picking up a bit of discomfort on their parts? But why?

She glanced over her shoulder toward Brad, who was exchanging low words with Paul. He didn't meet her gaze.

"And this," Leslie Roberts said, holding onto Katie's hand after they shook and using that hold to draw her deeper into the room, "is my cousin, April Gareaux."

Katie stopped.

Stopped moving. Stopped breathing. Stopped thinking.

Stopped everything but staring at the young woman who had been in the news so much at the beginning of the year. The young woman so many people had said she resembled. The young woman in the magazine she'd looked at so many times.

"We're here shamelessly throwing ourselves on Bette's organizing skill to pull together our wedding," April said with a warm smile. "I'm so glad it's also giving me this opportunity to meet you."

Katie looked into her mind searching for a reaction and it was an utter blank except for one fact. Brad had brought her here. To a house where April Gareaux was. *Brad.*

Movement caught her attention, finally breaking her immobility to focus on it. Now she was staring at the man who'd come to stand behind April, one arm going around her.

"Hello, Katie," said Hunter Pierce of the State Department's Security Service. "It's good to see you again."

Hunter Pierce. April Gareaux. … *Oh, God.*

She turned away, half stumbled, found Brad's arms around her. "Katie. Listen, please—" She tried to escape from his hold, and almost went down completely.

"Sit here," Bette said, a hand on her shoulder as she guided Katie to an easy chair. Other voices were saying things, lots of things, all trying to sound reassuring, soothing, persuasive, she was sure. It took several moments for the sounds to begin to sort out to words spoken by individuals.

"We just want to talk to you," Grady Roberts said.

"That's not entirely true."

Katie's head came up at those words, and she met Leslie Roberts' gaze. "We don't just want to talk to you. We want you to listen. And afterward, we want you to agree with us that you should meet King Jozef."

Katie was aware of someone—she thought it was Tris Dickinson—muttering, "Way to ease into it."

But she appreciated Leslie Robert's honesty. It gave her an anchor. "No. I told him—*Him.*" She specified Hunter Pierce. "I'm not the right person."

"Katie." Brad was there, crouched in front of her. "This isn't going to go away. And—"

"C.J. and Carolyn?"

"It's my doing. If you're pissed at somebody, be pissed at me."

"But they know. That's why they pushed this trip. That's why … this whole weekend."

He was going to lie. She saw that. And then he didn't. "Yes. They know." He took both her hands in his and she was so numb she couldn't feel it. "Katie, you have to deal with this. One way or the other, it isn't going away. Face it and—"

"I don't—"

"We want you to meet King Jozef tonight."

Katie's head jerked up to April Gareaux, standing behind where Brad crouched beside her chair.

Brad's voice pulled her back. "I told you all no, not unless Katie agrees. You're not going to spring a king on her."

Spring a king. She almost laughed. Was that a sign of hysteria?

"And we agreed he would not be here," Hunter said. "To start."

April was directly in front of her now. It was almost like looking in a mirror. Except a mirror that knew how to do things with makeup and hair that were far beyond her.

"Katie, will you talk with me alone for a while? You won't feel as pressured, as you must now with so many of us and just you and Brad. If it's only you and me, then it's even, right? We'll leave the rest of them here and go into Paul's office and we can—"

"Not Paul's office," Bette said firmly. "You'll both have nightmares. Use mine."

There was a sputter of knowing laughter from several directions that broke the tension.

Katie glanced toward Brad. His blue eyes were intense and focused on her. None of the laughter had come from him. How odd. He'd been the one to spring this on her ... *spring a king* ... so she should feel betrayed. Yet his presence, his look gave her the security to say, "Okay."

In the office, they simultaneously slewed around on the love seat to face each other. It made her think of mirrors again. Only the mirror didn't play by the rules, because it arbitrarily changed just enough that it wasn't like looking in a mirror.

April's mouth quirked. "Weird, isn't it?"

Katie wondered if she and April sounded as much alike as they looked alike. They said you didn't know the sound of your own voice. She'd have to record her voice, listen to it, then listen to April's—oh, God, why was she focusing on this?

"Very. But you're so much prettier—"

The other woman snorted. "I am not. You have much better features than I do." She tipped her head. "I learned a lot about clothes and hair and makeup after Hunter asked me to…"

The way April said his name, Katie knew that was some of the difference between them. The other woman loved and was loved. Yes, that was a major difference.

April huffed out a breath. "The best way to do this is to start at the beginning and tell you about it. Hunter showed up at my office back in November and asked me to pretend to be a princess…"

The door Brad had been watching for nearly an hour, ignoring all attempts to draw him into conversation, finally opened, and then he wished it would have stayed closed.

Hunter dropped a hand on his shoulder. Reassuring? Or to be sure he didn't jump up, grab Katie, and run out the way he wanted to?

April gave Hunter a look that communicated … something, but what?

Then she looked around the room, taking everyone in, before focusing on him as she said, "After Katie and I discussed all this, or some of it, anyway…" She stopped, pulled in a breath than started again. "What it comes down to is I've called King Jozef. He should be here in twenty minutes."

"I agreed to meet you to say to you directly that I am very sorry for your loss—all your losses—but I am not your granddaughter." Belatedly, Katie remembered to add, "Your Majesty."

King Jozef of Bariavak had arrived moments ago.

He was medium height, straight-backed, with a precisely trimmed beard, and strong features. In an effort to not stare at him, she made herself notice the genuine warmth in the others' greetings to him.

The only jarring note had been Hunter frowning, and saying something low to a young American who'd entered with the king. The younger man answered, "I barely got him to let *me* come."

Bette had directed King Jozef to a seat near where Katie stood.

He'd sat at the other end of the small couch and gestured for all of them to sit.

Katie had remained standing to deliver her statement, not a trace of tremor in her voice.

"Please sit, my dear," the king said in response.

She hesitated. Now that she'd seen him, now that she'd said what she wanted to say—needed to say—what was the point in staying? She looked toward Brad.

He came to her, put a hand on her shoulder. As soon as she felt that touch, her knees gave way and she sat, with more emphasis than grace.

Without moving or making a sound, the king drew her gaze to him. "Thank you for your courtesy and bravery in agreeing to see me and to speak with me when you preferred not to. What has brought you to the conclusion you have reached that a possible connection between us is not worthy of exploration?"

How about the fact that there is nothing royal about me.

Look at the delicate way he had worded his question. She wouldn't have the first clue how to verbally glide so readily among the land mines.

"The knowledge that I am the daughter of a pair of immigrants of modest means," she said bluntly.

He arched one brow. His eyes were bright and shrewd. He didn't stare at her, yet she felt he saw everything. "That is the cover story that was created. The role they played. We have done extensive research—"

"I am their daughter. Katie Davis of Ashton, Wisconsin. That's who I am."

He ignored her interruption—she'd interrupted a *king* for heaven's sake—with supreme calm. "The research shows numerous tears and gaps in the fabric of the lives they fabricated. I believe Hunter has provided you with information pertaining to a few. There are more. We can go over those—"

"No." Great. She'd interrupted a king for the second time in a row. "The gaps don't matter. I know who I am and who I'm not."

"How could you know what might have happened when you were a baby?" April asked, as she had while they were alone.

It was a good point. Katie admitted that. But she said doggedly, "I *know*. Besides, there's the *fact* that I'm younger than the princess. I'm twenty-seven. She would be twenty-eight, like April."

"Birth certificate's not valid," said Michael Dickinson.

It was the first thing he'd said since their introduction.

"That doesn't mean…" Under his steady look she dropped her gaze to her hand resting on the couch cushion beside her. "You can't be sure."

"It's still being looked at, but it looks that way," Hunter said.

"It's not a certain the information on the certificate is false. But it can't be certain it's true, either." Michael's voice was unemotional and steady. "So you can't know how old you are. Not precisely. No one can. We rely on certificates." His pause added weight to the next words. "And what our families tell us."

Hunter picked up, "The move to Wisconsin would have made it easy to shave a year off your age. Taking you away from people who might otherwise have questioned your age, and plunking you down among people who could come to your third birthday party not knowing you'd already had your third birthday party the year before."

You're wrong. I never had any birthday parties, much less one twice. She kept her mouth shut.

"It doesn't mean you are the princess," Hunter added. "But it adds another piece to it being possible. Possibility or impossibility are all we can assess until—unless we test for DNA. Even then … well, testing to confirm maternal grandfather is difficult."

A jolt ran through her.

It was the same jolt as in the basketball office conference room, when he had brought up DNA testing. A swab from the inside of her check…

Maternal grandfather. A relative. A connection. A family.

"Why's maternal grandfather difficult?" Paul Monroe asked.

"Mitochondrial DNA and Y chromosome links are strong. But with a maternal grandfather there's neither the Y chromosome of the paternal line nor the mitochondrial DNA of the maternal line."

"Okay, I get why there's no Y chromosome involved, since neither the daughter nor granddaughter would have one. But what about the mitochondrial DNA, Hunter?"

"Mitochondrial DNA comes only from the mother. A man inherits mtDNA from his mother, but can't pass any of that on to his kids. So a maternal grandmother and a grandchild—male or female—*would* show the connection in the mitochondrial DNA. But not a maternal grandfather and his grandchild."

"So you're looking for something with DNA from King Jozef's wife or daughter?"

"After this length of time, it would mean—" Hunter's gaze flicked to the king. "—invasive measures. It would be a last resort."

Katie looked from Hunter to the king.

Disinterment. "To go through that when I know it's impossible. No," she said.

Hunter sidestepped "With advanced testing, they can look for stretches of identical DNA shared by potential relatives."

"I thought we all have a lot of the same DNA, with a small percentage of differences," Paul said.

"A small percent can still mean a whole lot of genes. Plus, as I said, they're looking for stretches of identical DNA that unrelated people wouldn't share. If the top experts say the results show a family connection, you can rely on it."

"It is the way to know with the greatest certainty available," King Jozef said in a tone that said the discussion was done for now.

The force of his will slowly drew Katie's gaze to him.

When their eyes met, he reached out a hand and covered hers where it rested on the cushion between them. "However, it would be certainty for you, alone. For me—"

She tried to move her hand. She couldn't. It wasn't that he held it. She simply couldn't move her hand. She couldn't look away, either.

"—I know. You are my granddaughter, Princess Josephine-Augusta Katrina Mariana Sofia of Bariavak."

CHAPTER TEN

At that name, she pulled her hand back. "You can't possibly know."

"Looking at you, listening to you, seeing you move. I know."

She opened her mouth to refute his certainty, not knowing what words she'd use. She was spared using any.

"Why not let the DNA testing do what it's supposed to do?" April asked reasonably.

"I couldn't possibly until after the third week of May," Katie said quickly.

Hunter's voice slid through murmurs of surprise. "The test takes hardly any time at all. A swab of inside your cheek—"

"I couldn't *decide* anything until after the third week of May."

They stared at her. All except Brad. "Katie, you know C.J. would understand and want you to—"

"I am not going to let this interfere with my job."

"You're not going to let finding out if you're a princess interfere with your job?" Grady repeated. He sounded more interested than disapproving.

"Why the third week of May?" Paul's eyes glinted with interest. "Basketball season ends in early April, and with Ashton having a rebuilding season, it's not likely to be playing in the Final Four. No offense, Brad."

"We could surprise people. But what Katie's talking about is when recruits can sign the National Letter of Intent."

"What is this? Recruits? National Letter of Intent?" King Jozef demanded.

"It's about college basketball, sir," Hunter said. "When high school players commit to which college they will attend."

"And it's important to the team's future," Katie added firmly. "Not to mention that Brad—and C.J., of course, and the others, have been working all year to find the right players for our program and then persuade them Ashton's academics and athletics and campus life can't be beat. It's a vital time for the program, and I need to have all my attention on my job. No distractions."

"Distractions," Paul murmured.

From the corner of her eye, Katie caught his wife nudging him, even as they joined everyone else in looking toward King Jozef. She hesitated, but only for a moment, then she faced him, too.

He appeared to be contemplating the heavy ring on his right hand. His expression gave nothing away.

"We shall expect your answer after the third week of May. However, we shall continue inquiries. In addition we shall pursue opportunities to develop our, ah, connection."

"If you show up in Ashton or if you're seen with Katie, the media will be all over it," Brad objected.

Hunter nodded agreement.

The king frowned.

"And I'm going to be very busy with work," Katie added.

"Nevertheless," he responded.

Which, she had to admit, was a good response. It held his position, yet gave nobody anything to argue with.

The room remained silent after Katie and Brad left. When Bette and Paul returned from escorting them to the front door, King Jozef watched Bette exchange glances with Tris and Leslie. Leslie then looked at April, turned back to Bette and gave a tiny nod.

"Tris and Michael, would you mind gathering up the plates and bringing them into the kitchen and help Paul and me clean up," Bette said.

Michael and Tris rose immediately. Paul got out one "But," then his wife steered him toward the kitchen, with Tris and Michael following with dishes.

"These women should be in the diplomatic corps. Or in espionage," King Jozef said with dark humor. It was gone when he said to Hunter, "We require the strictest security for her. At all times."

"Security would draw attention to her. That's why we agreed the approach could not be direct, why I first talked to her at the basketball office, why we asked Brad Spencer to help, why we are here, not at your hotel. Her best security is that her possible connection to you is not known."

"*Possible!* Pah. She is my granddaughter. The Princess Josephine-Augusta of Bariavak."

"She says otherwise, sir."

"Give her time." April spoke to him as she laid a hand on Hunter's arm. "See it from her view. You are telling her everything she's been told all her life is a lie. Everything she's been all her life is a lie. That's a lot to absorb."

Leslie Craig Roberts did not mince words. "Time might not be enough. In asking her to believe she is who you say she is, you're also demanding Katie accept that the people who raised her are not who she—"

"*Them.* Those people are the filth who caused my daughter's death when they stole her baby, who killed outright my son-in-law as well as Hunter's father and many more. The filth who—."

"Raised Katie Davis in Ashton, Wisconsin as their own." Leslie's calm voice as much as her words brought him up short. "Sent her off to school in the morning with a bag lunch, and gave her a snack and a desk to do her homework when she came home. Yes, *home*, sir. To accept your account of events—even to submit to the DNA test— requires that she considers they might, indeed, be the filth you claim. That's a difficult hurdle."

"My mother was irresponsible and selfish, and it took me a long time to reconcile the opposing emotions I had about her," April added.

The king was aware of Grady taking Leslie's hand, of both of them looking on the young woman they'd helped raise with a combination of protectiveness and pride. He had come to feel the same things about her.

April leaned forward, meeting his gaze and holding it. "I can't imagine how difficult it would be to grapple with the idea that the people who raised you not only weren't your parents, but had purposefully caused you such harm. If you want to have a future with Katie, you must let her reconcile the past."

"Are you okay?" Brad asked, the first words spoken in the half hour since they'd left the Monroes' house in Evanston.

"Yes." She continued staring out the passenger window, knowing they were passing restaurants, shops, houses, and other buildings of a busy metro area, but reducing them all to blurs before unfocused eyes.

"Are we okay?" His voice was deeper, rougher. "Are you going to hold this against me forever?"

"Possibly."

"Don't blame C.J. or Carolyn. I made the decision. If I hadn't thought it was necessary for your—"

"My own good?"

"I was going to say for your being able to move ahead."

She said nothing.

He cleared his throat and when he spoke she could imagine a faint glint of amusement in his eyes. "You know most people would think you're crazy. A quick test to check the DNA. If it says no, it all goes away. But if the DNA proves you're his granddaughter—"

"I'm not."

"How can you be so sure?"

She turned to him. "How can you be so sure you're Brad Spencer?"

"I don't have someone telling me I might be—hell, that they're *sure* I am—the King of Siam."

"Siam doesn't have a king. It's not even Siam anymore."

"Katie—"

"So you think I'm crazy?" she demanded belligerently.

He shot her a look, but said, "No. I just wonder why you're so adamant you won't take this test."

She shifted in her seat. "I'm tired. I'm going to take a nap."

Pretending to nap was exhausting. She finally pretended to be awakened, and sat up in the passenger seat.

Then regretted it when he immediately said, "You're awfully positive you're not this princess, but how could you possibly know for sure, Katie? You only have what your parents told you. Maybe you don't want to challenge those family stories. I know they can mean a lot. But DNA would—"

"There were no family stories."

"Your folks didn't talk about how they grew up or about moving to the U.S. or when they met or why they decided to come here or their families?" She shook her head at each. He didn't give up. "C'mon, everybody has family stories. What you were like as a baby. When you started walking and talking. Your first words. How you tried to trade your sister for a basketball."

She stopped mid-head-shake and looked at him. "You tried to trade your sister for a basketball?"

He shrugged. "I was twelve. I had a lot more use for a basketball than a baby sister."

She smiled, because how could she not? But it faded quickly. "No stories about any of those things. It wasn't that kind of household."

"What kind was it?"

She looked away from the softness in his voice, in his eyes. "I wasn't abused, if that's what you're thinking."

"That's good to know." Then, shifting to an easier tone, he added, "You once told me something about your parents."

No she hadn't. She couldn't have. She didn't talk about her parents or have pictures of them. That should prove she was their daughter—

she was just like them.

Her silence didn't deter Brad. He said, "You told me neither one could raise one eyebrow."

She turned to look at him. Not just her head but as much of her as could shift under the seat belt's constraint.

"Are you nuts? Those people were talking about me being a long-lost *princess* and—"

"Heir to the throne of Bariavak."

"—you're talking about my parents not being able to raise one eyebrow without the other rising, too?"

"Yup."

"Why on earth would you—?"

"Because you can raise one by itself. And so could King Jozef of Bariavak." He turned his head. Their eyes met.

"Left eyebrow for both of you, too," Brad said.

CHAPTER ELEVEN

Brad turned into her street. From here, the house was a dark void, the trees absorbing what light was emitted by the small fixture near the front door.

Yours is curb repel.

The trees had been there as long as she could remember. Her mother once said her father chose the house because of them.

But when she was young they hadn't yet blocked all the sunlight from the front room. She'd liked the sun patterns in her bedroom at the back of the house. How old had she been when she decided she'd wanted to see what designs it made in the bigger room?

Bob Davis had stopped short as he came in. "Close curtains. They see in."

"But, Father, the sun—."

"Close them, stupid girl." The roar had hurt her ears.

Her mother had slid past Katie and to the windows, drawing closed the curtains as she murmured, "We don't want that people know our business."

Brad's car bounced on the rough connection between street and driveway, then stopped.

She unhooked her belt and reached for the handle.

"Katie."

She could have kept going. She should have kept going. Leaving without a word, closing the door on not only the meeting at the Monroes' house, but the entire trip. The time, the talk, the … yes, connection.

She looked over her shoulder at him. He leaned toward her, light painting the strong bones of his face. He was close. Six inches, no more, and his mouth would be on hers.

"Don't let anyone bully you. And if you need backup…"

He leaned closer, closer. He was going to kiss her. He was going to kiss her. *It was about damned time*, he was going to kiss her.

"You can always count on me, Katie."

His lips brushed her forehead.

She jolted out of the car, propelled by something she later decided was anger. This might even be worse than the finger down her nose and calling her "Squirt."

She tried to wrest her bag from him when he removed it from the trunk. He wouldn't relinquish it. If she had held the bag she might have slugged him with it. But she muttered something resembling "Thank you," and got inside the front door before he could do more than say another concerned, "Katie?"

Yes, she was angry, she decided as she leaned against the inside of the front door. Angry. Or as Maura would say, she thought with a shaky half laugh, she was *royally pissed.*

How long had he been telling himself she was a kid?

Since the day she'd arrived in the basketball office? Maybe.

Or had it been the second day when he'd turned from looking at Katie Davis and met Coach C.J. Draper's eyes?

There was no question about the message in his boss' gaze. *Hands off.* Perhaps because of Carolyn's role, or perhaps because of Katie herself, Coach was particularly protective of her.

And Brad couldn't blame him. Not one bit.

Not because he'd ever been as bad as his reputation, even when he'd been dating a lot. But because Katie was … *a kid.*

Sure she'd had boyfriends—worthless jackasses as far as he was concerned, but she'd figured that out eventually—but that didn't change him viewing her as a kid. A fifteen-year-old could have a boyfriend for heaven's sake. That didn't mean he'd view her as anything other than a kid.

Katie's not fifteen. Wasn't even on that first day, and now she's twenty-seven.

His cell rang, bringing him back to the airport gate area, where he waited for his next flight.

Katie.

No.

Hunter Pierce, according to the phone.

He knew what the man wanted. As if he had influence with Katie these days.

So maybe Katie wasn't a kid anymore. Maybe the buzz he'd felt the first time he'd seen her would be safe to let out of its box now.

Except she just might be a princess. And if that wasn't out of reach, what was?

In other words, the rules he'd lived by regarding Katie Davis were still in force.

That didn't mean he couldn't help her, be her friend.

In fact, he'd had a thought, though it would have to wait until after the season. He ignored Pierce's call and placed another one.

Katie was grateful she had no time dwell on the weekend's events, since Senior Night was Tuesday. The seniors deserved a great sendoff.

Those first days set the tone. Over the next weeks, work was her salvation. It occupied her mind. It left few hours and little energy for brooding.

It also kept Brad traveling and too busy when he was around to do much more than give her searching looks.

The same went for C.J. and, to a lesser extent, Carolyn. But for some reason their searching looks didn't slice as deep.

The team won twice in the conference tournament, which put the Aces into the National Invitation Tournament. Not the vaunted NCAA, but good experience for a young team. After a couple wins there, Ashton lost. The coaches went to NCAA tournament games for networking. Plus, these were the final weeks of an active recruiting period. Keeping track of which coach was where, making and changing arrangements took all her attention.

And then it was over. The NCAA championship game had been played the night before. C.J. was already back in Ashton, taking the day off to spend with his family, since the elementary school was on spring break. The other coaches would be returning over the next twenty-four hours. They'd each take some time off, too. She might not see … any of them for several more days.

Maura gave a deep sigh from her desk. "It all seems kind of flat, doesn't it? With the season over, I mean."

"Recruiting, summer camps, the Europe trip, preparing for next season." Katie ticked off the main chores ahead of them. "We've got plenty to keep us busy."

"The routine stuff, sure. But I mean the *drama*. There's so much inherent drama in sports and the basketball season can be divided into the classic three-act structure."

Drama was the last thing Katie wanted. But saying that would start Maura on how essential it was to the furtherance of humanity and how much of our lives followed dramatic structure. Katie looked forward to the end of the screenplay class the intern was taking.

Katie tried another tack. "I saw the notice that this weekend is Ice-Out Festival."

The Ice-Out Festival was a rite of spring no self-respecting member of the Ashton University community would miss. Since it depended on the weather it was never scheduled more than a week ahead.

Maura brightened. "I know. Like Mother Nature giving us the turning point we need right when we need it."

"We can push back the clean-up sessions to next week."

Katie had paid interns to do spring and fall yard clean-ups for years. The yard had improved a lot, especially the tangle in the backyard—no matter what some people thought.

They'd picked this weekend, but earning extra cash surely couldn't compete with the Ice-Out Festival.

"Scheduling's always a gamble, isn't it?" Maura said. Wisconsin weather wasn't known for its predictability, which meant Lake Ashton's ice break-up varied from year to year and so did the festival. That drop-everything-and-celebrate aspect was no small part of its appeal to students ... and faculty. "We talked about it, and if it's all right with you, we'll do most of it Thursday afternoon and finish up Friday before anything starts. That way we'll have plenty of money for the whole weekend."

Katie smiled back. "No studying in your schedule at all?"

"On Ice-Out weekend? No way. Nobody wants to miss a second."

Katie sent up a silent hope one person would decide to miss the whole thing. She wasn't ready to face Brad Spencer.

Katie knew her mouth was hanging open as she got out of her car after work Thursday.

Shock.

She'd had a few encounters with it lately so she knew what it felt like, and this was it.

Leaving the other interns spreading mulch, Maura practically skipped toward her. "Doesn't it look *fabulous*? It makes all the difference in the world. When we finish this, we're going to wash the windows and you'll have so much light inside."

"What have you done?" Her voice was a croak. She swallowed. "What on earth have you done?"

Maura's beam dimmed. "But...? You wanted them down. You wanted to open things up."

A voice behind her said, "I ordered the trees taken down."

CHAPTER TWELVE

She spun around, and there was Brad, as somehow she'd known he would be from the instant she'd caught sight of her bare, exposed house spotlighted in the late afternoon sunlight.

"You. Had. Them. Take. Down. My. Trees."

"Oh, *that's* what's bothering you," Maura chirped. Those trees were way too big and scary for us. Coach Spencer had professionals come in and take them down first thing. They were about done when we got here after morning classes. The tree guys said it was good timing, too, because a couple had a blight or something that was spreading. It would have been awful if one of those huge trees fell on your house. We've been doing the cleanup, and working on the new beds."

"Too scary," Brad murmured. "Told you."

She glared at him. "You had no right—"

"Oh, no, you *are* mad."

At the dismay in Maura's voice, Katie gave Brad one more dirty look, then adjusted her expression as she turned to the girl. "Coach Spencer got carried away. But you all have done a fantastic job. As you always do."

"Oh, this is way, way better than last year or the year before," Maura said. "It's been amazing to see what a transformation it's made. It's like one of those TV makeover shows."

"Curb appeal," Brad murmured.

She shot him a glare over her shoulder, then turned back to the intern.

Maura swept her arm wide like a magician's assistant. Katie's eyes obeyed the gesture, looking from one side of her property to the other.

It truly was a transformation. In fairness, she could understand Maura's excitement over that. But she couldn't completely suppress a shudder, either. It felt like her house had had all its clothes ripped off.

"It might look a little bare," Maura continued.

"A little," she muttered.

She jerked her head around at the sound of amusement from Brad. He held his hands up in a placating gesture. If he could read her murderous mind right now, that gesture would be one of supplication.

"We got more plants—well, Coach Spencer did." From the corner of her eye, Katie caught Brad making a "cut it" gesture with his hand by his throat. Maura picked up, "These plants will grow and fill in, and you can add in more of what you like. Give it a couple of years."

"The lawn already looks happier," Trevor said, brushing his hands on his jeans as he came up to join them.

"Yeah, and it's not like we didn't leave you any trees," Brad added.

One Norway spruce remained at the corner of the lot. It had barely been noticeable before in comparison to the mass of trees in front of the house. Now it looked … regal.

"Had to take out some dead branches at the bottom," Trevor said, apparently following the direction of her gaze.

"It looks airier, doesn't it?" Maura said. "And look over there, you have lilac bushes."

"I do?"

"That's what the tree guy said. He said they probably won't bloom this year but with the trees gone they'll be a lot happier and he said you should get blooms next year for sure. Isn't that cool?"

She was aware of Brad watching her. She carefully did not look at him. "If I'm going to feed this crew, I better get busy."

She'd finished frosting the sheet cake she'd made before leaving for work this morning. She started the pasta when they began washing up at the back spigot so there'd be no delay. The spaghetti sauce was getting a stir when the interns began trooping in.

Brad was the fifth one in the door.

"You're staying for dinner?"

"Thanks, I will." He picked up a bowl and got in line.

"That wasn't…" But she let it die. She'd have to be a lot ruder than she would be in front of the interns to get him to leave. Now, if they were alone…

Somehow the idea of their being alone didn't make her more comfortable. She didn't have to worry about that while the interns ate heartily from the spaghetti pot, then started on the cake. Although she was aware that Brad, sitting on the floor, was leaning against the side of the overstuffed chair she sat in.

Two interns stood, saying they had to leave to go study. Four more got up, including Trevor. Their departure would leave the room sparsely populated.

"You're not going already," she protested.

Trevor shook his head. "Heck no. More cake."

She relaxed too soon.

Brad shifted, making room for two of the crew to get past. From this new position, he twisted his neck to look up at her, saying in a low voice. "Are you really pissed?"

"About the trees or the plants you obviously bought?"

"Uh, start with the plants. They're smaller."

"Yes," she said with maximum sternness. "I'm paying you back for whatever you spent. For the trees, too. Even though … Anyway, I'm paying you."

"You could take it as a gift."

"No."

He sighed. "Okay, go ahead, hit me with the next one. Tell me if you're really pissed about the trees."

"That you did it without permission? Yes. That the trees are gone? I don't know yet."

He grinned. "Honest Katie." He turned more serious. "The trees had serious problems. The arborist's a guy I know from the summers I worked landscaping, and he knows his stuff. I left his report on the kitchen table. It's got his phone number if you want to call him to be sure I didn't forge it."

She clicked her tongue. "I can't imagine why you'd go to that extreme. In fact, I can't imagine why you did any of this."

"Can't you, Katie?"

She was saved from answering—or considering his question—by the interns returning with slabs of cake.

CHAPTER THIRTEEN

Friday at the office, Katie didn't look as if she'd slept particularly well the night before.

Sure couldn't blame him for that, Brad thought. He wouldn't have minded being to blame for it if—No. He'd decided not to go there with Katie.

That's why he'd left her house last night along with the last two interns. His reward for that restraint had been seeing her relief, which did a lot for a guy's ego. Reminding himself—again—he'd decided not to go there with Katie was no help. Dammit.

So he wasn't to blame. And there hadn't been much left to clean up, so that didn't explain her low energy, either.

Maybe her tiredness today was because she was being run ragged. The Ice-Out Festival drew visitors and a high percentage of them thought it would be a good idea to drop in and introduce themselves to Coach C.J. Draper.

Between fielding phone calls from slightly more realistic visitors and needing to be polite to drop-ins—some of whom could not take a direct statement, much less a polite hint—Katie's smile was flagging and he was about ready to throttle the next one who was a jerk to her.

Considering his mood—no sense examining the source of that too closely—he was sort of hoping the next jerk showed up soon. That's why he was propped against the doorframe of a fellow assistant coach's office door, barely listening to his colleague. This gave him a great view of anyone entering from the hallway.

The door opened to a well-dressed couple. They looked far too pleasant to draw a throttling, dammit.

"Hey! That's my mug." Katie half stood from her desk.

Beyond her, Maura let out a muffled screech.

Brad was already in motion, going after the slouchy student he'd noticed enter before the well-dressed couple, but had dismissed, since students knew better than to try to get in to see Coach without an appointment.

He vaulted the corner of an unoccupied desk, withdrew all throttling thoughts about the well-dressed couple when the woman stepped out of his way, the man said "Close the door" to the third member of their party, who'd come in last, and that third party did what he was told.

It wouldn't have made a difference, because Brad already had the back of the mug-stealer's collar, but he appreciated the quick-thinking and cooperation.

"Thanks," he said briefly as he pulled the kid out of their way. He addressed the kid, "What the hell are you doing?"

"Nothing."

"Stealing a coffee mug isn't nothing."

"Oh. Mr. and Mrs. Bridge, it's so good to see you. And Eric." Katie was beside him now, sending him messages with the significance in her voice and eyes. Message received: The trio was Eric Bridge, the top sophomore prospect, and his parents. "We're so sorry about this. Please, let me take you right in for your appointment with Coach Draper. This sort of thing never happens at Ashton. Truly."

Mrs. Bridge smiled. "If this is the worst thing that happens at Ashton, it's a truly remarkable place."

"You're Coach Spencer, right?" Eric asked. "You've got some moves."

A flicker of understanding passed between Brad and Eric's father—both recognizing that the unspoken rider on the teen's praise was *for an old guy.*

"Thanks." He extended his hand. "Nice to meet you. Thanks, too, for the quick reactions, all of you."

"Well, I'm going to be mighty dull after this introduction to Coach

Spencer," C.J. drawled from behind him. "But I hope you'll forgive me for that and come on in for a chat before your campus tour." As he introduced himself and escorted them toward the conference room, he also managed to make a damping motion with one hand, cueing staff members who'd come out of their offices in response to the commotion to act casual. He introduced the Bridges to the staffers, as if this gauntlet were an ordinary welcome.

As C.J. closed the door to the conference room, he sent a look over his shoulder at Brad that combined a wink, a frown, and questioning eyebrows.

Still holding the kid's collar with one hand, Brad wrapped another around Katie's arm. "My office."

"I have to answer—"

"Maura can handle it."

"I will. Don't worry, Katie."

Inside his office, Brad gestured her to his chair behind the desk and sat the kid in the chair against the far wall. The kid would have to go through him to get out of the room.

He pried at the kid's fingers clutching the mug. When the kid realized he was going to lose that battle, he released the mug and flopped back with sneering disinterest.

"It's no big deal, man. It's just a crappy coffee mug."

Brad set the mug on the desk. "Why did you want it, then?"

"Haven't you ever heard of a college prank? Or was that too long ago for you to remember?"

Brad stared at the kid, knowing his own face gave away nothing.

The kid started fidgeting about thirty seconds sooner than Brad had expected.

Then he swore.

Then he said, "Just because some guy said he'd pay me fifty bucks to get her coffee mug—"

"*Mine?* Why on earth—" She snapped her mouth closed.

Clearly her speculation on one likely "why" matched his.

"Who?" Brad demanded.

"I don't know. I told you, some guy. Never seen him before."

"What's he look like?"

"I don't know. Old. Like he'd work in a garage or something."

"Where are you supposed to meet this guy to get your money and when?"

Apparently at the reminder that he wasn't going to be collecting fifty, he slid lower and mumbled with his chin against his chest, "I don't have to tell you anything."

"You're going to have to tell a whole lot of people everything. If you cooperate it might get easier as it goes along. If you don't, it's going to get harder and harder." He paused, then added another, "And harder. The real question might be who you want to tell your parents about this—me? Campus police? Ashton police? Or worse?"

The bravado cracked at the mention of telling his parents.

"All right, all right. You're making a federal case out of nothing. Geeze. I'm supposed to be at the library loading dock in half an hour with her stupid coffee mug." Brad growled "Stay put" at the kid and left.

He stuck his head in the office next door and said, "Corston, will you keep that kid pinned in my office while I make a call?"

"Sure, Spence," said the strength and conditioning coach, who could keep almost anyone on earth pinned when he put his might to it.

Katie came out before Corston reached the door. She was right behind Brad as he entered C.J.'s office, unoccupied since C.J. was with the Bridges in the conference room, and pulled the door closed.

She propped her hands on her hips. "You're not going to call campus police. He's a kid."

"No." He'd found what he was looking for on his phone and punched the button, telling her, "I'm calling Hunter Pierce of the State Department."

"What? No. There's no reason to—"

But he'd already heard the other man answer.

"Hunter? This is Brad Spencer from Ashton University. A kid, probably a student, tried to steal Katie's coffee mug. He said some guy he'd never met before offered him fifty dollars for delivering her mug to him."

"Tried to."

"I stopped him."

"Katie's okay?"

"Yes. The kid's in my office, being watched. So's the mug. He's supposed to deliver it in half an hour. Less than that now. Maybe fifteen, twenty minutes."

"Damn. The man's seen the kid, right?"

"Yeah. I might be able to get another student who could go, say the first kid got held up and asked him to deliver it, but I don't like—"

"No, me either."

"Then I'm going," Brad said flatly.

"No," Katie breathed. He kept talking into the phone, "If I get campus police, they could hold onto the guy—assuming I find him—at least for a while."

"Any description?" Hunter asked.

"Kid said he was old—which could be anything over twenty-two—and looks like he works in a garage."

Hunter's silence indicated he was thinking it over. Twenty seconds later, he said, "No. This doesn't—No. Don't get the campus police involved. I'm in Chicago, so I'll head up there right away, but it'll be a couple hours. Don't do anything stupid."

"I won't do anything stupid." Brad spoke into the phone, but his words were more for Katie. "Figured I'd stay out of sight and take pictures on my phone."

"Good idea. Remember to turn off the ringer."

"Advice from a pro, huh?"

"Prime advice," Hunter confirmed.

CHAPTER FOURTEEN

Katie protested.

With time running out, he said he was going. Period.

"At least take Tony," she said.

He started to say no then thought better of it. "Good idea. If you'll keep an eye on the kid and let Brewster keep an eye on you."

So he and Tony Corston took off jogging across campus, while Martin Brewster sat with Katie in Brad's office.

They cut through the library because it was the most direct route to the loading dock. He stationed Corston within hollering distance but out of sight, grabbed a jacket that looked vaguely groundskeeperish and snagged a push broom and wheeled garbage can from nearby.

He kept his head down as he swept up the sloped ramp toward the outside, while keeping his peripheral vision on the lookout for "just a guy."

Nothing. He kept sweeping, stopping to pick up the accumulation and dump it in the can.

He was two-thirds of the way up when a man arrived, nearly five minutes late. He gave Brad a sharp look, then seemed to dismiss him. Brad kept sweeping and dumping. Only now, as he dumped with one hand, he shot as many pictures as he could with the other, shooting under his arm to mask the phone from the guy.

At the top of the ramp, they were only ten feet apart. Brad had to be more careful taking pictures, but surely some would be useable. Slowly, he started back down, stopping to resweep areas, still shooting.

The guy paced, looking around at every sound.

With Brad nearly back to the bottom, the guy swore loudly and strode off.

Brad could see Corston, his eyebrows raised, asking a question. Brad shook his head and kept up his charade for another minute—the time it took to complete his task, and to disappear from view of anyone who happened to be looking down the ramp.

"You take the path toward the lake, I'll take the path toward town," he told Corston as he pulled off the jacket. "Give it twenty minutes. If you don't spot him, go back to the office. If you do, call me, I'll do the same."

As he moved quickly along the path, Brad swept through the photos, sending three good ones to Hunter and emailing himself the complete set.

But maybe that cost him some time, because he never spotted the guy. Even going beyond campus and over the twenty minutes, walking up and down streets, ducking in to a couple garages, trying to spot the man.

Finally admitting defeat, he turned and headed toward the basketball office across campus.

He made use of the time to call Corston, who was back at the office and hadn't seen anything. "Uh, Katie would like to know where you are, when you're getting back, and what you're doing."

"Tell her I'm heading back. Everything still calm with the kid?"

"Yeah. She's been feeding him, and hearing his life story."

Brad muttered, "Don't let her adopt him before I get back."

Next he called Hunter and reported.

"Good work, Spencer. Got the photos you sent. Don't recognize him and initial review shows no links. A detailed review is going on now. I should be there in thirty or forty minutes."

Brad checked his watch and whistled. "Air traffic control know you're around? And how did you look at the photos driving like that?"

"I'm not the one driving."

But Hunter was alone when he eventually knocked at the locked basketball office door and they let him in.

Brewster and Corston had left as soon as Brad returned, but C.J. said he wasn't going anywhere. They sat with Katie and the kid, whose name was Tim and who'd clearly enjoyed a generous picnic all over his desk.

When Hunter arrived, they left Tim where he was and updated Hunter in the main office.

At the end, Katie declared, "You can't hold that boy indefinitely."

Hunter spoke over Brad and C.J.'s arguments to hold on to the kid. "Not indefinitely. I'd like to have a word with him. But first, I have a favor to ask you, Katie. Will you please go home right now?"

"I don't see why I—"

He leaned down and said something into her ear, too quietly for anyone else to hear.

She clearly wanted to keep protesting, but didn't. "That," she said to Hunter, "is dirty pool."

She got her purse from her desk, stood, and walked out.

C.J. let out a soft whistle. "Can you teach me that trick? I've never won any discussion with Katie, much less one so short."

Amusement came into Hunter's eyes, but didn't reach his mouth. "Maybe later, Coach Draper. Right now, I want to talk to this young man. Brad, I'd like to have you in there as a witness, but you can't say anything. Understood?"

"I don't like Katie going home alone. You can say it's Ashton and the kid only went after a coffee mug, but—".

"You stay, help Hunter," C.J. interrupted. "I'll follow Katie home then head home myself if that suits you, Hunter."

"Sure."

"That good enough, Brad?"

He nodded, because the feeling that it damned well wasn't good enough was irrational and he knew it.

"Call if you need anything, Hunter." C.J. took off. His long legs would make up enough time on Katie that she'd be in his sight before she reached the parking lot.

Hunter cleared his throat.

"Brad, unless I hear something unexpected from this kid, I don't see a serious threat to Katie's safety. I have a good bit of experience with this, plus I ran it by my boss on the phone on the way up. I'm telling you this to try to put your mind at ease, not because we aren't going to pursue it full-out. We are.

"One more thing before we go in there, would you mind giving me a ride to Katie's house when we're done?"

"What happened to the car you came up in?"

"It's not here anymore."

Which gave Brad a strong suspicion of how Hunter had gotten Katie to go home. He'd bet she'd gone to meet April, who'd dropped off Hunter, then driven to Katie's house.

Brad's suspicion was confirmed in a little over an hour. A rental car was parked in front of the house. He and Hunter found April Gareaux inside.

Katie let them in and gestured toward the kitchen. They'd probably have gone there without the gesture, drawn by mouth-watering smells.

"Oh, good," April said immediately. "Now that you're here, we can have an early dinner, then go to the festival."

"Festival?" Hunter repeated with disapproval.

"It's the Ice-Out Festival. It's to celebrate when Lake Ashton's no longer iced in—get it? Katie's been telling me about it. That's why you couldn't find a hotel room."

"That's right. No rooms anywhere." Hunter turned to Katie. "Any chance you can put us up tonight?"

"Of cour—"

"She's putting us *all* up tonight," Brad said. It wasn't that he didn't believe what Hunter had said about this not being a serious threat, but that didn't mean he was letting her out of his sight.

"I'm happy to have you stay here, April and Hunter. But I don't need security," she added pointedly to him.

"What you need is a dog," April said. "They're great security."

Hunter coughed.

"Okay, so ours aren't great guard dogs, but they'd discourage someone from trying to break in."

"Nobody's going to break in," Katie protested. She swung back to Hunter. "After talking with Tim, I'm sure you know—Oh, did he give you more information? You didn't get him in trouble with campus police, did you? Most students would have been tempted to make some money from a harmless prank. He's a kid—"

"A kid who scared you and invaded your privacy," Brad said.

Katie ignored him.

Hunter said, "We let him go after he went over the details. We got his contact information, and, uh, emphasized the need for absolute discretion. More people, more leaks, more attention focused on you. Low-key is best. Coach Draper knows, but the other coaches—"

"They won't say anything," Katie said.

"Corston and Brewster don't know much to say even if they wanted to." Brad lifted the lid off a slow cooker, the source of some of the good smells.

April chuckled, tipping her head to direct his attention toward Katie, who frowned fiercely at him.

"Hey, I'm not saying they *would* say anything, I'm just being practical. What is this?"

"Beef stew Katie made. Biscuits should be done soon," April said. "And after dinner we can go to the festival."

Before Brad could say what a lousy idea he thought that was, Hunter said to April, "Remember, the reason you came straight here to Katie's house was to stay out of the public eye."

"Unless that was a ploy to get me out of the office," Katie inserted with a glint of mischief.

"It was not," Hunter said firmly. "If April's recognized it'll stir up talk about how much you two look alike. Do you want that, Katie?"

"No," she conceded.

But April was saying, "Oh, we've got that covered." She pulled a blonde wig and oversized gray hoodie from a bag. "Isn't this perfect? Katie had the wig from Halloween. And with the hoodie pulled up nobody'll see much of my face. And I have some truly awful makeup planned. You'll hardly recognize me."

Hunter eyed the items, but all he said was, "No sense chewing on this until we have more information." He cracked the oven door. "Though I wouldn't mind chewing on something."

April laughed. "Subtle, Pierce."

Katie went into overdrive, preparing fruit salad with April, directing him and Hunter to move the table out from the wall and bring more chairs. Soon they were digging in.

Conversation about anything but food flagged, not resuming until they'd each had a healthy wedge of apple pie with cheese on it.

Hunter received a call as he finished and went outside to take it. They were cleaning up when he returned.

"Nothing definitive," he said in response to their questioning looks. "So far, there's no indication anything more serious than trying to snatch the mug was involved."

"Good. Then we can go to the Ice-Out Festival," April said.

"No way," Brad said.

Katie frowned at him. "It was no—"

"It *is* a big deal. What if whoever hired your pal Tim also hired other people to come after you?"

"Good point, Brad," Hunter said. "But that's a reason for us to go—to flush out any more Tims, we're both on hand. If Katie stays out of sight all weekend, we leave, then she returns to work next week, someone could try then."

He muttered.

There was no way Katie could have heard what he'd said, but she must have figured out the gist because she declared, "I am not going to lock myself inside. And I am going to work Monday and every day after."

"Okay," April said with great cheerfulness while he and Katie frowned at each other, "well, I'm thrilled we're going to the Ice-Out

Festival. What—"

"In disguise," Hunter interposed.

"—I want to know is how it started?"

Hunter groaned, but also put his arm around her shoulders and squeezed. "Of course she wants to know the history."

Katie told April, "I have no idea. It's been around as long as I can remember."

"Started in the 1800s," Brad said. "Both tracking the Ice-Out date and the festival. They still don't take fancy scientific measurements or anything. They go strictly on observation, so it's a more accurate comparison of now and then. In the 1800s, the day they could row a boat from a tavern across the lake to the Ashton campus was officially Ice-Out. That's how the tavern owner delivered booze to campus, while avoiding officials. The first day in spring his employees could get across with the against-the-rules booze was a big celebration."

April had stopped drying the glass bowl the fruit salad had been in to listen to him. "That's fascinating. How do you know all that, Brad?"

"I took a class."

"On climatology?"

"On local festivals."

Katie's laugh came first. He turned toward the sound—toward her. Suppressing a smile, he pretended pique. "It was a real class. On how festivals reflect a community—ethnic groups, industry, geography, weather. All that."

April said, "Well, I'm glad we're going to honor the great tradition of the Ice-Out Festival."

"Uh-huh. The tradition of celebrating sneaking in illicit alcohol to probably underage kids," Hunter said.

April stretched up and kissed him on the cheek, then said fondly, "My Mr. Law and Order."

CHAPTER FIFTEEN

Hunter was eventually satisfied with April's disguise—"only because it's dark"—and they walked to the Meadow, where celebratory bonfires in safety fire pits along the shore blazed high enough to hastened the ice's melting.

Dancing and singing certainly were melting the students' winter restraints.

No one showed the least interest in their foursome. So they all tried Slapshot (getting the puck in the goal), which Brad won, and Bowling (using snowballs to try to knock down small pins), which Hunter won, and they agreed they were too old and too smart to attempt Bobbing for Ice Cubes.

Fireworks over the lake capped the official festivities, though ad hoc parties could be heard all over campus.

Walking back to the house, Brad was aware of April and Hunter holding hands, while he and Katie walked beside each other in silence.

He was also aware, lying on the couch, looking at the night sky through the window no longer obscured by giant trees, of Katie down the hall in her bed. Warm and tousled and—

No. That wasn't why he was here. That wasn't why he was in her life.

Brad was up and out before the others stirred. He left a note on Katie's kitchen table saying when he'd be back.

He swung by his place for a shower and change, tossed necessities in a duffel and headed back.

He could see Katie and April at the table finishing breakfast as he walked to the front door. On impulse, he tried the door without knocking. It opened and he walked right in.

"I locked that door when I left. Why isn't it locked now?"

"Oh." Katie put a hand to her heart. "You startled me. I guess I didn't lock it when I got the newspaper."

"Somebody else might have done a heck of a lot more than startle you."

"If there was any cause for concern, Hunter wouldn't have sent me back here to the house by myself yesterday."

"Coach followed you home."

Her triumph deflated. "C.J. did?"

"Yes, and reported back to us that you and April were okay, which he could tell through the wide open windows."

He was aware of April watching them like an absorbed fan at a tennis match.

"If you're criticizing me for having wide open windows, you shouldn't have cut down the trees."

"Curtains work, and you can open—or close—them."

She made a face, but before she could say anything, Hunter entered from the back.

"News?" April asked.

He hitched one shoulder. "Let's all sit down." When they had he said, "The short answer is we found the guy who was going to pay Tim for the mug. He really is a mechanic. In Milwaukee. Seems like an upstanding citizen other than this. Heard from a customer that someone was offering a thousand dollars for a sample of a woman's DNA. We're tracking down the customer and we'll keep working this end. We're working from the other end, too."

"What other end?" Katie asked.

"Who's willing to pay to get a sample of your DNA. Presumably it's someone interested in knowing if you're the lost princess of Bariavak."

"King Jozef—"

"No," April and Hunter said in unison.

"He's too good a politician to do anything so clumsy," Hunter added.

April frowned at him then said to her, "He would never do that to you—not only scare you that way, but take the decision away from you. He wouldn't. He wants to spend time with you, to get to know you. He wouldn't want that if he were going to force the DNA issue."

"Then why hasn't he spent time with Katie?" Brad asked.

"He's got other issue's he's juggling." Hunter held up a hand. "Yes, April, I'll tell them the rest. And in fairness, I keep telling him it will bring down the media on her, so he's held off."

"Eliminate King Jozef, and there's still someone who wasn't worried about scaring Katie," Brad said. "Someone plenty clumsy enough to hire cheap and inept help."

"That's exactly the clue we're following up." A glint of a smile showed in Hunter's eyes. "I'll keep this short, but you need to know that Bariavak's situation is a little complicated. With the death of King Jozef's daughter and the disappearance of his granddaughter, he was left without an heir. He instituted a provision that said he could name his heir from among a trio of family connections. His nephew by marriage, Prince Vatche, thinks he has the best chance, but he's the one Bariavakians dislike the most."

"With good reason," April said. "That's a personal opinion, not the stance of the Department of State."

"State has no stance on the matter."

"Of course not." April added to Katie and Brad, "He's smarmy and—"

"April."

She raised a hand in surrender, but slid in one last word: "Slimy."

"One of the other two connections made Prince Vatche look good. But Prince Stefan Carlos got himself killed not long ago in a jet-ski accident—"

"His fault," April said.

"—and that ended that line. So King Jozef has had to dig deep to track the descendant of the third branch."

"International intrigue," Brad muttered, with a glance at her.

"Have you found this third candidate?" Katie asked.

"Yes. But there are, uh, issues."

"Issues?"

"Let's just say the third candidate would be happy if you prove to be Princess Josephine-Augusta. So for now we relax here and let good people work the situation. I suggest we play a game of cards. Poker?"

"Do not play poker with this man," April warned the others. "He can bluff you out of your last possession or your last toothpick."

"Well, I have toothpicks, but no cards," Katie said.

Brad and Hunter gaped at her. "No cards? What games do you have?"

"I don't. I didn't play games as a kid and—Oh, wait. Carolyn's and C.J.'s kids brought over a game and left it here." She went to the sideboard and pulled out a rectangular tin triumphantly. "Dominoes."

Hunter received one interim report that added more weight to the suspicion that King Jozef's nephew by marriage was behind the mug-snatching effort.

By that time, the dominoes competition had become fierce. Each game's loser had to serve the others drinks and snacks.

Katie and Brad had tied for last on the just-finished game, so they were in the kitchen getting popcorn and drinks. "I should have said this before, Brad. Thank you for everything you did yesterday."

"You're welcome. And I'm impressed you didn't add anything on about none of it being necessary."

"Don't tempt me."

He grinned and she grinned back.

"You *were* awfully hard on Tim, though," she said.

"As hard as I had to be to make him stop being an ass."

"Yet, I'd think you'd understand."

"Are you saying I'm an ass?"

"No! I didn't mean—" Then she saw the humor in his eyes. "Although at times ... But I meant because you had a tough time as a kid, dealing with your mother remarrying, having a step-parent and then half-siblings. You rebelled."

He snorted. "I was a brat." He considered that a moment. "*And* an ass. Who's been telling you I had a tough time? I can't believe Andy—"

"She didn't say much. And C.J. was—"

"C.J.? *Coach* told you I had a tough time as a kid?"

"Not in so many words, but—"

He laughed. "I'll bet not in so many words. Ah, there you go again with the left eyebrow climbing."

"Did you know that raising one eyebrow can be learned? It's a matter of training your muscles," she told him triumphantly.

"You should have read all the Google search results, Katie. That's what some people say, but there's strong evidence that the innate ability is inherited. Like wiggling your ears or being able to roll your tongue. Want to explore that?"

She froze.

Only for an instant. Then Hunter's voice came from the other room, "Hey, are you two growing the popcorn out there?"

They heard April shushing him, but by then they were gathering up the baskets and glasses and heading to the living room.

By Sunday, even Brad looked relaxed. Even though she knew that couch couldn't be comfortable for him to sleep on. She'd thought about him again last night. He'd have been so much better off in her spacious bed.

Instead of her. Sleeping. Alone.

Then, as she drifted asleep those thoughts intertwined with images of him in her spacious bed *with* her. Not alone. Not sleeping.

"Why are you blushing?" April asked, folding a dishcloth after lunch.

"I ... I wasn't aware I was."

April made a sound between a snort and grunt. It was disbelieving, knowing, and accepting. "C'mon, let's go sit on the couch and talk.

Brad will be back with the dinner groceries soon and Hunter's going to be off that phone sometime."

"Okay, but … the chairs are far more comfortable than the couch. Poor Brad…"

"Ahh. There's that blush again," April said as they settled into the chairs. "Okay, okay, I won't give you grief about that. But there is something else I want to talk to you about. Remember how I said when we were talking in Bette's office that I'd thought I had my life all figured out. Then my fiancé dumped me for his ex, I had nowhere to live, and I'd adopted Rufus, so I had a dog I was responsible for. Oh, and Leslie and Grady were gone and I was fed up with myself for relying on other people. So I took a leap."

"A leap?"

She nodded. "Not as much about being a pretend princess as trusting myself. And now I'm going to trust myself by asking if you'll come to our wedding next month in D.C. Please say yes."

"I, uh, I'm honored, but—"

"I know we haven't known each other long, but…"

Their eyes met and Katie nodded. Yes, they had a connection.

April gave a tiny nod back, then smiled radiantly. "I know it's usual to wait for the RSVP until you get the invitation, but there's another reason I want to know right now if you'll come. We have this tradition in my family—Actually, Paul started it when he and Bette got married, but I consider them family. Anyway, some of the people closest to the couple get together before the wedding and spend time together doing fun things, and I want you to come."

"But … but…"

"Please, Katie. You see, before I met Hunter I'd let all my friendships wither. I probably would have let my relationships with my family—all of them, like the Monroes and the Dickinsons, but even Leslie and Grady and the kids—wither, too, but they wouldn't let me. They'll all be there and I'll have a great time with them but I want—" She looked a little shy, then determination pushed it aside. "I want a girlfriend, you know? If you can't stay a full week, I understand, but maybe you could come in, say, the Monday before the wedding?"

"Monday?"

"Yes, that's great! We'll have a lot of fun. I already know a bunch of places I want to take you. And—"

Panic welled in Katie. She'd said Monday as a question, not a confirmation. "April."

"—things we can do. It'll be so much fun to—"

"April."

"—do them together."

Yes, they had a connection, but she barely knew this woman, much less what April seemed to expect of her. She'd never had a girlfriend—

You don't think you're any good at having friends do you?

Katie swallowed, "I'm … I don't know what to say, except thank you."

April hugged her and Katie hugged back.

The guys returned just then—Brad with the makings for dinner and Hunter with an update.

Hunter said King Jozef had come down hard on his wife's nephew. "There won't be any more efforts to collect your DNA until you say the word, Katie."

"So let's make this dinner a celebration," April declared.

CHAPTER SIXTEEN

"Katie?"

"Hmm."

She was only a few minutes away from having three full days of a normal work-week under her belt. That was good. Great, in fact. She welcomed normalcy.

April and Hunter had left Monday morning with admonitions about keeping her eyes open, just in case. Brad had left before she'd even gotten up, traveling to see prospects in Tennessee. So she'd only had C.J. and Carolyn being over-protective.

True, there had been a phone call Tuesday. It was King Jozef. He added his assurances to Hunter's that she would not be bothered again.

He next said he regretted that for security reasons he would not be able to visit her in Ashton as he'd planned to. Before she recovered, he suggested she come to Bariavak.

She quickly declined, citing her work responsibilities.

"Ah, yes. Then I must hope an opportunity presents itself."

That left her a little uneasy, but he didn't push, so perhaps it was paranoia.

Brad had returned by noon today. He and C.J. had been shut up in C.J.'s office. Probably going over the prospects Brad had seen. That was another part of normal, although the door had been closed again. There'd been some raised voices, but that was normal too in discussions of players. And it left her in peace to get her work done.

Until now, when they exited the inner office for the main area where she was the last one left, and C.J. spoke her name.

"There's something you should be up to speed on," he said.

She looked up from the computer screen, finding both him and Brad standing beside her desk and watching her. C.J. looked very laid back. That got her attention, because he didn't usually work that hard at looking at ease. Brad didn't look laid back at all.

"Okay," she said cautiously.

"There's been a slight change of plans with the trip," C.J. said. "The one to Europe this summer."

As if she could forget about that trip.

"It won't mean more work for you," C.J. continued. "The travel company's handled it all. Administration's real happy about it, too. So it's all set."

"That's good." She looked from one to the other. "Isn't it?"

"Yeah. It's good—better than good. It's great. Great opportunity for all of us. An experience."

"Tell her."

She had never heard Brad issue an order like that to C.J. Draper.

C.J. shifted his weight. "We've added a couple games and a series of workshops. The thing is…"

"They're in Bariavak," Brad finished.

It took an instant to make sense. "What? *What?* No—"

"It's all set. You don't have to do a thing but come with," C.J. said. "All the arrangements are made. The administration thinks it's great, even the NCAA's happy about it after Hunt—uh, the State Department nudged them. Good for international relations. No team's ever been there."

Brad bit off a curse. She heard him come behind her chair, but didn't see him, because a dark haze was narrowing her vision to a tunnel. She felt the pressure of his hand gently but firmly pushing her head forward. "She's going to faint."

"Oh, God." C.J. crouched at her side. "Katie, Katie. Can you hear me?"

"I can hear you. I can't *believe* you." She snapped her head up. The fuzzy black walls of the tunnel shuddered, then retreated. Brad's hand ended up at the nape of her neck, but she couldn't dwell on that now.

"What were you *thinking*, C.J.? How could you do this?"

He tilted his head to glare up at Brad. "Thought you said she was going to faint."

"Not now. She's too pissed to faint now."

"Tell her you think it's a good idea, too," C.J. said, still looking at Brad.

"Stop acting like I'm not here, C.J.," Katie demanded, "and get up before your knee causes you trouble for a month and Carolyn has my head for—Does Carolyn know about this hare-brained scheme of yours?"

C.J. rose with enough reliance on the desk that she knew she was right about his knee. "She knows. And she doesn't think it's hare-brained. It's a few days in Bariavak. Some games, some clinics. From what I can tell about their basketball program, they need all the help they can get. In the meantime, it'll give you a chance to look around. Get a little familiar with it, spend time with King Jozef—What are you doing, Katie?"

She had turned off her computer and stood. Now she gathered her purse, took out her keys.

"It's the end of my workday, C.J., I'll see you tomorrow."

"But the trip—?"

"I'm not going."

"Katie—"

C.J.'s plea was sliced in half by Brad. "Yes, you are. You won't let C.J. or the team or Ashton down by not going." His voice changed as he added. "You won't let yourself down by not going."

"I'm not going," she repeated. "Good-night."

Brad pounded on her front door. Where all the neighbors could see and hear him because of that wonderful, welcoming curb appeal, damn him.

"Go away."

He'd barely given her time to get inside the house. Much less time to assess this new twist. If she simply kept refusing to go on the trip—

"You know I won't leave," Brad shouted from outside her door.

She did know.

She yanked the door open, then walked away.

He came in, all easy-going reason now that he'd gotten his way. "You seem upset."

That might have been the wrong thing to say.

Brad gathered that from the glare Katie pointed at him.

"I left work after my official ending time. I came home like I always do. Didn't take a single step on the campus paths," she added pointedly. "So you have no reason to say I seem upset."

Katie was battling to hold onto calm.

A calm he needed to do something about if he was going to find out why she'd nearly fainted at the idea of going to Bariavak. If he was going to find out the true reason she'd built walls up against the idea of testing whether she could be this lost princess.

"You know, this reaction worries me more than when you went berserk that first day Hunter showed up."

"I did not—" She bit it off. He watched her breathe, breathe, breathe.

"Let's talk this through. There's got to be a way—."

"No. I don't want to talk about it. Understand?"

"No. I don't understand. Nobody does. I told you before it's downright weird that you're putting off finding out if you're this Princess Josephine-Augusta."

"I'm not a princess."

He sliced his hand through air. "Okay, forget the princess part. But you'd know if King Jozef is your grandfather. And going to Bariavak—"

"What purpose could that serve? That baby was taken when she was months old. She couldn't possibly remember anything."

"Maybe not. But aren't you curious? It's not natural not to be curious. You can go and—"

"If I go, I can't come back—No." She turned away.

But he'd already seen how much she regretted the words she'd snapped out. They were getting closer to whatever was tying her in knots.

"What do you mean you can't come back? Even if you *are* his granddaughter, King Jozef can't make you give up your life here. You're—"

"It's not him."

"—an adult. You can make your own choices. What do you mean it's not him?"

"Never mind. Forget it. Forget I said anything."

"The hell I will. Katie, tell me what this is about."

"Go away, Brad."

"You know I won't. Tell me, Katie."

She didn't. Instead, she turned and headed deeper into the house. After an instant, he followed her.

CHAPTER SEVENTEEN

He wasn't sure if she was heading somewhere or trying to get away from him when she swung open a door off the kitchen he hadn't seen opened before. Either way, he was going after her.

As she started up steep stairs beyond the door, he decided she was, in fact, heading somewhere.

The attic, he realized when his eyes came above the floorboards into an area lit by three light bulbs hanging from the ridge pole.

She walked down the center of the space to under the last light bulb and sat on the floor. He followed, crouching to avoid hitting his head, then sat beside her.

"Katie?"

"After the first of the year," she said in a voice that remained scary calm, "when there were all those stories about April and King Jozef, with everyone telling me how much I looked like her, I remembered this suitcase. I came up and searched. It was way back in a corner with things from my childhood. Things my fa—Bob never would have bothered with. I was about to give up, thinking I'd dreamed the memory of this suitcase. Then I found it. And found…"

A shudder passed through her. She drew a battered suitcase in front of her crossed legs and flicked open the clasps.

First, she removed what appeared to be tattered and yellowed tissue paper.

She set that aside and he saw the next layer held something wrapped in fresh, crisp tissue paper.

She carefully folded back the sides of the paper, so they fell down on either side of her palm. Resting there, not much larger than her hand was a piece of fabric.

"What is it?"

"I think it's a corner cut from a larger piece." With her other hand she pointed to the difference between two finished edges and two that looked frayed.

"Are those letters written out in thread?"

"That's embroidery. Silk, I think. The fabric and the threads. I looked up about the gold thread. It's called goldwork. The thread can have real gold in it, not only the color."

He looked at her as he pursued the question she hadn't answered, "You mean the gold where it looks like letters."

After a pause, she murmured, "Uh-huh."

"That second letter's an A. The first one … If I had to decide, I'd say a J."

Josephine-Augusta.

He concentrated on drawing in oxygen to lungs that suddenly felt as if he'd been playing one-on-one for hours straight.

He forced himself to continue. "And up here?" He pointed without touching. "A crest, right? Bariavak's?"

Her silence was an answer.

A princess's monogram embroidered in silk. In an attic in Ashton, Wisconsin. In Katie's attic.

"My God, you really *are*. You are a *princess*."

No longer a kid … now a princess. Even more untouchable.

But that was for him to deal with. Now was about her.

"Knowing this, why on earth are you holding back from taking the test? To let the world know—your grandfather—"

"I also found this," she said evenly.

With her head still down, she covered up the fabric piece again, then retrieved a folder from beneath another layer of new tissue paper and handed it to him.

He opened it to see what appeared to be Katie's birth certificate on top. Next, he found yellowed newspaper pages. Not complete editions, but a few pages from several dates. Nothing to do with the rebellion or the missing princess, which had been his first thought.

These were obituary pages. Faded circles marked at least one notice on each page. The circled notices were all for babies. All girls. On the third page he spotted Katherine Mary Davis, two months old, daughter of Robert and Annette Davis.

He checked the date of the paper, subtracted the two months and came up with Katie's birthday.

When he looked up, she was staring at him, tears glistening her eyes, but not falling.

"Now do you understand?"

He was beginning to.

He had to think this through. For her sake. No sudden leaps. Step by step.

"You think they gave you this baby's identity? Your par—The people who raised you."

"I don't know."

"It sure seems reasonable as a working hypothesis. Though why they'd keep these newspapers … The embroidery, maybe, if they wanted to prove someday that you—" He bit it off after a glance at her. "But why the newspapers?"

"It was her. My … Anna. He didn't know she'd kept any of this. I'm sure of it. The one time she got really angry at me was when I tried to get in this suitcase. But I think it wasn't me seeing it that made her that way, but that *he* might have seen."

He sat back on his heels.

"You've known this since *January*. Before Hunter Pierce ever showed up, you'd seen all this, you'd known … Why haven't you told—" He shifted in mid-question, suppressing the word he wanted to use and substituting, "—anyone?"

"I don't *know* anything. It could be nothing. It could be coincidence."

"Coincidence? That's stretching it, Katie. What about this crest. Did you look it up? It's Bariavak's, isn't it?"

The smallest nod possible confirmed his supposition. "According to the Internet, anyway."

"DNA would tell you for sure."

"It might not. You heard what Hunter said that day at the Monroes'. And I've looked it up since then. It might not provide a definite answer. So I could be nobody—"

"Bull. You're Katie. You'll always be Katie."

She'd let his voice override her, but now she said, "Nobody with no country."

The despair as much as the words brought him up short. "Of course you have a country. Hell, you've got two. Bariavak and here—."

"No." Her head jerked in a sharp shake.

Then he saw it. "Illegal. You think you're illegal."

She nodded. "If this—" She gestured toward the folder still in his hands. "—means what it seems to mean, then I wasn't born here. I was brought here as an illegal alien, presumably smuggled in by two other illegal aliens who stole an identity for me."

"Through no fault of your own. You had no way of knowing—"

"It doesn't matter. I've talked to three immigration lawyers and they all agree. I'm not a citizen. I'm here illegally. I could get kicked out any time."

"Only if someone has a reason to dig into—"

"*Someone?* A *reason?* Like the State Department or King Jozef's people or the media or the king's nephew or someone else who's interested in whether I'm this lost princess? And that's if Ashton's travel office doesn't find out first."

"Travel office? Why would—?" He breathed out a curse. "Your passport."

She nodded. "The passport I don't have and I'm afraid to get."

"This is why you've been trying to hold everybody off? This is why you've been so adamant you're not the princess?"

"I sat up here in January and thought it through. I decided I would never tell anyone about any of this." Her gaze flicked to him, then away. "The day Hunter first came I was up here preparing to destroy it all when you showed up at my door with Chinese food. Afterward I decided to wait. I've kept stalling, and now they'll find out without this."

"You're worried they'll find out your documents are fake?"

"They already suspect. Michael Dickinson said it flat-out that day at the Monroes'. How long would it take an expert to confirm it? That would mean I'm not a citizen. Worried? I'm more than worried. Wouldn't you be?"

"Yeah, I might. Even if you get the passport and get to Bariavak, if something comes out about your being here illegally…"

"I would have to stay in Bariavak. Whether I belong there or not. Whether I'm … It's not that I don't think King Jozef would be kind, but I couldn't come home. Ever." Her voice broke on the final word, but no tears fell. "And even if I went and came back okay, I'd know that at any moment…"

She'd been carrying this alone for months. Building the wall of worry higher and higher with each new bit of information she'd found.

He wanted to give her hell for holding on to all this. He wanted to take her in his arms and rock her.

Both reactions would have been for himself. They weren't what she needed.

"I know you're worried that if a DNA test proves you are Josephine-Augusta that you'll lose your U.S. citizenship, but you can't stall forever, Katie. Not even for much longer. The king's nephew sending somebody after your DNA shows others are interested—really interested—in whether you're the heir to the Bariavak throne. But there's another reason—you have a grandfather."

"I *might* have a grandfather. It's not like you and Andy, Brad. He's a stranger. And he's a king. It's risking my home, my job, my country on a gamble that we might get along."

He started to argue, but stopped himself. If he'd had the experiences she had with what she'd thought was her family would he be willing to risk everything he knew on the chance of more family?

"Katie, those immigration lawyers you talked to. Would they remember you?"

"I don't know. They might remember the scenario I asked about, with a baby brought in illegally, now grown, and did he have any standing in the U.S."

"Did you disguise yourself at all? Use another name?"

To his surprise, she smiled. "I not only used another name, I used a pre-paid phone I'd bought with cash in Milwaukee. They never saw me and I made up a name."

He grinned back. "Good for you, Ms. Mata Hari Davis."

At the use of her last name, her smile faded.

"I shouldn't have told you, Brad. It's not fair to ask you to keep this quiet when you could get in trouble—"

"Yeah, right. I'm going to run right out and report you."

"You should," she said, but he could see what it cost her. "I shouldn't have involved you—"

Her head dropped forward. He scooted closer, using a hand at the back of her neck to bring her head against his chest. His other hand stroked her back. He kissed the top of her head. With his lips still on her hair, he pledged. "You're not alone in this anymore."

"You can't tell C.J. or Carolyn. The university—"

"Don't worry. I won't tell a soul. You and me, we'll figure this out, Katie. We'll figure it out."

"How?"

"I don't know yet, but I swear to you we will. There's always a way."

CHAPTER EIGHTEEN

Katie heard his familiar footsteps coming down the hall outside the offices Friday afternoon and prepared herself.

Forty-three hours since Brad had left her house.

They'd talked a little more without arriving at answers, because there weren't any. He'd insisted she go to bed early, and with her head fuzzy from crying that had been a relief.

She'd slept better than she had since … well, since January. Not only Wednesday night, but also last night. Even though she felt so guilty for putting any of this mess on him. But apparently she could sleep through guilt.

Brad breezed into the office.

Officially, he'd taken personal days yesterday and today. Since he had piled up enough to take a couple trips to Mars and back, no one objected.

Except her. Inside her own head.

She'd called three times. And hung up twice. The third time she'd left a vague message that no one could possibly ever use against him.

Telling someone to forget that you'd involved them in your potentially illegal immigration status was not something to say on the phone.

"Brad, I have to talk to you," she said as soon as he walked in.

"No time now. Get your purse. I need you to come help me with something off-campus."

"Off-campus?" He'd thrown her completely off. "Did you get my message? You took—you accidentally kept some, uh, papers that I need back."

But he hadn't even slowed down as he passed her desk. He was already sticking his head into C.J.'s office and saying, "I'm going to steal Katie for a while. Could have her back in an hour or so if you need her. Or we could call it quits for the week."

"Call it quits. No problem. Is this something I need to worry about?" That was C.J.'s standard question.

"No." And that was Brad's standard answer.

"Okay."

"C'mon," Brad said to her, returning to her desk.

"I'm not as easy as C.J. What's this about? And did you get my messa—"

"You'll see. I thought this was the drawer where you keep your purse."

"No. Get out of there. It's not in a file for heaven's sake."

"Well, where—? Ah, here it is." He slung the strap on his shoulder. "Let's go."

"You are not walking out of here with my purse on your shoulder."

But he was and she scrambled to catch up with his long-legged stride. Out of the office, out of the athletic building, and toward the parking lot.

"If you want your purse, you have to come with. Forget the Pied Piper, I'm the Purse Piper."

"You look ridiculous," she said as sternly as she could with an entirely unexpected chuckle gurgling in her throat. Was this the first step to hysteria?

He angled one leg, looking down at the purse. "You don't think it matches my outfit? Too informal for the rest of my attire?"

His attire consisted of a slate gray shirt tucked into chinos. He had gone more formal than usual by wearing loafers instead of basketball shoes. "I think it looks like a peanut hanging from a string on a giraffe."

"Ah," he said wisely. "The proportion's off."

He opened the passenger door, slung her purse in, then stepped back for her. She supposed she could dive in, grab her purse, then retreat, but that seemed overdramatic.

She settled for "Where are we going?" once they were both in the car and he was driving out of the parking lot.

"You'll see. Hey, guess what I got in the mail today. A real surprise."

"An offer to headline a Vegas comedy act."

"Whoa. That's spooky. How'd you know?"

Despite herself, she laughed. Then more seriously, she said, "An offer to be a head coach."

In fact, she said it far more seriously than she'd intended. She looked away from him, realizing they were heading toward Ashton's business district.

Of course an offer for a head basketball coaching position would not come by mail or as a surprise. He *should* be moving up, even though it meant leaving Ashton. She wanted that for him. She did.

"Better. Got an invitation to April and Hunter's wedding."

"You did?"

"Yup. The wedding being talked about in all the gossip magazines and yours truly's going to be there."

"How do you know it's being talked about in gossip magazines?"

"I have my sources," he said mysteriously. "Heck, they were talking about it at the barbershop last week."

"I don't believe—Why are you parking here?"

He'd pulled into the parking lot behind the copper-domed county courthouse at the center of town.

"Because we're going into the courthouse."

He was out of the car and around to her door, opening it before she had a chance to ask, "Why?"

He put out a hand and she automatically put hers into it. He drew her up and out of the car easily.

"Because," he said as he swung the door closed behind her, "we're getting a marriage license."

Still holding her hand he started to head toward the entrance. She stopped. "No. No. Absolutely not."

She'd let him lull her. With his humor and his charm and—yes, admit it, with her pleasure at being in his company. She'd trailed along, not questioning. But not now.

Brad kept going until their arms were fully extended, his grip tightening, preventing her from pulling free.

Two women who'd gotten out of a van parked a row behind them, looked at them with interest. A man walking between cars turned to watch.

No notice. Draw no notice.

"Brad," she pleaded.

"Just because we get one doesn't mean we use it." He sounded as at ease as always.

"You planned this. You knew—this is why you took that bir—the papers."

"I thought it might come in handy. And it will. We need it to get the license."

"No. What if they spot—"

"They won't. It got you all through school. It'll do fine here, too."

Then she realized how selfish her objection sounded—how selfish it *was*. "You don't want to—We can't—"

"We'll get the license and we can argue about it later."

"This is insane."

"It's a solution. The quickest, easiest, best solution. Of course you could have a kid born in the United States and that would—"

The women had stopped, openly listening. The man was craning he neck to keep watching them. A couple with a toddler hushed the child, apparently to hear better.

"This is not funny," she said, pitching her voice low. "And don't talk so loud."

Never taking his eyes off her, but in a tone only she could hear, he said, "No, it's not funny. And having a baby would take nine months. I don't think you can put off King Jozef for nine months, do you?" He narrowed his eyes. "I don't think you want to, either. I think you want to know."

"But—"

"But you don't want to risk losing everything. So this is the best solution. It gives you the security about being able to come back that will let you take the DNA test."

"Brad, I can't do this to you—"

"You can go inside with me now and get the license. Nothing permanent. Heck, if we don't use it in time, it dries up and blows away. So we'll get it, and we'll have dinner and talk about it."

The pressure of all the eyes watching was too great. She relieved the tension of their arms by stepping forward, toward Brad, toward the courthouse. "I'm not agreeing to use the—it."

"Understood."

"I'm paying for my own dinner."

"You can pay for mine, too."

Only after they'd done the paperwork did she wonder if the pressure she'd felt of the watching eyes had come mostly from Brad's blue gaze.

Brad took two more slices from the pizza box sitting on the coffee table, folding them together for a better bite.

Yes, she'd bought the pizza. That was the only dinner treat he'd allowed her. He'd insisted they eat at her house. "Because we don't want anyone overhearing the things we've got to talk about."

He had a point.

His long legs stuck out from where he'd plopped himself on the area rug.

Once he sat on the floor it had seemed unnecessarily stiff to remain primly on a chair, so she'd slid down at the other end of the coffee table. It made it easier to reach the pizza box.

Brad used the base of the couch as a back support. Somehow it didn't look as bad with him sitting against it.

"So, we can wait the six days—" he said. She chewed faster. She didn't want to be at a disadvantage by being caught with a mouthful of pizza. "—or I can go back and pay for a waiver and we can get married immediately. But I think—"

She swallowed. "No, wait. I haven't said I—"

"No, you haven't said you will, but you know it's the best we're going to do with the circumstances we've got."

"These are *my* circumstances. There's no reason you should have to—"

"Sure there is. I promised."

"I am not holding you to that, Brad. This is serious. If officials found out you married me so I would be a citizen, you can get in a lot of trouble."

"That's not likely. Really, this is an insurance policy. Gives you a fallback position so you can get your DNA tested without risking being a person without a country. Now you know you'll always have a home."

"Brad, I can't let you—"

"We're in this together, Katie. I signed those license papers, too."

"I haven't agreed—"

"I know, and it's getting in the way of making plans. I say I call that woman back in the morning and say, yes, we'll take the opening in the judge's schedule next week."

"But—"

"You're not going to get superstitious on me and say it's bad luck because that couple canceled, are you? You don't believe in that stuff. You won't even humor C.J. or the guys about their superstitions before a big game. Besides, next Friday's perfect. We can both take the afternoon off. I'll call Frank and Thomas to be witnesses," he said of two of his former teammates. "All I have to do is tell them it's for you and they'll be here like a shot. I'll even let you have Frank be your witness and I'll take Thomas."

"But—"

"I know you'd probably like Carolyn and C.J. but under the circumstances, that wouldn't be a good idea…"

"No, we can't let Carolyn or C.J. be involved, because if it comes out they could get in trouble. With the law. With the university." Dismay washed over her. "But that means you—"

"That's why no Ellis, either," he said of the remaining member of C.J.'s first recruiting class. "Lawyer that he is, he takes that officer of the court stuff real seriously, so we won't put him in a bind. And we won't tell Frank and Thomas anything that could come back and bite them."

"You're worrying about everybody except yourself. If you're worried about what the university could do to C.J. or Carolyn, what about you?" She put down the remnants of her pizza slice. "No. I won't ask this of you. I can't. It's not fair when—"

"You're not asking me. I'm doing. If it comes out, we'll say I got you drunk because I was afraid you'd say no—with good reason, considering the way you keep saying no—and I was utterly besotted with you."

"Right. They'll really believe that."

"They should."

"What do you mean, they should?"

He ignored that. "Do you trust me, Katie?"

"Yes. But—"

"Trust has no buts. Close your eyes and let the ball fly, Katie. It's going to swish right through the basket, you'll see. I promise."

CHAPTER NINETEEN

How many times in the days that followed did she tell him no way on earth was she going to let him do this?

He'd nod, and say, "I'm going to have to move some things in to your place. Don't worry, I'll sleep in the guest room. To most people, it'll look like we're dating, involved. But if there're questions later it can also look like we've been married."

"Brad—"

"Just a precaution. And I travel enough that I won't get in your hair a lot."

"There is no way on earth I'm going to let you do this."

He'd nod and say, "It's all lined up with Frank and Thomas. As soon as I said it was for you, they were in. And they won't ask too many questions. Unless you have someone you think would be better?"

"No. Because there is no way on earth I'm going to let you do this."

He'd nod and say, "We'll take them out for dinner after. I thought Angelo's. To people outside it would look casual, but if there were official questions about it later, it would seem natural we went there for sentimental reasons. Unless you want someplace better?"

"No. Because, there is no way on earth I'm going to let you do this."

He'd nod and say, "I thought I'd wear my new suit. Because if I don't wear a suit, Gordo and Abbott would get suspicious. Do you need a bouquet?"

"No. Because, there is no way on earth I'm going to let you do this."

He'd nod and say, "We're taking lunchtime tomorrow to look at rings. Unless you trust me to pick them out."

"No. Because, there is no way on earth I'm going to let you do this."

Yet here she stood, pressing out creases from the dress she'd bought tonight, spending the evening at the mall two towns over, telling herself she would get something new only if she could wear it to April and Hunter's wedding in two weeks. Despairing she'd find anything that could possibly work for that … and something else.

Until she did.

And, yes, they'd gone one lunchtime to a jeweler who was a major fan. It had felt surreal, with Brad acting like this was for a real wedding and her trying to spot the prices. They'd settled on simple matching bands for tomorrow.

If there was a tomorrow—at least if there was a wedding tomorrow.

When she was done with the iron, she was going to hang up the dress carefully. No sense getting wrinkles in it, no matter what came later.

She'd work the morning, as usual. Only after lunch would she have to decide whether she was going to come back here and be ready for Brad to pick her up at three.

Or to finally say no and make it stick.

This was either the best idea he'd ever had or the worst thing he'd ever done.

Brad watched the only couple remaining ahead of them being ushered to the courtroom by the clerk. The glass doors closed behind them.

He wouldn't let it be the worst thing he'd ever done. He'd protect Katie from the potential downside for her in this … which happened to be him.

He'd lived by the rules of keeping his hands off Katie all these years. He could keep it up for as long as he needed—as long as *she* needed—even if they were spending a lot more time together. Even if they were married.

The previous couple had taken three minutes and forty-two seconds, probably because they'd had a dozen spectators. The one before had taken three minutes eighteen seconds. The first one had been three-twenty-seven.

Oh, the couples' time in the courtroom lasted longer than that. Even with the efficiency of the operation, there were formalities, then they allowed a few minutes at the end for congratulations from the onlookers. But counting from when the judge started officially addressing the not-yet-married couple until the end when he declared them married, that's how long it had been taking.

Why was he timing it?

Three minutes and change, and two people were married.

So what. That wasn't such a big deal. He'd seen games turn around in seconds. Teams come back from seemingly insurmountable odds. Spin from surefire loss to glorious victory.

Why was he thinking about comeback wins? Why was he thinking about basketball at all? This was no game.

He sure as heck didn't know one millionth as much about it as he knew about basketball.

He'd been so sure this was the only solution. When Katie argued with him it had made him all the more certain. But now they were here—now *she* was here. Not arguing, but actually going through with his idea to give her security by marrying him. The security she needed to explore another life so far beyond him that—

That didn't matter. She was a princess for God's sake. That was her destiny. That's what she deserved.

Besides, it wasn't like they'd have a marriage, even if they were married.

"You're not going to throw up, are you?"

He glared at Thomas Abbott.

"Just wondering. Because I made the reservation at Angelo's like you asked and I don't want my appetite ruined."

"You didn't tell Filomena—"

"Will you quit worrying about that? I didn't tell her anything except there'd be four for dinner and we'd like the small back room."

"Good, because remember, you're not supposed to tell anybody about this. Not anybody. Especially—"

"Coach or Carolyn. I know, I know. Don't understand why you and Katie wouldn't want them to know. But I also don't understand why Katie wouldn't want a real wedding with all the trimmings like every other female. That's half the reason I haven't gotten married yet. All that hoopla."

"Yeah. Somebody shy and retiring like you would melt under the spotlight. I feel for you."

Abbott grinned, but gave the obligatory objection. "I am sensitive. Very sensitive. That's why I decided against law school and politics."

"That and you realized you'd make more money in business."

"That, too."

With the important issues covered, Brad grumbled, "Why the hell would you ask if I was going to throw up?"

"You used to before big games, so I thought—"

"I did not."

"Yes, you did."

Frank strode over to them, deserting Katie where she stood by a tall window.

Brad couldn't stop looking at her. She wore a straight-lined dress in a green that was so pale it was almost white but wasn't. It was a nice green. Calm. Sophisticated.

He should have gotten her something other than daisies. Not even a real bouquet. Just a bunch tied with a ribbon by the lady in the florist shop.

"Can't leave you two alone for a minute," Frank said.

Brad was still looking at Katie. The dress had something over her shoulders that were a cross between small sleeves and wide straps.

She had great shoulders. Why had he never noticed that before? Was it possible he'd never seen them? She didn't wear sleeveless tops to the office, much less strapless. But surely he'd have seen her shoulders sometime over the years.

Shoulders weren't the only thing that dress showed off. The front curved down in the middle. Not revealing too much—that wouldn't be Katie's style—but enough to remind you ever damned second that there was plenty to be revealed.

She wore a necklace that curved several inches above the top of the dress. It was a gold chain with white pearls spotted along it.

It was pretty enough. Delicate, which suited her long neck and smooth, pale skin.

He hated it.

Which was stupid. Why would he hate a necklace? He didn't care about necklaces. If Katie liked it, why shouldn't she wear it?

Because it should be his necklace she wore. Because he wanted only a necklace he'd given her to slide against that delicate, pale skin. Because he wanted nobody and nothing to touch it except him. He wanted everyone on earth to know that only he—

"I was saying he used to throw up before big games and since this is a helluva lot more pressure than a game—"

"Why don't you go talk to Katie, Thomas. I'd like a word with Brad."

With something like relief, Brad jerked his attention from Katie and thoughts that might have been okay for a guy really getting married, but for someone in his position were downright nuts.

He flicked Thomas' shoulder and warned him, "Don't go telling her lies about me throwing up before big games."

"But you did, so—"

Frank nudged Thomas toward Katie and took Brad's arm to steer him toward the opposite end of the room. "You did, you know. Not every game, but some."

Brad shook loose. "You, too? What is this?"

"We're concerned about you—both of you. You and Katie. Brad."

He waited until Brad looked up to meet his eyes. "I know it's something—"

"I don't know what you—"

"—don't try to tell me it's not. Not when you don't have Ellis or Coach or Carolyn here. But I'm not asking you what. Some people made the mistake of thinking you were a flibbertigibbet—"

"*Flibbertigibbet?* What are you? A hundred and fifty years old?"

"—but I was never one of them," Frank finished serenely. "Especially not the way you feel about Katie."

"I don't—." He bit it off because he didn't know what he *didn't*. Especially what he didn't feel about Katie. But he had to say something because Frank was looking at him the way he did sometimes because he was two years older than the rest of them, which you'd think he'd have gotten over since they were no longer college kids, but apparently not. "Katie's part of the team."

Frank's brows went up. There was surprise in the expression, but something more. If it had been Thomas, he'd have said mocking, but Frank didn't mock.

"She is," Brad insisted. "She didn't come on until later, but she's still part of it. Like you and Ellis and Coach and Carolyn and Thomas."

Frank looked over his shoulder toward Katie, then to him. Brad braced for a challenge that "teammate" was not how he viewed Katie.

Instead, Frank said, "You almost always had good reasons for what you were doing. You almost always did them for the good."

Brad had nothing to say to that.

"Almost always," Frank repeated. "So, tell me this, Brad, do you have a good reason for what you're doing? A reason that's good for Katie?"

"Yes."

"And good for you?"

"Yes." Because it was good for Katie.

"Are you doing this for the good?"

"Yes."

Frank continued to look at him before slowly nodding. "Okay."

He heard that low sound Katie made in her throat when she was trying not to laugh. He turned, seeing her grinning up at Thomas, who was trying to keep a straight face. He supposed he needed to be grateful to his old teammate for easing Katie's tension. But mostly he wanted to go grab her and pull her away.

That thought hadn't even finished when the clerk said, "Davis and Spencer."

Their eyes met. He gave one small nod, strode toward her and held out his hand. She'd hesitated an instant, so when they met he'd gone more than halfway. But she put her hand into his as if it belonged there and they walked into the courtroom side by side, with Frank and Thomas behind them.

CHAPTER TWENTY

"Please stand here," the judge said after the introductions and other preliminaries.

"What are you doing?" Frank asked from behind them.

"Getting ready to take video," Thomas said.

"Video?" Katie looked around, apparently alarmed.

"Oh, everyone wants a video, dear. Someday you'll be glad you have it," said the woman who'd escorted them in.

"Sure," he said, hoping Katie caught both the warning lift of his eyebrows and the humor in his voice. "We'll be glad we have it someday."

"Oh. Yes. Thank you, Thomas."

They turned back to the judge.

The three minutes and thirty-four seconds that followed were flashes for Brad.

We are gathered here in front of these witnesses…

The judge was talking and Katie was watching him with such intense concentration.

Love, honor, comfort, and cherish as long as you both shall live.

The judge asking, "Will you join right hands?"

He reached across and took her hand in his. For half a heartbeat he thought she'd balk, pull back. Instead, she shifted toward him, reducing the stretch of their arms and settling their hands together more comfortably.

"I, Bradford Alan, take you, Katherine Mary, to be my wedded wife

"From this day forward

"To love and to cherish till death do us part."

Forsaking all others.

"I, Katherine Mary, take you, Bradford Alan, to be my wedded husband

"From this day forward

"To love and to cherish till death do us part."

The rings were there, in his hand when he needed them, though he had no recollection of Thomas handing them to him.

"As a symbol of our constancy and a token of our vows, with this ring, I thee wed."

Her rings glided on—the wedding band they'd selected together and the diamond engagement ring he'd gone back for.

"Brad," she whispered, surprise, admonition, and was there the tiniest bit of delight?

He held the rings there at the base of her finger, looking at them, at their joined hands until the judge cleared his throat.

Katie's hand shook as she went to put the band on his finger. But when it didn't slip right on, she concentrated and the shaking stopped.

"It's good it's a tight fit," the judge said with a smile, "because you don't want it falling off."

Katie smiled back at the judge.

"Now, by the authority vested in me by the state of Wisconsin, it is my pleasure and my privilege to pronounce you husband and wife. You may kiss the bride."

Katie's eyes came to his. He gave her a small nod of reassurance, cupped her shoulders, his hands sliding under the loose fabric there to rest on her warm, smooth skin. He leaned down and she looked up.

Their lips brushed softly, gently. Parted. But only by a breath before they came together again.

Then they both stepped back.

There was more, but the next thing Brad heard that formed into words was "Congratulations. Okay, we'll go sign some paperwork and make this official."

He and Katie were married.

Angelo's wasn't the best restaurant in Ashton, but it was the best-loved.

It offered the quintessential red-checked tablecloths, candles in wine bottles, Americanized Italian cuisine, and the warmth of staff that had been there as long as the doors had been opened. It had been the scene of celebrations and consolations for the basketball team and those connected to it for more than a decade.

They had just ordered when a stir at the doorway of the private room introduced a new arrival, a dark-skinned young man with intense and intelligent dark eyes behind stylish glasses.

"Did you really think I wouldn't find you?"

"Ellis!" She, Frank, and Thomas greeted the newcomer with delight. Brad demanded, "How'd you know?"

"Frank, of course."

Brad swiveled around. Frank shrugged with an unabashed grin.

"You didn't think you were going to keep this gathering from me, did you?" Ellis Manfred asked, reclaiming Brad's attention. "Or what it is celebrating. Yes, I know that's not for public consumption. I seriously doubt it's a lack of faith in my discretion that explains why I was excluded from both the event and the news. Though I have a fair idea why you might have wanted to exclude me." He gave Brad a hard look.

"Why?" Thomas demanded.

"Because," Ellis said in measured tones, "he knew I'd try to talk Katie out of it because we all know she's way too good for him."

"Well, that's true," Thomas said.

"Oh, yeah, like you're such a great bargain for Amanda," Brad shot back at Ellis. "And you're too late to tell Katie anything."

He slid his hand under hers, displaying the ring.

Katie's accelerating heartbeat made her lungs burn.

"Then, first, I'll kiss the bride." He kissed her soundly on the cheek. "Second, tell you that you're one lucky son of a gun." He slapped Brad on the back with more force than absolutely necessary. "And, third, be glad that I already told Filomena I'd like the broiled trout, green beans, and house salad. Because that means I can sit here next to Katie and let you try to explain why you didn't want me to know you two were getting married."

Silence.

"It's complicated," Katie said. Even to herself she sounded breathy and uncertain.

"It always is with Brad."

"No, no, none of this is his fault. He's helping me."

Brad chuckled. It wasn't bad, either, though she heard strain in it. "They'll never buy that, Katie. They know I don't put myself out for anyone else."

"That's true," Thomas said. At the same time Frank said, "That's not true."

Ellis looked from her to Brad and back. "What do Coach and Carolyn say?"

"They don't know. They can't know," she added quickly. She touched Ellis' hand. "Please."

"Why can't they know?"

"You know. Nepotism in the office and all that," Brad said. "Once we've shown we still work together without our, uh, relationship causing problems, then we'll let them know."

When Ellis finally spoke after a pause, she was aware of Brad releasing a breath. "How long do you think that will take?"

She turned, but Brad didn't look at her. He shrugged. "We'll play it by ear."

Ellis considered him, then asked Thomas, "Do you know what's really going on?"

"Nope. You think Spencer would tell me and not you? Well, I guess he did about today, didn't he, huh? Maybe it's something he thinks you'd disapprove of."

Ellis turned to Frank. "Do you know what's going on, Gordo?"

"No. Brad asked me to come, so I came. But you know Brad

wouldn't do anything to hurt Katie. Besides, you heard—she's the one who said Coach and Carolyn can't know."

"Good point." Now Ellis' gaze came to her. "The way you've got this set up, is it something that can hurt them?"

"No." She cleared her throat and got it out with more volume on the second try. "No."

Then, as if she could hear his thoughts, she knew Brad was telling her not to explain any more. He was right. If she said they weren't telling C.J. and Carolyn in order to protect them, Ellis would be even more suspicious, and probably never stop digging until he knew the whole story. And the more people who knew the truth, the more vulnerable Brad might be.

She closed her mouth.

Once again, Ellis looked from her to Brad.

"Then I guess all that's left is to tell Katie every secret I picked up in four years of trying to keep you in line so you wouldn't freelance your way into a world of hurt."

While the others laughed, Ellis' gaze sharpened. She followed the direction of the look and felt a jolt to realize Brad still held her hand. Only it wasn't solely Brad holding her hand. Her hand held his as well. She started to withdraw, and Brad held on.

Their eyes met, and she saw a hint of warning in his.

She produced a smile and did her best to relax her hand, as she turned back to where Thomas and Frank were telling Ellis about the brief ceremony. She even contributed a bit, though not much contribution was needed when these four got together.

She was relieved when the server brought their salads so Brad released her hand. Certainly it was relief that brought a slight coolness where Brad's warm palm had heated her skin. Yes, relief.

"So what are you going to do?" Thomas asked as they ate.

"Do?"

"You know, like where are you going on your honeymoon?"

Katie couldn't look at Brad, yet knew if she looked at any of the others they'd see the utter blank that had taken over her mind. She grabbed her water and started drinking seriously.

"We'll only take the weekend." Brad sounded so calm. "We'll plan a honeymoon later."

Thomas nodded. "So are you moving in with Katie? Or is she moving in with you?"

"We're not going to rush into anything—"

"Except marriage," Ellis murmured.

"—my lease runs a while longer and of course the house is Katie's. So we have time to decide."

"Sell both and get a place that's yours together," Frank advised.

Thomas jumped on that. "Better yet, get a new place for the two of you—it's a good time to buy—and keep Katie's house to rent it out."

That started a conversation on real estate, interspersed with teasing about Thomas' mogul tendencies, that lasted throughout dinner.

Along with dessert, came another stir at the doorway.

C.J. and Carolyn, being escorted in by Filomena, Alberto's wife and the ruler of the restaurant.

CHAPTER TWENTY-ONE

"Thought I spotted you guys in here when we walked in," C.J. said.

"But Mr. Coach C.J., you called first to see if—" Filomena's sentence was smothered when C.J. wrapped her in a hug. Since she was about a foot and a half shorter than him, her face was pressed into his shirt.

Katie recovered first. Under the table, she took his left hand and tapped the ring.

Trying to mask his movements, he pulled the snug-fitting ring off.

"We hope you don't mind us crashing your party and joining you for dessert," Carolyn said, with only the slightest hesitation before "party."

Katie transferred both her rings to his palm. He slid all three into his pocket. "Of course not," Ellis said. "Here, you want to sit beside Katie, so you two can talk."

"No, no," Carolyn protested with a hand to his shoulder.

Brad heard Katie release a breath, but he thought her relief might be premature.

Sure enough, Coach and Carolyn went around to the other side of the round table where they could look directly across at Katie and him.

Released from C.J.'s hug, Filomena forgot everything except chastising a new waiter for dropping a dessert fork. She quickly had the desserts served and bustled the unfortunate waiter out.

"Did I ever tell you guys we came here the first time Carolyn agreed to come out to a meal with me?" C.J. asked, digging into his cake.

"We went to that prime rib place first on the way to watch a game," his wife corrected.

He grinned at her. "Ah, but you didn't agree to go there with me. I sprung that meal on you, because I was still having to trick you into spending time with me."

Interesting. Coach had had to spring things on Carolyn to get their relationship rolling.

"You came here for your first date?" Frank asked.

"It wasn't a date. It was a working dinner," Carolyn said primly. "Oh, all right. It was a date. Though we did mostly talk about you guys."

C.J. chuckled. "Boy, have we ever corrupted her—she started referring to players as 'individual students who happen to be involved in this peculiar pastime involving a sphere.' Now it's 'you guys.'"

"I was never that..." Carolyn let the protest die as she looked around at their grins. "Okay, Coach Draper. Shall I tell them about what you did at that dinner?"

"Me? I was a perfect gentleman."

"He spoke to the waiter in Italian."

They groaned. "Way too obvious, Coach," Thomas said.

Ellis shook his head. "You've got to be subtle to impress a girl that you'd played in Italy."

"*Now* you tell me. I might have gotten somewhere with that babe if I'd had you guys to coach me," C.J. said dryly, tugging Carolyn close to kiss the top of her head. "Hey, speaking of foreign travel, the team's itinerary this summer's been expanded. Final paperwork went through today. We're also going to Bariavak."

Beside him, Brad felt Katie stiffen. He slid his hand under the tablecloth to take hers. He squeezed lightly, reminding her they had this covered. It would be okay.

Brad had told his friends they were taking the weekend. What he hadn't said was they were taking it for manual labor in her yard.

They'd all stayed at Angelo's, talking and laughing until after midnight. She'd been exhausted, but she couldn't leave—Brad had driven her to the courthouse and the restaurant. The two of them leaving together would surely have started remarks that would have made C.J. and Carolyn suspicious ... if they weren't already. Plus, it would have cleared the way for C.J., Carolyn, and possibly Ellis to pump Thomas and Frank.

So she'd silently supported Brad's choice to stay until everyone left.

Brad put their rings in a small box she gave him and left it on a kitchen shelf.

Saturday morning she heard him in the shower, but he was gone when she got up. He soon returned with supplies ... and a list of tasks a mile long.

If his goal was to work them both so hard neither of them had time to get uncomfortable, he succeeded. She fell into bed so exhausted each night that she barely was aware of him sleeping in the other room. Barely.

Early Monday he left for a week on the road, scheduled to return Saturday, she knew because she'd made the arrangements.

He was right. They certainly didn't trip over each other. Except she kept thinking about him. But she could hardly blame him for that.

There were also his usual phone calls to the office from the road. He teased. She handled business. It was almost like it had always been.

Except nothing was as it had always been.

She decided to clean Saturday morning. Because the house needed it. Not in anticipation of his return.

She was vacuuming the living room with a bandana around her head. The front door opened, Brad walked in, dropped his bag, and stood looking at her.

She couldn't look away. He hadn't shaved, the stubble darker than his hair. He looked tired, a strain around his eyes.

It might have been half a minute before she remembered the vacuum and turned it off.

"You're not supposed to be here yet."

"Caught an earlier flight. Would have knocked, but your neighbors were watching from across the street—yes, I know that wouldn't be an issue if the trees were still there—but it seemed a good time to use my key."

She answered his slight smile with one of her own. "Wouldn't have mattered, I wouldn't have heard you over the vacuum."

"Katie—"

Her cell phone rang.

For another beat they looked at each other, then he nodded toward her phone sitting on the coffee table.

She picked it up. "It's April."

He frowned, but said nothing as she turned so he wouldn't be in view, produced a bright smile, and accepted it as a video call.

"Hi, Katie, we're both here," came April's voice. Hunter added a hello from beside April, though he appeared distracted by a computer screen to one side. "We wanted to see how you are and, uh, how things are going."

"No change," she said brightly. "Everything's fine. Busy at work. Very busy."

"But it should be lighter now, right? And you're still coming to Washington next week, right?"

"Yes."

"That reminds me," April said, "I hope you don't mind, we invited Brad."

She almost said she knew, but with Brad listening, she substituted, "How could I possibly mind anyone you choose to invite to your wedding."

"She was afraid you might not bring him as your plus-one."

"Hunter," April scolded. Then she grinned. "Though that is the truth." Before Katie recovered, April's grin changed to a frown. "Please don't tell me you were going to bring someone else."

"I'm not bringing anyone."

April's smile returned. "Great. Somehow I forgot to include the plus-one option on Brad's invitation, so no worries there about needing to change table arrangements."

"Again," Hunter muttered.

"April, I think you might have the wrong idea." She'd *really* have the wrong idea if she knew they were married.

"Don't worry, we like Brad, and we want someone here who'll have your back just in case."

Hunter said, "I think Katie's more worried about you butting into her private life, April."

"I would never do that," April said. With that peculiar feeling she was looking at a slightly distorted image of herself, Katie wondered if she was as bad a liar as April was. "I was checking because if we change the guest list again Bette would have our heads."

"*Your* head," Hunter said. "I haven't changed my list since the beginning."

"He's so disciplined," April said admiringly.

"And too smart to get on the wrong side of Bette."

Katie brought them ice water then Brad got her to sit on the couch, beside him but not too close. No, he had little hope of her sitting too close.

He'd worked them both hard last weekend to avoid awkwardness. But that, combined with his trip, meant they'd had no chance to get comfortable with the situation, either.

It had been a long week. The snippets of conversations with Katie had not been nearly enough. The thoughts about her had been too much.

They were married.

Married.

You may kiss the bride…

She was a princess.

Abruptly, he said, "You know you'll be around King Jozef next week in D.C., spending time with him."

"I suppose."

"You know they want you to have that DNA test. And now you

can."

"I … I don't know if I want to."

That was progress, wasn't it? "You don't owe the people who raised you a damned thing, Katie. When I think about what they stole from you—"

"I was *lucky*. Truly. Since I found those things in the attic, I've read about kids taken from their families and the things they endure … I was fed and clothed, warm in the winter, cool in the summer, sent to school. And after…" She straightened. "It sounds awful, but after he died things improved. My mother supported my going to college."

"Financially," he said. "Did she ever say she was proud of you? Or that you'd done well? Or that she loved you?"

"She wasn't that kind of woman. But she worked very hard to support me. I can't forget that."

"You said once you had no family stories, Katie, but there *were* family stories. At least implicit ones. That they were your parents. That you were born in Portland. Your birthdate. Your age. That they moved to Ashton for opportunities. Those stories were lies. They stole your birthright, your family, your future."

She looked down.

He swore sharply. That brought her head up, her eyes wide with surprise.

"What burns me," he said, "is how they closed you off, kept you hidden—Worse, they taught you to keep yourself hidden. You're wrapped in that gray shroud even when you're not wearing it. You're still living behind those damned trees even though they're gone."

He reached to her, stroking the back of his fingers down her cheek.

"Don't hide, Katie. Don't…"

You may kiss the bride.

He had. Just enough to taste her. To know there was fire between them.

Her breath hitched.

His mouth was on hers.

Her lips parted. His tongue slid between them.

Their teeth clashed. He couldn't remember the last time that happened to him.

He changed the angle, one hand pushing off the scarf she wore so he could slide his fingers into her hair, cupping her skull. His hand wanted to shake, but it couldn't now, not when it was needed to support her head as he kissed her deeper and harder.

She adjusted with him, her tongue meeting his. Her fingers slid into his hair. Her other hand gripped his wrist.

He drew her closer. His hand on her thigh. Was he imagining the faintest vibration under his palm? He'd felt it, too, when he'd put a palm on her leg under the table that day at Andy's.

A frequency of what stretched between them?

Or could that be a tremor? Was he rushing her, not leaving her time to show reluctance?

Was she holding onto him because he'd rattled her?

He released her mouth. Pulled away, even as he brought her upright with him. Then he needed to shift to the side to put some space between them. Because she was too close.

Temptation. So close.

The next county might be too close.

Her fingertips went to her lips. He saw the rub of his beard against her skin, the swelling of her lips from the pressure of his.

He had to look away. Had to. Before he did even more.

"That ... that isn't friendship." She paused, then added, staring straight ahead, not focused, "Is it?"

Her flat voice carried little or no accusation, but it didn't need to. He could supply plenty of accusation himself. He'd broken his own rules.

"Sorry. Sorry, Katie."

He grabbed his bag on the way and closed the door behind him.

CHAPTER TWENTY-TWO

She remained on the couch, trying to sort out what had happened.

That kiss hadn't been friendship. She'd been sure of it. And for an instant, the flare of hope had seared her, tightening her throat, immobilizing her muscles.

Then he'd apologized and left.

He'd regretted kissing her. That was the only thing that made sense. He'd regretted kissing her the way a man kissed a woman. The way a husband kissed a wife.

He regretted it, this man who had put himself and his career on the line for her. She owed him so much. The only thing she could do to repay him was to accept his regret and protect him from it.

It was early afternoon before she resumed cleaning. Even later when she got in the shower. And then, with the afternoon nearly gone, her cell rang. She answered before the first ring ended. Not because she'd been looking at her phone, considering calling him. Not at all.

"I need your help."

"Brad?" Of course it was Brad. Caller ID said so. Her ears said so. Her heartbeat said so.

"Yes. I need your help. At my place. Right now. You know where it is?"

"I have the address." She had addresses for all of the staff.

"Good. Get here now. It's an emergency."

Emergency. The word had her out of her chair, grabbing her purse, making sure she had her keys. "Are you okay?

"I am now, but I won't be."

The address was close to the center of town, a block off the main street. It belonged to a large, two-story stone house with stacked bay windows on each side and a double door in the center that must have been built around the same time as the courthouse.

The front door had four buttons. She pressed 2A—Spencer—and was immediately buzzed in.

The big door opened into a two-story hallway with a wide staircase. Upstairs, she turned left and saw 2A next to a door already opening.

"Damn. You're here already." Brad showed no sign of injury. He'd shaved, but wore the jeans and shirt he'd had on when he left her house, now with a green and blue striped kitchen towel decorating his shoulder. "I was about to call to ask you to pick something up at the store on your way."

"The store?" The small entry way opened to a living room to the left and a dining room to the right, with the kitchen further to the right, and tucked back. "But—you said it was an emergency."

Even with the sun nearly set, the front bay window and another good-sized window at right angles to it provided lots of natural light. Beside the second window a bookcase system covered most of the wall. The large center area held a generous but not outrageous TV screen, with other electronics below it. Narrow sections held CDs and DVDs. Other than that, there were books.

A leather couch sat across from the TV. An upholstered chair and a floor lamp occupied the bay.

"It is. Doesn't matter how great the recipe is if you don't have the ingredients."

She'd been to bachelor pads. This wasn't one. He even had art on the walls. In frames—and not a basketball picture among them. A framed photo of Brad's grandmother, mother, stepfather, and two half-sisters had a prime spot on the shelves. "Ingredients? You called me for a *cooking* emergency?"

"C'mon back to the kitchen. I've got something on the stove." The dining room was divided from the compact kitchen by an island with stools on the dining room side and a cooktop on the kitchen side. He went to the working side. "Speaking of which, remember we can't say anything when they get here."

"Who gets here? Say anything about what?" Her head hurt.

"About being married."

"We're not saying anything about that to anybody."

"I know. But it'll be harder with Andy. She has a way of sucking words out of people that they had no intention of saying."

"Andy?" But he was halfway inside the fridge, moving jars and containers around like beads on an abacus. "What are you doing?"

"Hoping against hope I have heavy whipping cream stashed in the back of a shelf where I'd forgotten about it."

"If you've forgotten about it, it would be moldy and gross."

"Not in my refrigerator." That was the most arrogant she'd ever heard him. "Damn. None."

She retrieved her purse from a stool. "Okay, I'll go to the store for whipping cream."

"*Heavy* whipping cream. That's what I need for this killer shrimp and garlic dish. But there's no time. They'll be here before you could get back. And you do not want to deal with Andy when she's hungry, which she will be, since they're getting here at seven and she usually eats at six-fifteen on the dot. At least I don't want to deal with her. I need to figure out something else."

He closed the fridge and faced her. "Think. What can take the place of heavy whipping cream?"

"Uh, yogurt?"

"Of course, why didn't I—?" He pulled a container out of the fridge, but his shoulders slumped. "Strawberry."

"Shrimp, garlic, and strawberry yogurt."

"If you keep laughing, I'll tell Andy you're the reason for this and leave you to your fate. Think, Katie, think."

"Okay, okay." White. Soupy … "What about vanilla ice cream?"

His head came around to her but his gaze was unfocused. "Vanilla ice cream. Too sweet for … but … Leave out the sugar and … Yeah, that'll work." He took ice cream from the freezer, put away a couple spices, pulled out others, adding them to a skillet on the stove.

"So you were worried about Andy knowing you didn't have heavy whipping cream?"

He grinned.

Bradford Alan Spencer's grin should be banned in forty states and against the rules in the rest of them. It wasn't fair. It wasn't ethical. It was dangerous.

She turned away, devoting great attention to the dining room. It had a second bay window out the back. A door replaced one angled window, leading to a deck. It was a great apartment. "Nah. Worried she'll know I haven't been here and then she'll want to know why. She'd left a message on my landline. She knows my cell's the way to get me with my traveling and she uses it all the time. But once in a while she'll leave a message like this on the landline. It's like she's giving me a pop quiz, only I don't know what the subject is. Or, maybe … Well, anyway she left this message saying her neighbor is driving her up to some gardening thing they're going to tomorrow in Madison. They'd stop in and have dinner with me here unless I objected. And then she says, 'So if I don't hear from you by tomorrow, we'll plan on Saturday night.' I don't even know when 'tomorrow' was. Could you do something else for me?"

"Something with cooking?" she asked doubtfully. She felt safer on this side of the island.

He grinned again. "I might ask you to stir this. But first, how about setting the table. There are mats and napkins in that drawer." He tipped his head toward the buffet on the far side of the dining table. Then he jerked his chin down near his hip. "Silverware's around here. And if you want to wash your hands, the bathroom's down the hall." This time he tipped his head backward.

Down a short hallway the first door was to the bathroom. An open door next to it showed his bed. The comforter was pulled up and pillows in coordinating shams stacked at the top.

She returned and gathered silverware, mats, cloth napkins. "You have a very nice place."

"It's the clean towels in the bathroom that get the girls," he said wisely. "Direct quote from Coach. You know how he always says being a guy doesn't mean you're automatically a slob. He hammered that in to us."

"Did he also hammer at you being able to cook?"

"Nah, Coach is a strong believer in restaurants. Cooking was Andy."

She considered her handiwork, remembering Carolyn and C.J.'s festive table whenever they had people over for dinner. "Should there be something else on the table?"

"Salt? Pepper?"

"Something decorative."

She turned, watching him. He moved quickly, easily. Hands so sure and powerful handling a basketball now deftly whisked ingredients in a bowl held at a dangerous angle. "Good idea. Look for a vase on the bookcase, but I don't have anything to put in it."

She eyed the columnar dark blue vase currently separating two stacks of books. "Too tall. Nobody could see over it. How about that plant?"

"Sure, though the pot's not much."

"I have an idea. Do you have a rubber band?" He pointed to another drawer in the kitchen. She collected the rubber band, the pot, a cloth napkin and got to work. "What kind of plant is this?"

"Shamrock. Got it for St. Patrick's Day two years ago."

"So you can also grow plants, not only order them to be cut down?"

"Hey, you admitted the house looks a lot better without—"

"I never said 'a lot.' "

"—those behemoths. Besides, I added plants last weekend—Looks good, Katie."

The rubber band secured the napkin around the pot. The excess fabric flopped down to cover it. He stepped to the end of the counter to stand beside her, putting an arm around her shoulders.

The squeeze seemed to urge her to turn toward him, and then it was so natural to look up. Was he…?

No.

He kissed the top of her head.

He released her quickly and returned to the cooktop. "Got to stir this so nothing sticks on the bottom."

The doorbell sounded.

Amid greetings and introductions, Andy pulled Brad's face down to kiss him on the cheek. Katie shook hands with Andy's friend, Viola. Releasing Brad, Andy opened her arms and engulfed Katie before she could think or hesitate. She returned the embrace, smiling.

Stepping back from the hug, Andy's eyes sharpened. She turned and squinted up at Brad as he hugged Viola, who said, "It smells heavenly."

"It should," Andy said, moving to the pan and peering at it. "It's my recipe."

"With a twist." Brad edged into the kitchen between the two older women, reaching over Viola to give the pan a stir, then checking the rice. "We'll see if you can figure out what's been done to it."

"Oh, I have a pretty good idea what you've done," his grandmother said dryly.

CHAPTER TWENTY-THREE

Even as they enjoyed the meal and chatted easily, Brad could see his grandmother plotting to get Katie to herself for a dose of Andy cross-examination.

He was torn between throwing himself in front of the truck with no brakes that was his grandmother when she was on a mission and letting events play out.

The important thing was he and Katie appeared to be mostly back on an even keel.

If hashing out what had happened this morning would have helped, he'd have hashed as long as it took.

But it wouldn't have. It would have made her more uncomfortable. Far better to demonstrate that things could be light and easy between them again. And it appeared to have worked.

As long as he kept his hands off her.

His grandmother interrupted his thoughts.

"Viola heard a noise in her car driving here. Will you take a look at it for her, Brad?" Andy asked—if a general giving an order 'asks.' "Katie and I will do the dishes."

Brad didn't miss Viola's surprise at hearing her car needed looking at. But he didn't fight. Better to get it over with.

"How are you and Brad progressing, dear?"

Katie sucked in a breath at the direct question. "Mrs. Spencer—Andy—I'm afraid you misunderstood about me coming with Brad back in March—"

"No. I didn't misunderstand. Brad had spoken of you many times before he brought you to meet me and for me to meet you. He's done that with very few women."

"We work together, that's all. Truly—"

"No." She tipped her head. "At least not on his part. I don't know you well, Katie, so I can't be sure of your feelings. Brad's are a different manner."

"He can't have said—"

"He doesn't need to say. Not to me." She smiled. "You know he was once engaged."

Brad engaged. Planning to marry someone. Was this the "until" Carolyn had mentioned? Had he backed out? Had she broken his heart, this phantom woman? How did he feel now—

"No," she said, as much to her rampaging thoughts as an answer to Andrea.

"His senior year at Ashton. She broke it off right after he wasn't drafted to the NBA. Could she have been any more obvious? But I knew she wasn't right for him the first time he brought her to see me."

"You shouldn't be telling—"

"He was helping her off with her coat by the front closet—you know how tight that can be—and she practically knocked me over in her rush to get away. Brad didn't follow her. He stayed back there hanging that coat up like it was a military operation. So I knew. And I could have told him, but no man will listen to such things." She snorted. "So I kept my mouth shut. Then watched while Brad realized what was what. At least he knew it before she broke off. Sure wasn't disappointed when it ended."

Katie waved from the front window as Brad walked Andy and Viola to the car—which was working perfectly—for their hour's drive to Madison. Then she resumed the cleanup.

"Whatever Andy said to you when she wrangled time alone, forget it," Brad said as soon as he walked in the door. "Hey, you don't have to do that."

She gently scrubbed at a spot on a pan that had been soaking in the sink. The glasses, dishes, and silverware were already in the dishwasher. "This is something I know how to do in the kitchen."

"I've had your spaghetti and stew and cake—you know how to do plenty in the kitchen."

"Staples. Nothing fancy, like you made. In fact, I know almost nothing about fancy food or fancy anything."

"Just a different recipe to follow. Hand me those covers, they go in the dishwasher. Find a recipe and dive in. Nothing to be scared of."

"I've been scared of so many things." She kept her eyes on the pan. "Clinging to the ledge of what I'd always known. You're trying to push me off the ledge."

"So you'll soar. Even more." The smile she heard in his voice was gone with his next words. "You're a princess. An honest to God princess. You have a future ahead of you that's nothing like your past."

"Did I mention scared?" she asked wryly. "Heck, I'm not even sure about this trip to Washington for the wedding. I hardly know these people, even April—"

"You can handle it. You can handle anything. Now give me that last pan to dry, and then I'll take you for ice cream."

CHAPTER TWENTY-FOUR

April had instructed Katie to call her cell when her plane landed at Washington's Reagan National Airport. She'd barely exited the terminal when she heard a beep and spotted April waving from the back of a town car.

A driver took Katie's luggage with professional courtesy that didn't quite mask his curiosity.

After giving Katie a quick hug, April announced, "This is Rupert, Katie. He drives for the embassy. Rupert, this is my friend, Katie Davis."

"Ms. Davis," the man said with a slight accent she couldn't place.

She said hello and even smiled.

A driver. For an embassy. What do I know about this kind of life? Nothing.

She'd told Brad that Saturday night. He'd passed it off as nothing to worry about. Then he'd distracted her with ice cream. Then kept her busy Sunday with yard work until it was time to change and go to dinner at Carolyn and C.J.'s, who had wanted to know all about this trip.

Early this morning had been jam-packed with details for work … and now she was here. With no idea what to expect.

"I wanted to drive, but Hunter got all protective," April said. "I haven't taken evasive and defensive driving classes, so he thinks I can't drive."

"Miss April is an enthusiastic driver," Rupert said neutrally.

April laughed. "Just for that, Rupert, I'm closing the privacy barrier."

Katie could see the man's smile in the rearview mirror as he repeated, "Yes, Miss April."

"Now," April said with a satisfied sigh as they merged into traffic on the George Washington Parkway, "we're going to have some just-us-girls fun."

Katie didn't know which had her more off-balance—the two stops they'd made, the clogged traffic, or the street signs packed with "or," "only," and "but not" clauses. She didn't want to think about April's "enthusiastic" driving in these conditions.

The first stop had been a posh Georgetown salon. April breezed in with Katie in tow and went right to the back, where the proprietor reigned.

Feeling as if her head were still in the clouds she'd watched from the airplane, she listened to Etienne and April discuss how, despite their physical similarities, Katie needed a different hairstyle from April's. She didn't even try to have a say.

Etienne waved April away, ordered Katie's hair shampooed, then circled her again with her hair wet and straight. The first cut made her gasp. She closed her eyes and kept them closed until he called April back in.

"Oh," April breathed.

"Perfect," Etienne proclaimed.

"Yes," was all she got out. The almost structural lines of the cut gave her a sophistication she had never thought possible. Yet it retained enough soft naturalness to be comfortable.

She listened to his instructions for reproducing this effect but doubted she'd pull it off. "Have your stylist call me when you go for a trim," he said in a low tone with astonishingly little accent as he tucked a business card in her pocket.

The second stop had been to an establishment with an austere exterior. Inside, April introduced her to Tonya, an elegant African-American woman who opened a hidden door, then led them down a hallway and into a dressing room ringed with mirrors.

"Your wedding dress," Katie breathed as she spotted the dreamy, elegant flow of white hanging high in front of a mirror.

"I'm not trying it on until you've tried some things. What do you think, Maurice?" April added as a man nearly as tall as Brad but much more slender entered. "This is Katie, whom I told you about."

"I think you are blackmailing her into trying on clothes. I approve." He examined her. "Etienne?" A lazy finger indicating her hair turned into a commanding gesture for her to turn.

"Of course," April said.

He chuckled, and a good part of Katie's discomfort ebbed away.

It was a good thing, because April, Tonya, and Maurice did not allow her much modesty, much less time to sort through what was happening. "I'm sure I can't afford these," she'd said to April in an urgent whisper.

"Don't worry. It's all set."

"But how—"

"Both Hunter and King Jozef insisted on paying Maurice for clothes he made for me last Christmas. And that's on top of the State Department covering the cost as part of the operation. I couldn't get either Hunter or the king to not pay and Maurice didn't even try. He said we'll work off that balance. Even with the wedding dress, it would take ages, so—"

Maurice swept back into the dressing room. "Next, a dress for April and Hunter's wedding."

"No." Katie said firmly. "I have a dress for Saturday."

Maurice looked at April, who shrugged. "Very well," he said, "bring it when you come for fittings Wednesday morning and the adjustments will be ready before you both return Friday. Now. It is time to see how your wedding dress goes, April."

It went stunningly in Katie's opinion. April looked elegant, beautiful, and glowing.

"Duchess satin," April said with a grin. "Closest I could come to a princess. I love the back, too." She turned to show how the rounded, off-the-shoulder neckline dropped to a V in back, with a modest train. "I didn't want anything too busy, especially with wearing the Craig family veil—all lace."

The hotel was all understated luxury.

The car pulled under a portico before the impressive entry. Discomfort was rising in Katie until a man in hotel livery who opened the door winked at her. Behind her, April chuckled and the man did a double-take.

"Winking at other women behind my back, Jorge?" April teased. "This is Katie, who's joining our group for the rest of the week."

"Welcome, Miss Katie. It is a pleasure to have any friend of Miss April's."

Katie's thanks were nearly lost in April's questions about his nephew's graduation and his mother's back. Jorge started to steer toward registration, but April said, "That's all set. Straight to the elevators, please."

On their way what seemed like a dozen hotel employees exchanged greetings with April. In the elevator, she said to Jorge, "What are you grinning about?"

"Mr. Pierce would not be happy at how long you have known so many."

"And there is no need for him to know," April said firmly. Apparently seeing the questions in Katie's eyes, she added, "I stayed here when Hunter was, uh, training me for you-know-what. He was paranoid about anyone knowing and thought—I'll tell you later, because here we are. Thanks, Jorge." She took Katie's elbow, and steered her off the elevator.

"My things," she protested as the doors closed with Jorge and her suitcase still inside.

April headed down the hallway. "Jorge will take them to your room and here's the key. But we're going to the suite where everyone's hanging out, and this is your suite key." She handed that over, then used another key to open the door. "Oh, good, you're all here."

For a dazzled instant, it seemed to Katie all of Washington might be in that room. And the crowd wasn't even as impressive as the view over the tops of trees to the White House. Almost immediately the crowd surrounded her, shaking her hand, pronouncing names, and welcoming her.

She said hello back to April's cousin Leslie and her husband Grady, greeted Tris and Michael Dickinson, as well as Paul and Bette Monroe, whose Evanston home was where she'd met April, as well as—Katie scanned the room.

"The king's not here," April whispered. "I told him to give you a chance to get settled."

A bevy of kids eddied into the room, including the two she'd met at the Monroes', followed by two dogs. "Rufus and Dragon," April said fondly, as the dogs danced around her.

"Oh," said one boy with vivid disappointment, "we thought it was Hunter."

"That charmer is ours, Jake," Leslie admitted, then introduced all the kids, promising at the end, "There won't be a quiz on names or affiliation. Sometimes I forget which ones belong where. "The door swung open to a chorus of "Hunter!" from the boys.

"He's the cool guy," Leslie informed Katie, "because he's not related to any of them and he carries a gun."

"And because he's just cool," April added before Hunter reached her, kissing her while stretched over a boy who said, "Eww."

"Some day, Nick," Paul said. "Some day."

Hunter grinned, dislodged a smaller boy from his leg and held out his hand to Katie. "Great to see you, Katie. I see April has already unleashed Etienne on you."

"*That*'s what's different." Tris looked from her to April and back. "It makes you look less alike. You see each of you as individually beautiful before noticing the similarities."

"Wait 'til you see what Maurice has in store for her," April said. "This one dress looks so simple, but—"

"Before you start on that," Hunter interrupted, "let me introduce my colleagues to Katie."

April immediately went to the two people who'd followed Hunter into the room and gave them each a hug. The African-American woman who exuded no-nonsense intelligence except for a wicked gleam in her eyes was Sharon Johnson, Hunter's supervisor. The good-looking younger man was introduced as Derek Kenton, Hunter's partner. April recognized him from the night she'd met King Jozef.

A knock on the door introduced an armada of room service carts and waiters. As they set out a buffet, Katie saw April give one a big hug. The waiter returned it, but kept a wary eye on Hunter.

The conversation was wide-ranging—including Washington sights to see, a piece of legislation Michael was working on, school progress for each of the kids, Leslie and Tris' efforts to preserve a historic mill in Connecticut, Paul appraising toys from an archeological dig in North Carolina, and, of course, the wedding.

April said everything was all set so they could enjoy these days before the wedding. "Bette's pulled this off even with the complications of security for King Jozef. But—" She grinned. "—we happen to have the help of security experts."

"She's talking about Bette, not me," Hunter said, deadpan.

"Grady's the miracle-worker," Bette said. "Couldn't have done it without him. Especially not in less than five months. He lined up the church and reception venue that are usually sold out years ahead."

April kissed Grady on the check, then rubbed out the lipstick mark. "We also have these amazing luxury buses—another of Grady's contributions—to take people to Charlottesville on Saturday for the wedding, and bring them back to D.C. at night. It saves all that driving—"

"And parking where there's no room," Leslie said.

"Charlottesville is where my mother's family is from and Great-Grandmother Beatrice lives there," April told Katie. "But we don't want you to wait until the wedding to see it. We—Hunter, Leslie, Grady, Bette and some others—have to be there Wednesday to work out final details. Thursday, we'll explore it with you. But no more for now. I'm going to roll out the rest of the week day by day."

CHAPTER TWENTY-FIVE

Tuesday morning, April appeared at Katie's door with a room service cart and breakfast for two.

"Oh, good, you're already dressed. We're going to pick up Hunter in the suite at nine for our first stop. Gunston Hall. It's the home of George Mason, who was a friend of Washington. He probably could have been as famous as the rest of those Founding Fathers, but he loved his home so much he didn't want to leave. Leslie and Grady took me there as a teenager and I tried so hard to be bored and indifferent, but now I love the place. But before we get Hunter, we can talk while we eat breakfast."

Katie chuckled. "Isn't that what we did yesterday? Talk and eat?"

"Sure, but I didn't want to hit you straight off the plane with your decision about having the DNA test and how you're feeling about King Jozef and whether you're getting your head around all this."

Katie resisted an urge to change the subject. "I don't know, I don't know, and absolutely not."

April gave her a shrewd look. "Someday you'll want to know what the DNA might be able to tell you. I'm not saying—" She held up a hand to stop Katie's response. "—when. Might be when you're old and gray. Set that aside. Next, how you're feeling about King Jozef."

"I'm concerned. By his certainty. And his expectations. He would expect a true member of his family. Oh, God, his *royal* family."

"Would there be expectations? Yes. But I'd worry more about Madame. Even though she's loosened up a lot."

"Madame?"

"She ran the embassy forever. Now she's sort of the king's, uh, right-hand woman. He probably listens to her more than anyone else. As for King Jozef, there are two factors. He's practiced with me on what a relationship with a granddaughter might be like. And—"

"But you said he knew from the start you weren't his granddaughter, so he never had expectations or hopes or—"

"Oh, yes, he did, crafty old statesman that he is. Although I will say they had more to do with Hunter than with his kingdom."

Katie groaned at the final word.

"But that's the other factor with King Jozef. He's had all these years since the rebellion, since his daughter's death, since the kidnapping to assess what he'd done right and wrong. He told Hunter—and I don't think either of them would mind my telling you—his regret was he didn't start earlier to honor his family by doing what they'd taught him was important. Life, love, and family."

"But his *family* isn't a normal family. It's—"

"*Is* there such a thing as a normal family? Some fortunate people have wonderful families, like the Monroes—oh, make sure I introduce you to Paul's mom and dad at the wedding, they're terrific—or Tris' family. The rest of us make up our families. A relative here, a friend there, piecing them together to create what's important to us."

"I don't know about families of either kind. My upbringing was … distant. I have it on good authority I don't let people be my friend."

"Oh, I don't know, I think you're making progress." April grinned and she couldn't help but grin back.

"Maybe I am. But not on the other part of this—King Jozef's family is *royalty*. I'd have no idea who Princess Josephine-Augusta *is*. How could I possibly be her?"

"You've got it backward. You wouldn't have to worry about being her. She'd have to be you." April folded her napkin and set it on the table. "We can talk about this later. Right now, c'mon, let's get Hunter."

April was right. Katie loved Gunston Hall.

There was something about the brick house and its grounds that struck a chord. She'd been fascinated to learn both about the man who wrote the Bill of Rights for Virginia, which became the basis for the federal version, and about life on a Potomac River plantation.

She and April were talking about the river being the plantations' primary thoroughfare when Hunter exited the parkway. Katie didn't know the area well, but this exit—

"We're swinging by the airport," Hunter said, unnecessarily, since road signs proclaimed that. He met Katie's eyes in the rear view mirror. "You can ask April while I go inside."

April suddenly had a lot of directions to give Hunter, keeping her too busy to talk until he'd pulled up to the terminal, Hunter got out, and April took his spot behind the wheel.

"April—"

"Wait until we're in the cell phone lot. Drivers get crazy here."

After she'd parked, April turned off the engine and swiveled in the seat to face her. "Hunter's gone in to get Brad. I told you we'd invited him."

"You—I thought you meant to the wedding." And he'd never said a word. "Oh, no, he'll be here the rest of the week, doing all the fun stuff with us."

"April, I don't want you to think Brad and I are…" She had no idea how to complete that sentence.

"Dating? Oh, I know that." Something in her overly breezy tone made Katie edgy.

"April—"

"It won't be you two alone together all the time like on a date. But even if it were, how could you object? He's a great guy, fun and smart and so attractive, though he is awfully tall, and I wonder about … Besides, you can't tell me you're not interested in him."

Her head jerked up and she faced April's knowing smile. She tried anyway. "Where did you get that idea? That's—"

"I got that idea from how you reacted—or didn't react—to Derek Kenton."

"What?"

"I watched you with Derek. He's very good looking. And nice. And he has his fair share of The Jaw."

"The what?"

"I'll tell you later. Let me finish this first. Derek gave you a little of the once-over but there was no reaction from you at all. On the other hand, I've seen you light up when Brad walks into a room—heck, when he stumbled into your kitchen after a night on the couch, looking far, far less than his best. So, that was one clue. Plus the Kenton Test. If I'd been more attuned to my own feelings I would have realized right off that having no reaction to the Kenton Test showed I'd fallen for Hunter. Of course, Hunter is the perfect specimen of The Jaw."

"That again."

"Okay, let me tell you about my theory of The Jaw. I have to admit a couple women I've told my theory to have not gotten it at all. There was a former neighbor…"

It was only much later—long after she'd concurred with April's theory of The Jaw, as well as long after they'd picked up Brad and Hunter at the terminal, and also long after her heartbeat had nearly returned to normal after its first-sight-of-Brad sprint—that Katie realized she'd never straightened out any lingering misconception about her relationship with Brad.

That was because she'd been thoroughly distracted by April's casual comment to Brad on the way to the hotel that they were all having dinner tonight at Leslie and Grady's house … and King Jozef and Madame would also be guests.

"Who's Madame?" Brad asked.

"A force of nature," April said. "And, it turns out, she's related to Hunter. So you should ask him."

"April."

"Okay, okay. I'm clearly being told not to say anymore. Except I'll repeat what I told Katie—Madame *has* loosened up a lot in the past six months."

Katie had to fight to keep her jaw from dropping at Leslie and Grady's three-story brick home in Old Town Alexandria. She might have thought they'd stepped back to the era of Gunston Hall when Grady opened the door for them.

"This is … stunning," she said, trying to see everything at once.

"It's all Leslie's doing," Grady said.

"He doesn't mean that as a compliment," Leslie said, coming toward them down the hallway beside a magnificent stairway. "Good to see you, Brad. So glad you both could come join us tonight."

"It's a pleasure," he said. "This is a great place."

"Thank you both. Can you believe a developer wanted to gut this interior and make it all modern?"

"Oh, no," Katie breathed.

Leslie hugged her. "Exactly what I said. I had to save it, even if it was a little more work."

Grady and April snorted simultaneously and grinned at each other. "A little more work," April muttered.

"Okay, a lot more work and a lot more money," Leslie conceded. "But worth it."

"Worth every penny," Grady agreed, squeezing her shoulders. "Especially when we put on the addition so we didn't have to cook in a fireplace or make guests use an outhouse. C'mon, Leslie will give you the tour. Sometimes I think she invites people in off the street to tell them about preservation."

Leslie conducted Katie and Brad around the eighteenth century structure, restored to its original elegance with its modern infrastructure cleverly hidden away.

"Katie's restoring her house in Ashton," Brad said as they started upstairs to see the next floor.

"How wonderf—"

"Nothing like this," she objected. "Small house, paint, a few little changes. A work in progress and—"

"It looks good," Brad said.

"You just like the curb appeal now," she said and he grinned.

Katie became aware of Leslie watching them. "Leslie, this staircase is amazing."

Leslie chuckled knowingly. "I get it—your topic of choice is architectural features."

The tour ended on the ground floor of a three-story addition that T-d off the original building. This was clearly the nerve-center of the home—updated conveniences and comfort beautifully married to mellow history in a kitchen and gathering room for an active family.

Bette, Tris, Michael, and Grady were cleaning up a table near the bay window overlooking a back yard enclosed by a red-brick wall. Paul herded the gathered kids toward French doors and a smiling dark-haired teenager holding it open. "Everybody out to play. Do what Marc tells you. And do not bother the nice men with earpieces and sunglasses standing outside the wall," he said.

Leslie propped her hands on her hips. "Where's Arancia? If you ruffians have scared off the most important person tonight, I will have your heads."

"Relax, Les," Tris said. "She's doing a final check on the dining room. Said dinner's right on track."

Hunter came in from another doorway. "They'll be here in two minutes."

Leslie patted his arm. "A hostess's dream. You truly mean two minutes. Not one, not three. Front door or garage?"

"Garage."

"Okay, everyone, let's adjourn to the front parlor."

Most of them did, while Hunter and Grady went in another direction. After two minutes, Derek Kenton walked in, surveyed the room then exchanged a nod with Grady behind him. In another breath King Jozef entered, accompanied by a woman of a similar age. Straight-backed and dignified, she wore a black dress that wouldn't consider stooping to being fashionable.

"Your Majesty, welcome to our home. I believe you know all the other guests," Leslie said. "Madame, may I introduce Katie Davis and Brad Spencer. Katie and Brad, this is Madame Sabdoka."

Madame Sabdoka's gaze pinned Katie with concentrated focus.

No notice. Draw no notice.

And then there was Katie Davis, working so hard to not be noticed…

She straightened and extended her hand. "It's a pleasure to meet you, Madame Sabdoka."

The older woman hesitated for less than a blink, took only the tips of Katie's fingers and dropped her head slightly. "Miss."

Katie was aware of a zing of looks going around the room, but didn't have time to sort out what they meant.

"It is very good to finally see you again, Katie," the king said.

"And you, Your Majesty." That sounded stiff. She felt stiff. She surely looked stiff. How could April possibly think she could—

Brad stepped up beside her. She knew it even before she felt his hand encircle her arm above her elbow. She doubted his hold was visible to anyone else, but she felt its warmth and support.

"Madame Sabdoka. Your Majesty," he said.

"One greets the monarch first," Madame Sabdoka sternly told him. "It is protocol."

Brad grinned. "Maybe in Bariavak. But in the house where Andrea Colecchi Spencer rules, *one* greets a lady first."

King Jozef made a sound that might have been the start of a chuckle. Madame, though, was not amused. Even so, the moment eased the tension. The others guests greeted the new arrivals with cordial respect and champagne was passed out for a toast to the soon-to-be-married couple.

Katie relaxed as the evening went on. It wasn't much different from many of Carolyn and C.J.'s dinner parties. Perhaps the conversation did trend more toward national and international topics than basketball, English literature, and university politics. But the underlying current of affection and respect among those present was similar.

Except for the King of Bariavak being on hand, along with unspoken tension about whether she was or wasn't his granddaughter and whether she would or wouldn't take a DNA test that might or might not prove it.

That was all.

At his farewell, the king held her hand and her gaze for two extra beats before simply bidding her goodnight. Madame's look was assessing. And it included Brad.

When they left the room, once more accompanied by Hunter and Grady, Katie released a long breath.

April patted her shoulder. "You did great." She gestured and they sat on a loveseat at right angles to its twin.

"I doubt Madame would agree with you," Katie said dryly. "So that's loosened up?"

April chuckled. "Compared to six months ago it is. Really. She's mellowed."

"Does it have to do with her being related to Hunter?"

"I'm going to jump in here to say the less than discreet thing so April isn't tempted," Leslie announced as she and Bette joined them, sitting on the other loveseat. She turned to Katie. "I suspect it has to do with Madame and King Jozef, ah, re-establishing a rapport they enjoyed as young people. Now, there, wasn't that tactful?"

"You'd be an asset to the diplomatic corps." Michael took a nearby chair. "Hope you don't mind my crashing your group. My wife's arguing basketball with Paul and I don't want to give him the satisfaction of knowing I agree with him, so I've left Brad to referee."

"You are a wise man, Michael," Leslie said. "Now, proving the diplomatic corps overlooked a gem when they didn't beg me to join, I am going to adroitly change the subject to what I want to talk about. Katie, you must agree to April's plan to show you and Brad around Charlottesville on Thursday. It is an absolute tradition that the about-to-be-married couple gets to boss their special guests around at will the week before the wedding, isn't it, Bette?"

"Those were certainly the rules my dear husband established when he started this tradition," she replied with dry humor.

"Have you ever been to Thomas Jefferson's home—Monticello?" April asked Katie.

"I haven't and I'd love to, but we can't impose on you any more than we have with all you have to do for the wedding Saturday."

April chuckled. "I can hardly believe it myself, but it's pretty much all done."

Grady walked in, smiling to all, but going directly to his wife and resting a hand on her shoulder. Her hand automatically came up to meet his.

"We're talking about Katie and Brad coming to Charlottesville on Wednesday night to meet up with April and Hunter for touring on Thursday." Leslie tipped her head back to smile at her husband. "All the rooms are spoken for at Grandma Beatrice's with this crew staying overnight, but surely we can recommend places for them to stay."

For a moment, Katie thought Grady was so absorbed in looking at Leslie that he wouldn't respond. But then he nodded. "Great idea. In fact," he slanted a grin at his wife before addressing Katie, "we know a place on the way to Charlottesville that we highly recommend."

Leslie sat up, turned to him, and put both hands around his. "Oh, what a fabulous idea, Grady! Perfect." She faced Katie. "We'll make all the arrangements."

"There's no need—"

"It would be our pleasure."

"But—"

"Good, it's all settled," Grady said. Katie had a feeling it had been settled for him the instant Leslie voiced her enthusiasm. "We'll get it set up and I'll get the directions to Brad."

CHAPTER TWENTY-SIX

After early fittings Wednesday at Maurice's, April left for Charlottesville, while Katie met Brad at the hotel to walk the few blocks to the National Mall, goggling at the White House on their way.

"Why didn't you tell me you were coming?" Her question appeared to surprise him less than it surprised herself. "You've known for weeks and you kept it to yourself."

"I could say because you didn't ask." He turned his head toward the Ellipse and away from her. "Truth is, I wasn't sure I was coming. Maybe I shouldn't have. There are plenty of folks here to look out for you."

"I can look out for myself."

"I can see that." His grin flickered then was gone.

"But none of that's any reason for you not to have fun, too."

His head came around, a strange expression on his face. "I suppose that's why I decided to come."

"I ... I'm glad you did, Brad."

His smile banished that strange expression, but she thought some lingered in his eyes.

They went in the Museum of American History to see the Star-Spangled Banner that Francis Scott Key had been watching the night he wrote the anthem's words. But mostly they walked outside, enjoying a perfect spring day and marveling at the iconic images before them whichever way they turned—the Capitol Building in one direction and in the other the Washington Monument, with the Lincoln Memorial beyond it, and Arlington Cemetery rising on the hills across the Potomac River.

"We better get going," Brad said. "The rental car will be at the hotel, and you know what Hunter said about beating the traffic."

"I know. It's … I'm coming back here someday. And I'm going to visit every memorial and every museum and every monument."

For an instant, she thought he'd say something again about her future being somewhere far away. Instead, he said, "Count me in if you're looking for company. I'd like to do all that, too. So you're having a good time?"

"A wonderful time. I'm glad to have April as a friend."

He cut his eyes to her, probably checking if she recognized that topic. She gave a small nod of acknowledgement.

"Turn right," Katie read from Grady's instructions.

"Onto this cowpath?" But Brad was already making the turn.

"It's not quite that bad. It *is* paved."

"Are you sure you didn't miss a turn somewhere or add a couple?"

But she knew he was joking. Mostly, anyway. They definitely were not on the express route to Charlottesville.

"I'm sure. In fact—look. There's the sign. Tanner Inn. There's the drive. See it? And—oh my gosh, these bushes lining the drive are rhododendron. Amazing."

"You plant these in front of your house and it'll be almost as bad as that spruce fortress."

"They wouldn't grow to this size in Ashton or—Oh, it's lovely."

The drive had opened to a circle in front of a white frame building with a riot of flowers across its front, interrupted only by wide welcoming steps leading to a two-story screened porch.

"When Grady said this was on the way to Charlottesville, did he mean by way of Denver?" Brad grumbled, but good-naturedly, as he braked to a stop.

Katie was out of the car, turning around to take in all the plants and gardens around them.

"Welcome!" called a woman as she jogged down the porch steps, gray curls bouncing. "You must be Katie and Brad. I'm Karen Tanner."

"It's a pleasure to meet you, Mrs. Tanner. What wonderful gardens you have."

"Please, call me Karen. And I'll be sure to tell Marty—my husband—what you've said. I do the fun part—the planning and buying—but he handles all the manual labor and a little flattery can ease the aches."

Karen led them through the porch, past open doors and into a gracious hall with parlors on either side, a stately stairway and, against the opposite wall, a breakfront fitted out as a reception desk.

Karen Tanner chatted away as she signed them in, then took Brad's credit card payment first. Most of her comments centered on the theme "Grady and Leslie Roberts are such a special couple."

As Katie reached for her wallet to make her payment, a thin man with only a gray border holding out against baldness came toward them from the other end of the hallway.

"Hello, dear," Karen said, "these are the young people Leslie and Grady sent us, Katie and Brad. This is my husband Marty. Oh, and Marty, Katie's been saying such lovely things about your gardens."

"*My* gardens." He winked at Katie. "I'm the beast of burden. Karen's the visionary."

"My visions wouldn't come to anything if you didn't do the work," Karen said firmly. "Now we have you all set for your room."

Room. Singular. Oh, no.

Katie had never even considered Grady and Leslie might assume she and Brad...

"Two rooms," she said. "We want two rooms."

"Speak for yourself," Brad muttered.

Heat flashed across Katie's cheeks. She didn't know if either of the Tanners had heard him. They gave no sign if they had. "We need two rooms," she said firmly.

The couple looked at each other.

"Oh, dear. I'm certain Grady made the reservation for one room.

We discussed it, because he asked which one I recommended. They take the separate cabin when they have the children. Otherwise, Leslie and Grady have a sentimental attachment to a room at the back of the house that belonged to our son before he went in the Air Force. That's where they stayed the first time they came here. Such a rainstorm that night. A regular deluge, and here they came rushing in, needing someplace—any place—to sleep. And we only had Teddy's room. Not at all what we like to provide our guests. Not like the Albemarle Room we have for you." She beamed at them. "It's a lovely room."

"I'm sure it is. And I'm certain Brad will appreciate it. I'll be happy to have your son's room. Truly."

"But my dear, it's not available. We renovated years ago, and it's spoken for, like every other room. We're going to be absolutely full up as soon as the Crawfords arrive. That won't be until after dinner, but of course that doesn't help you any."

Nothing was going to help her any. That was quite clear.

She was going to share a room with Brad.

She did her best. She smiled. She remained calm. She reassured Karen.

But apparently she hadn't been as convincing as she hoped, because Karen apologized again while giving them a tour of the grounds and a third time when they arrived in the dining room for dinner.

Karen hesitated a moment before seating them, glancing toward the remaining unoccupied table for two, then steering them toward a long table with a mix of groups. The dinner was delicious, the people convivial, and the conversation interesting. After peach cobbler for dessert, the couples at the individual tables, while everyone from the long table, joined by Karen and Marty, went to the porch, talking and laughing as the sunset sky dragged its feet through red and purple, then orange and rose splashes before finally relinquishing the stage to star-glittered night.

The innkeepers excused themselves to deal with inn business and soon after, the others departed in pairs or family groups.

"I'm going up," Brad said after a spell of quiet. "Unless you want me to sleep down here."

"Of course not. There's nowhere you'd fit."

She did fine until they were both in the room with the door closed behind them.

"Don't look so worried. I'll take the couch, Katie," he said. He dropped down to sit on what was barely more than a loveseat.

That left her to stand, which seemed awkward, or to sit, which presented other kinds of awkwardness. The bed was high enough to require having a step stool on hand, plus there were certain connotations...

All those calculations took less than half a breath.

She sat on the somewhat less than half of the loveseat not occupied by Brad. As close to the arm as she could get without making a spectacle of herself.

"You are not sleeping on this," she said. "Your head or your feet or both would dangle off the ends."

"I'm glad you feel that way. We're adults and I promise—"

"I'll sleep here. You sleep in the bed."

"Katie." His voice held strain and something more. "That's not necessary. I won't—"

"It's not a problem. I'll curl up here and be perfectly comfortable."

He sat forward abruptly, elbows on his knees, hands clasped and looking straight ahead. "You have reason not to trust me, but I swear, Katie—"

"Not trust you? Of course I trust you. After everything you've done—"

The sound he made held no amusement. "Yeah, everything I've done. What I did Saturday morning."

"I know you were trying to make me feel better."

"Make you feel better? Right. I scared the hell out of you."

"How can you think that, Brad? You've never scared me." What she felt for him, oh, yes, that scared her. Scared her mightily. But Brad himself? Not possible.

"Oh, Brad, you really thought—? No. Never."

He turned to her. She brushed hair back from his forehead. Instinct brought her lips to the spot.

His hand grasped her wrist, stilling the hand in his hair.

"Katie."

She heard in her name his question, his warning. But heard more than that. She heard desire.

Longing, even.

It was a seduction—unknowing on his part—she could never resist.

She shifted lower, taking her lips to the corner of his mouth.

His breath went ragged and she liked that. She liked it a lot.

"Katie," he said again. Everything was there in his voice again, only stronger now.

"Brad," she answered evenly. Then she flicked the tip of her tongue along the seam of his lips.

She held her breath. She had to *show* him now that he didn't scare her. Not him. Never him.

Watching her face, he drew her wrist up, around his neck. He released his hold, and she tightened hers.

Heat and more flickered across his eyes.

Slowly, she closed the last inches between them. She kissed him softly. Felt his lips cling to hers.

Then his mouth opened, and his hand splayed across her back, so warm and sure.

The relief of it was so strong.

He was dizzy with it.

Relief, hell. He was dizzy with her. With the taste and touch of her.

He slid his hand down the side of her throat. It nestled under the fabric of her collar.

And he made a welcome discovery. The v-neck of her top was far more accommodating than it appeared to be. Specifically, it accommodated his hand, allowing it to skim across her shoulder, his fingers brushing her bra strap.

The tip of her tongue flicked at his lips. His tongue matched hers. Brief, light meetings becoming longer and deeper and sweeter.

His hand returned to her shoulder, fingers underneath the bra strap this time, absorbing the smooth warmth of her skin. Then seeking more of that smooth warmth with a slow slide down. He felt the beginning rise of her breast, the cadence of her heartbeat— accelerating.

The strap slid off her shoulder, opening his way. He swept lightly along such incredible smoothness, his fingertips feathering the tips across her nipple.

She made a sound. A small, moaning sound, into his mouth. He wanted more of that. Much, much more. Would she make that sound as he entered her? When they moved together? When she climaxed? When he did? Or would her sounds be different? Less restrained?

Discovering Katie was becoming an obsession.

He cupped her breast with his large palm, feeling its sweet weight and the nudge of her hardening nipple.

She made that sound again. And he might have groaned.

Then another sound. Not from Katie. Not from him, either. It tugged at him, nagging that he identify it, when all he wanted was to sink deeper into the sensations of Katie.

Knocking.

Someone was knocking on the door.

Katie gasped and jolted, pulling up her bra straps and tugging her shirt together.

"Aren't you going to—You have to answer it," she said.

He looked down to his lap. Her gaze followed, then bounced away. "I'll answer it," she said quickly.

He grasped her wrist to stop her from standing, called out to the knocker, "Just a minute," then said to her in a low tone, "You can go in the bathroom—"

"I'm okay. I'll answer."

He shook his head and rose. It wasn't the most comfortable he'd ever been and he pulled the other side of his shirt out for more cover, but he made it to the door and opened it.

"I hope it's not too late," Karen Tanner said with a worried smile.

"Not too late," he reassured her. Another few minutes and then, yeah, it would have been too late. "C'mon in."

"I wouldn't disturb you but I know how set you—." She looked toward Katie then back to him. "—were on having a second room, so I wanted to let you know the Crawfords just called to cancel. Their flight was delayed so they missed their connection in Atlanta and won't be here until tomorrow."

Apparently Katie was as devoid of a response as he was because this announcement was met by such absolute silence that the insects outside could be heard despite the closed windows and air-conditioning.

"Th—that, uh, means we have a room available. Two in fact, though, of course you don't need…" Karen gave her head a little shake. "As I said, you were so set on a second room, Katie, and I don't want you to be uncomfortable under our roof."

What? The innkeeper thought he was some ravening satyr?

Well, maybe she wasn't too far off.

To ease the concern in the woman's kind eyes, he said, "It's okay, Karen, we're—"

"Delighted to have the second room," Katie interrupted. "It's so kind of you to let us know this late in the evening."

"Not at all. I can leave you the key or—"

"No, no, I'll go with you now." She picked up her unopened bag. "Good night, Brad."

He responded to both their good nights automatically. Most of him was preoccupied with mentally damning the Atlanta airport.

And himself.

Rules weren't enough. He needed to keep her out of his reach.

CHAPTER TWENTY-SEVEN

Brad was already having breakfast when the Tanners ushered Hunter and April in to the otherwise deserted dining room and insisted they eat, too.

As soon as the three of them were alone, Brad asked Hunter, "How fast could the results of that DNA test be back."

"A day. Less."

He nodded to mask his need to swallow. "Fast."

"For something like this, yes," Hunter said.

April said quietly, "You've encouraged her to take the test, haven't you."

"Yes."

"I'm glad. Are you … Are you hoping it comes out one way or the other?"

His mouth twisted. "When this started what I wanted was for her to be Katie Davis for sure and for good." Now he knew too much to hope that. "Now, I find myself hoping it gives her—I was going to say answers. That's not right. Because she thinks she *has* the answers. It's not even different answers. It's … A shakeup. She needs a shakeup in order to start seeing straight. To see herself."

"A shakeup?" Hunter frowned.

"Like I got when C.J. suspended me sophomore year because of my grades. I thought I had things figured out. C.J. and Carolyn had other ideas. They decided I could do more, want more, and get away with a whole lot less. They'd been saying that, but I hadn't been listening. It took the jolt of being suspended and not getting to do what I liked best in the world to open me up to a new view."

"Well, if she truly is Princess Josephine-Augusta, she's going to get one heck of a shakeup," Hunter said.

Hunter and April were with Brad, finishing breakfast at one end of the long table when Katie came down. She hadn't slept well. She kept being awakened by dreams. Of Brad.

Of what they'd started. In her dreams it hadn't been unfinished.

As Katie ate, April explained that Leslie and Grady had dropped her and Hunter off so their foursome could get an early start.

After farewells and thanks to the Tanners, they headed into historic Charlottesville in the rental car. "Where's the church where you're going to be married?" Katie asked April.

"Oh, you'll see that Saturday. We'll look around The Lawn and Rotunda on campus—you know Jefferson designed the University of Virginia—then we'll widen the circle. First to Montpelier—that's the Madisons' house. Do you know about Dolley? She's really fun. Then Monticello for the Jeffersons. We'll finish up at Highland. Later owners called it Ash Lawn, but when the Monroes were there it was Highland."

"You talk like you know these people," Brad said.

"She does." Hunter grinned. "Just wait. Hey, I almost forgot." He dug into a pocket. "Special delivery's part of our super fast-track service. So you know you have it for the basketball team's trip."

The sealed envelope Hunter held out to her was a little larger than a passport.

She thanked him and slipped it into her purse. She couldn't help looking toward Brad. But he didn't meet her gaze. He was looking at her purse.

Katie had had a lovely day and she was certain April had, too. The guys had gotten their fun from arguing at dinner who would have made a better basketball player—Jefferson or Monroe. Madison was let out of the running because he was too short.

Now the four of them were back in the rental car, with Brad driving toward Washington by the same route they'd come.

"This is the way Grady directed you, huh?" Hunter commented from the back seat.

From the corner of her eye, Katie thought she saw April poke him. But she'd been preparing to look out her side window—to ensure she wasn't looking at Brad when they passed the entrance to Tanner Inn—so she couldn't be sure.

Brad's next words convinced her *he* hadn't been thinking about last night at the inn. "You've got a reservation to fly back home Sunday afternoon, don't you, Katie?"

"Yes." *Why?* Buzzed in her head, but she didn't speak it.

"So tomorrow's the last day you could have the DNA test here."

She breathed slow and even. Once, twice, a third time. "I could have the test in Ashton, couldn't I, Hunter?"

"Yes."

"It's not now or never," she said to Brad's profile.

"You told that man back in March that you'd make up your mind by now whether to take it or not. There's nothing keeping you from taking it now." He shot her a glance, holding her gaze for a flash before returning his attention to the road. "With the basketball office, I mean."

He didn't mean that at all and they both knew it. He meant now that a passport in her married name—his name—had come through.

Was he tired of this charade? Want his freedom? She couldn't blame him. How unfair of her to hold on to him this way.

Thanks to Brad and the passport, she had the safety of knowing she could return home to Ashton, no matter what. That's what held her back. Only that. So, as Brad said, there was nothing keeping her from taking a DNA test now.

She looked out the passenger window again, chewing on her lip. There'd been something else in what Brad said ... *That man*—not King Jozef, not the king, but *that man*. A man who'd lost his family and had a right to know ... whatever there was to know.

"I'll take the test as soon as you can arrange it, Hunter."

She heard April release a breath. She thought Brad sucked one in.

Hunter said, "I want you to be clear about this, Katie. There might not be a slam dunk answer. The most likely result is a sliding scale of probability, not anything like a certainty."

"You already warned me, Hunter. That first afternoon at Bette and Paul's house."

"Listen to it again, because I've got to be sure you know there's little chance this will bring you a definitive answer. If the test hits one end or the other of the scale, the experts will give high or low percentages that you and King Jozef are related. But there's a whole lot of territory in between. If your results fall in there..."

"Then there's no way of knowing. I get it. It's okay, Hunter. It won't be any less uncertain than it is now."

April said, "King Jozef is certain. If anyone should know, he should."

"But DNA—" Katie started.

"Think about what Hunter's saying, Katie," Brad said.

She chuckled, a little rusty but not bad. "Now you're saying *not* to take the test?"

He remained serious. "I'm not saying that. But think it through. You might be moving from certainty to uncertainty. One alternative is to accept King Jozef's certainty now."

She shook her head. "This can't rely on his belief. It has to be as sure as it can be one way or the other."

Hunter broke a silence. "Okay. Let me make a call."

Before they reached the hotel he had the test set for the next morning in Katie's room.

For all the thought, concern, uncertainty—drama, even—the test was entirely anticlimactic.

A swab dipped into the inside of her cheek, swirled around and that was it. Oh, they did it a couple times with multiple swabs, to be sure. And, granted, there were officials there—Hunter representing the State Department, Madame silently representing Bariavak, and three employees of the testing company on hand to make sure nothing went awry.

April was also there. And so was Brad.

The experts packed up carefully and left. Madame gave her a long look, dropped her head, then departed wordlessly. "Well, that's done," April said with only slightly forced cheerfulness. "Katie and I have to go, or we'll be late for Maurice's final fittings. And if we're late for Maurice, we'll be late meeting Bette and Tris and Leslie at the spa. And if we're late for that we could be late to the embassy for dinner. And then we'll have Madame on our case."

"Your case, April. I'm not coming to your rehearsal dinner," Katie said.

"It's not a rehearsal dinner. We did that Wednesday in Charlottesville. You're coming." April spun around to Brad, who'd opened his mouth to say something. "Both of you."

Hunter chuckled. "Give my regards to Maurice. If you need us, call. We'll be at—"

"I know. The ball game. Have a great time." April stretched up and Hunter met her for a kiss.

Their movements left Katie looking right into Brad's eyes.

"C'mon." April tugged on her arm. "We've got to *move*."

As the front of the group began to exit the Ambassador's office to head for the next stop on Madame's tour of the Embassy, Bette rested a hand on Katie's arm and said, "We're so glad to be here with you tonight, Katie. We've all grown quite fond of King Jozef."

There were undercurrents in that statement that Katie feared could drag her under.

But the other woman showed her diplomacy or her innate niceness or maybe both, by squeezing her arm and skirting a clot of kids to catch up with Paul at the doorway.

Katie watched the group move away. For an instant it seemed to her a special glow surrounded them. One made up of all the talking, the joking, the love.

"Lucky kids, aren't they?"

At April's question she looked up quickly. April also was looking after the departing group.

"*All* of them are lucky. Kids and adults," Katie said.

"There was a point in my life when I thought families like that and especially kids like that were an alien species, one I had absolutely nothing in common with."

It was as if April had read her mind … and her memories. How often had she watched other kids and felt a distance, a difference she thought could never be bridged.

"That was after my dad had died when I was little. My mother…" April sighed. "Maybe she was the alien species, doing the best she could on a planet where she didn't belong. You know?"

Katie met the other woman's eyes. "I think I do."

April nodded. "I think you do, too." She rested her hand on Katie's wrist, an unexpectedly consoling touch. Then the touch turned to a tap, repeated three times, which felt like an exhortation to both of them to shake off this mood. "The thing is, these folks didn't get handed happiness—well, maybe the kids have been, but not their parents. To look at them you'd think they'd all had ideal families. Michael once said to me—his parents have been married to a slew of people each and he's got so many step-brothers and step-sisters he'd have to a hire bus if they all wanted to drive somewhere together. Anyway, Michael says you don't have anything to say about the family you're born into but you're entirely responsible for the one you create.

"That's what they've done. All of them. Created a family. The three best things that have ever happened to me are loving Hunter, having Leslie, Grady, and Great-Grandma Beatrice take over my upbringing, and being included in that." She gestured toward the group, now mostly out of the room. "My family."

Katie's eyes burned.

April gripped her arm. "You have a chance to create a family now."

"The *Royal* Family of—"

"I know that part sounds daunting. But it's still family. *Family.* And you'll decide what to make of it, between the two of you."

"King Jozef and I aren't—"

"Oh, I wasn't thinking of King Jozef," she interrupted with a sly look. "Guess I should have said the three of you."

Katie took the only safe way out. "We'd better catch up before Madame comes back for us."

"Heaven forbid." April gave a mock shudder. As they started along the hallway, she added, "I don't want you to think I missed how you changed the subject." She looked ahead to where Brad was standing holding the door to the next room, waiting for them. "Changing a subject doesn't make it disappear, you know."

The Saturday departure for the wedding in Charlottesville went off like clockwork. As each guest boarded the bus, all electronic communication was turned over, sealed in an envelope with the guest's name and filed alphabetically in bins, part of the special security.

Katie joined Sharon Johnson and her family on the bus. She'd met Sharon's husband Ross at the embassy last night. Now they chatted easily.

She saw Brad find a seat with Derek Kenton, clearly off duty today, and from a few words that floated her way, their conversation immediately settled on basketball.

With the suburban houses barely starting to spread out beside the highway, they exited to rendezvous with a third bus, which had loaded up here for those who opted out of the downtown pickup. They entered what could have been an airplane hangar, stopping alongside two other buses. In front of them were three more identical buses. The buses in the front row started pulling out.

"I thought all the guests fit on three buses," Sharon muttered. "What are they up to?"

Bette stood up next to the driver and spoke into a microphone. "We hope you'll forgive a bit of deception. As you know, media interest in this wedding—legitimate and not-legitimate media—has raised security issues. So, we arranged a decoy event in Charlottesville. Decoy buses are heading there now. We'll stay here a bit longer to be sure any followers—and there were quite a few—continue on after the decoys. We, on the other hand, are returning to Washington for the wedding and reception."

A buzz rose from the guests. Bette answered a few good-natured questions, then started down the aisle for individual conversations. When she reached their row, Sharon asked, "What about April's great-grandmother?"

Bette laughed. "We offered to have her driven into the city last night, but she insisted on staying in Charlottesville this morning to throw off suspicion. Right this minute her helicopter should be landing, then she'll be whisked to the church. I think she likes the drama."

The drive back to D.C. brought them to a historic church across from their hotel. The trip was quick, cheerful, and full of camaraderie.

The church wore its status with respectable reserve, rather like Hunter. But it brimmed with flowers as bright and welcoming as April. Shortly after the other two busloads of guests filed in, the music struck a bridal chord.

Hunter came from a side entrance to stand at the altar, with Grady beside him.

Grady and Leslie's children, Jake and Sandy came down the aisle first, followed by Leslie, as matron of honor.

Then came the flourish that announced the bride and all turned to see April on the arm of King Jozef of Bariavak. The bride appeared to float.

Katie's throat closed and her eyes filled, and she couldn't have said what part of her reaction was for April and what part was for her own whirling complex of thoughts about grandfathers, weddings, brides … and most of all grooms.

Her gaze, following April's progress toward Hunter, caught sight of Brad, across the aisle and a few rows behind her.

For an instant she thought—No, she couldn't read the emotions in his eyes. Though she thought the emotions there were strong.

She jerked her head back to the front of the church.

Nearly at the altar, King Jozef took April's hand and kissed it. Grady stepped forward for the final steps, while the king went to stand with Hunter. The two men had beautifully shared the honors of escorting the bride and of best man.

There was not a dry eye to be seen.

Not then and not as April and Hunter exchanged their vows of love and hope, then put on the rings that symbolized those vows.

Katie found herself rubbing at the empty spot on her own ring finger. She clasped her hands together hard.

Pronounced husband and wife, Hunter and April were invited to kiss and accepted with gusto.

Brad's lips on hers. For the first time during their wedding. Then a week ago on her couch. At the inn…

She shook her head, concentrating on the scene before her. When April and Hunter were presented to the guests as an officially married couple, both grinned widely. So did their attendants, who followed them back up the aisle. Pew by pew the guests joined the progression, every one of them smiling.

When it came to Katie's turn, she exited the pew and saw those behind their row were also smiling.

With two exceptions.

A toddler who had fallen asleep on his father's shoulder. And Brad Spencer who looked almost grim.

She tried not to look at him, standing so straight and handsome in the same suit he'd worn at their—no. She wouldn't let her thoughts go down that path.

He was staring straight ahead, apparently oblivious to everyone around him.

She didn't see him outside the church or in the stream of people walking across the street to the hotel, where smiling employees directed guests to elevators reserved for those going to the reception at the top of the hotel.

Katie took another elevator to her room for a moment alone to repair her calm and her tear-damaged makeup.

And there, as she started back toward the elevators, was Brad, opening the door to his room, several doors down and on the other side of the hall from hers.

He was in the room, about to let the door swing closed when she reached the doorway.

"Brad."

She thought for an instant he was going to let go of the door. No, he held on, but for how long?

She stepped inside.

"What's the matter, Brad?"

He looked down at her, expression unchanging. "I'm sorry, Katie."

"Sorry? Why?"

"For robbing you of this."

"Of what?"

He jerked his head in apparent reference to the reception rooms above them. "All this. The church, the flowers, the guests. It's what you should have. It's what you deserve."

And then he leaned forward. And no thoughts could form except one.

He was going to kiss her.

He leaned closer…

…and kissed her on the nose.

On. The. Nose.

CHAPTER TWENTY-EIGHT

Squirt. His fingertip on the tip of her nose. Kiss on the top of the head. And now this.

"What I *deserve*? What I deserve is to not be kissed on the nose like a … like a *puppy*."

"A puppy? I didn't—What are you—Hold up, Katie."

But she was already out the door and turned toward the elevators. She was aware of Brad coming after her, but if she had to take off her heels and sprint, she'd get to an elevator before he reached her.

Then she recognized King Jozef coming toward her, with three people behind him.

Her determination to keep going wobbled as King Jozef neared and she saw his expression. This was the face of a king. Of a ruler. Of a man responsible for the welfare of many. A man who took that responsibility completely to heart.

Her own heart dropped.

The DNA test was in. His face told the result. He was so solemn because he was here to tell her the test wasn't positive enough. He would claim only the irrefutable princess as his granddaughter.

She'd worried so much about the other result that she hadn't considered this.

No family.

No history.

No one who had been looking for her all of her life.

Until this instant she hadn't known how she had counted on that in some hidden part of her.

She forced herself to straighten. "Your Majesty."

He was nearly in front of her. "You must come with us now."

"Come with you? To the reception?"

"To the airport. Immediately."

"What? No." The king reached for her arm. She stepped back. Directly into Brad. She knew it was his chest against her back, his hands gripping her arms to steady her.

"She's not going anywhere she doesn't want to," Brad said.

"Young man, you are no part of—"

One of the men behind King Jozef murmured something. The king's jaw tightened. "Yes. This is no place for discussion. We shall go into your suite, Katrina."

He strode past Katie to stand in front of the door.

"It's my room, actually," Brad said.

The king's face stiffened even more. Brad held his gaze an extra beat then unlocked the door, following it in to hold it open.

The king entered first. The older man—the ambassador—and Madame inclined their heads, indicating Katie should precede them. She joined the king by the windows, aware of those two, then Derek Kenton, his day off apparently canceled, following them in. As Brad let the door close, the king said, "We shall not detain you."

Brad turned to her. "Do you want me to go, Katie?"

"No." She shot a look toward the king, then back to Brad, and said stronger. "Please stay, Brad."

"Sure thing." He folded his arms across his chest and leaned against the wall.

"Katrina, this is not for outsiders—"

Brad interrupted. "I'm not going."

The ambassador gasped. King Jozef remained still for two breaths, his shoulder to her, which didn't allow her to see what was in his face. Brad's held unshakeable determination.

Abruptly, the king turned to her.

"We must waste no more time. The test you took is conclusive. A higher percentage match of DNA than even the most experienced expert had seen across two generations. You are—as I knew you were—Josephine-Augusta, daughter of Princess Sofia and Prince Leopold and thus the Princess Royal of Bariavak."

Katie didn't realize her knees had liquefied until Brad was there, holding her up. A small part of her mind wondered how he'd gotten there first when he'd been the farthest away. But most of her mind was occupied with spinning at a sickening speed.

"Great way to ease into it," Brad muttered.

"This is merely an added confirmation," King Jozef said, dismissively. "There is no surprise. As I have said, I knew, Katrina."

"I'm Katie." She caught the king's glowering frown, but that wasn't her top concern. "I don't know what to do. How to decide—"

"Decide?" The king's rich tones swelled. "There is no decision. We will depart on the royal jet immediately for Bariavak. You are Her Royal Highness, Princess Josephine-Augusta. You will do your duty to your country and your name. You will do as I command you."

"Command?" Katie repeated. Her knees no longer felt shaky.

"Yes. As your king. As your grandfather. My command is—"

Madame made a low sound, deep in her throat.

King Jozef glanced toward the two men who had accompanied him. "Leave us."

For a heartbeat no one moved. No one seemed to even breathe. Or maybe she thought that because she wasn't breathing.

"Your Majesty?" said the ambassador.

"Go." he repeated. Then more mildly. "Go to the reception."

They started out, but from the door Derek Kenton gave Brad a pointed look.

"Not going anywhere," Brad said evenly.

Kenton then said, "I will be right outside, Your Majesty."

The king raised a hand in acknowledgement and royal dismissal. It was an impressive gesture, giving way on this point of continued security without ceding one iota of his royal prerogative to have tossed them out of the room. Could she ever master a gesture like that if she were—

Not if she *were* a princess, because she *was* a princess. She truly was this stranger named Josephine-Augusta. And King Jozef wanted her to fly with him right now to Bariavak. As his granddaughter. As his heir.

The door closing snapped her thoughts back to this moment. She braced herself to not be overrun by the force of the king's will.

But he looked over his shoulder to Madame. "What would you say to me, Therese?"

Without any conscious intention, Katie found herself looking toward Brad for his reaction. His brows went up, his mouth quirked, and the blue of his eyes glittered as if amusement had electrified them.

"As Therese to Jozef?"

Katie admired the woman's tone. She asked for confirmation, not permission.

"Yes," he said.

"You would not allow anyone else to disrupt this day for April and Hunter. Would you do so yourself?"

"I shall simply withdraw with my granddaughter and depart. There will be no disruption."

"Sure," Brad agreed with such deceptive affability that Katie almost wanted to warn King Jozef. "Nobody will notice the most famous guest leaving with someone who looks remarkably like the media's previous princess candidate. And what? Motorcade out to Dulles Airport where the official royal jet gets cranked up in a hurry and an emergency flight plan is filed. Nah. Nobody will notice."

The king glared coldly at Brad. Madame cleared her throat.

"The young man's casual language is regrettable, but his points are valid," she said. "The media would surely speculate if you were to depart now."

Brad pursued the point. "Right now, no one has reason to suspect there's been a test, much less the result. No sudden moves and you won't startle the media into swarming. But if you rush Katie off her feet and spirit her away, how long will it take some enterprising journalist to put two and two together and go after the DNA info?"

King Jozef stared at the far wall for a long moment. "We can handle the media efficiently in Bariavak. However, I shall order the departure to be moved to tomorrow. One day before the schedule should not startle any journalists. We shall enjoy the wedding celebration today, then I shall take my granddaughter home to Bariavak."

His always resonant voice hit a deep note on those final words that stirred simultaneous empathy and determination in Katie.

"I have not agreed to go to Bariavak," she said simply.

"What!" the king roared.

Katie thought she heard a sigh from Madame, but was too focused on giving back look for look to the king to be sure.

"I will think about it and let you know if I want to visit Bariavak. And if I do, when I will go."

"You will—"

Brad interrupted. "She will do exactly what she said."

The stalemate broke only when Madame said, "Nothing will be determined during the time of Hunter and April's wedding reception."

Katie gave herself a little shake. "You're right, Madame. I'm going to the reception."

She was aware of Brad behind her. But he didn't try to catch up. He simply followed at a distance.

"You of all people, Therese—"

"Hah. Because I honor your rank with the respect it is due does not mean I am blind to your errors, Jozef."

"Errors? What *errors* have I made? I have allowed her to wrap herself in this cloak of independence all these weeks upon weeks when everything in me wanted—no, *knew* she should be safeguarded and the lessons begun for all she will need to know. She is a lifetime behind in this education and to waste even another—what? Now what do you sigh over, woman?"

"You. I know your heartbreak, Jozef. And I know that is driving you. But you are making mistakes a second time that you never should have made thirty years ago."

"Thirty? What has thirty years ago to do with this? It was twenty-eight years ago that those subhumans stole Katrina from us."

"And it was thirty and more years ago that you nearly drove your daughter away for good."

The king's shock at the truth delivered so bluntly let Madame continue.

"Sofia was your true daughter in spirit and stubbornness. It appears this Katie might also be your true granddaughter. Not in a way that blood and tests determine. But in the way a spirit responds to orders. To *commands*. You know your reaction. You know Sofia's. You cannot now be surprised if Katie feels the same."

"I obeyed. Sofia obeyed eventually. Katrina will, too."

Madame shook her head slowly. "You said you had learned from Sofia. But now you would assume your granddaughter is not like you in order to have your commands fulfilled?"

Katie felt a touch on her back, suppressed the instinct to jump, then saw it was Leslie. "Are you enjoying yourself, Katie?"

"It's was a wonderful wedding and it's a wonderful reception, Leslie. Absolutely lovely."

She smiled, looking around. "It's been a labor of love. Not to mention a monumental struggle not letting Madame on one side make it stiff and formal or Maurice and Etienne on the other side turn it into a grand blowout. Either of which would have made Hunter and April miserable." They both chuckled. "But I notice you didn't answer about you enjoying yourself, Katie."

"Oh, I don't want you to think I'm not. I didn't mean that at all."

"What I think isn't the issue, either."

"I don't know many people here," she said quietly.

"Bless your heart, about the only one who does is April. That's the thing about a wedding. It pulls people together from all the aspects of the bride and groom's lives. Course Hunter's been so one-track-minded about work his are pretty narrow. Although…" She scanned the room. "See there? See those two couples talking with Tris and

Bette?"

"Yes."

"The younger man is the son of the older couple and that's his wife. The older couple had another son who was in the Army. He saved Hunter's life when he was a little boy. Saved him and then was killed himself. Scotty's Army buddies got Hunter to the States to fulfill a promise."

Katie hadn't had any idea that kind of pain existed in Hunter's past. She'd seen only the happiness in his present.

"Hunter had stayed away from them, sure he'd remind them only of their loss. Stayed away until April got hold of him, that is. Ah," she added as Hunter approached the group. He extended a hand to the older man, who met it, then used that grip to pull him into a hug. Hugs from the rest of the group followed. Katie could almost think she saw tears in Hunter Pierce's eyes.

"So, you don't know anyone? Then you get to know them." Leslie stepped back, surveying Katie. "What you need is to throw yourself into having fun. You are entirely too serious. I know just the thing."

Katie got a first-hand taste of Leslie's organizing ability as the woman talked to the band, snared a dozen people, and began a conga line—all while holding Katie's wrist. Then Leslie swung their part of the line around and tugged Brad in to place behind Katie without losing a step.

Katie wasn't as lucky. She stumbled, and felt Brad's hands at her waist, steadying her. She had to move forward or break the line. She moved forward.

She saw Maurice and Etienne wincing, but April grinned as she grabbed Hunter and took the lead of the line.

But she was mostly aware of Brad's large hands connecting them … remembering how they had touched her other times.

The song ended, the line breaking apart with laughter and hugs. Brad pulled her back against his chest. She was aware of him bending his head. His lips brushed her shoulder where the sleeve had flipped up. This was better—far, far better—than the nose or forehead or top of the head. She shivered with the heat of the contact, relaxing against him.

With the line disintegrating around them, he released her. When she turned, he was halfway across the room.

"Champagne, miss?" one of waiters asked her.

"Yes. Thank you."

He stayed away from her after that.

Had to for his own sake.

Not to mention he was being glared at by a head of state. A king for God's sake … because Katie was his granddaughter.

Katie was a princess. It was over.

She deserved a prince … at the very least.

"I think this is in order." April handed Katie another full glass of champagne.

"To toast your happiness." Katie lifted the glass and took a good swallow.

April echoed her motions and gave her a significant look. "That's not all we're toasting."

"You know? How? Hunter—?"

"We can't talk about this right now or right here. But, actually, I've known a while. We all have. This was only a formality."

"You couldn't have."

"First, there was King Jozef's certainty. But the clincher was when Madame had to stop herself from curtseying to you Tuesday night. She sure never treated me that way."

Katie remembered the looks zipping around the room when Madame Sabdoka and she met at the Roberts' home Tuesday night.

"But how could she…"

"Never question the mysterious ways of Madame. Now drink up your champagne and let me introduce you to one of Grady's nicest employees who will dance with you, since Brad is staying on the opposite side of the room. Not that I blame him, with King Jozef glaring at him." She clicked her tongue. "Soon as I get you dancing, I'm off to de-scowl a king."

CHAPTER TWENTY-NINE

How had she let herself get married to a man she loved?

Katie almost giggled, then covered her mouth. The champagne was bubbling in her head, thoughts popping into nothing more than a pleasant impression. She had to be serious. This was very serious. She was married. To Brad. She'd adored him for years. He had never shown the least bit of interest in her.

Well, that wasn't completely accurate. But he hadn't shown the kind of interest in her she'd wanted him to show.

Except … he had kissed her. The wedding didn't count, since that was on command. But on her couch and at the inn, those counted.

She took another glass of champagne and downed half.

That's when she saw Brad heading for the elevators. Leaving.

Oh, no, he didn't. He wasn't going to go off to his room and get a good night's sleep while she wrestled with getting herself married to a man she loved and being a princess and … what *had* she done with her room key?

She was almost to the elevators, but he wasn't anywhere to be seen. Oh. Right. He'd gotten in one of the elevators.

So, she did, too. And pressed the button of her floor … *their* floor.

She knocked on his door with determination.

Then she had the horrible thought that maybe this wasn't his door. It was this side of the hall, but maybe it had been the next one down. She turned to judge the distance, trying to remember how far down the hall King Jozef had been when she'd seen him—

Oh, God, King Jozef. DNA. He'd proclaimed her as Princess Josephine-Augusta. What was she going to—?

"Katie?"

Brad had opened the door without her hearing.

"I want to talk to you," she said stridently.

"Okay."

She strode in. And came *smack* up against the memories of King Jozef delivering the news earlier today that she was—

"What is it, Katie?" The door closed and Brad approached.

"You've never said a word about my haircut," she champagne-blurted.

"It looks great."

The champagne wasn't done. "Did you notice my dress?"

What a stupid thing to say. She sounded like an actor in a badly dubbed movie, words grinding and jerking nonsensically.

"Yes."

Something in the way he said that calmed the panic and set very different flutters going in her stomach.

"It's the same one—" she started.

"You wore to our—at the courthouse."

"Yes. April's dress was so gorgeous and…"

"Exactly what people think of as a wedding dress."

Their eyes met for an instant. She looked down. "You didn't like—don't like—"

"I like it. What do you call those?" He stretched two fingers toward her, but stopped short of touching.

She looked down. "Cap sleeves."

He nodded slowly. "Cap sleeves look good on you."

She swallowed hard. She wasn't going to fall apart from one compliment. "Thank you."

"And what about—" His fingers sketched a scalloped line in the vicinity of her chin. "—that?"

"The necklace?"

"No." He sounded grim.

"You don't like my necklace? Carolyn and C.J. gave it to me."

"It's growing on me. But I meant the dress. That style."

Then he should have pointed significantly lower, she thought, mildly indignant. "It's lower now than at the courthouse—"

"I noticed."

"—because Maurice said the proportions were better. It's—"

"Maurice is a dangerous man."

"—called a sweetheart neckline."

"Sweetheart."

Her heart flipped.

Ridiculous. Absolutely ridiculous. He was simply repeating the word. Probably trying to commit it to memory to get a dress for one of his girlfriends.

Oh, wait. How could he have girlfriends when they were married? Not that that stopped some men. But Brad wouldn't ... Of course, they weren't really married, so there wasn't any reason he couldn't. *Oh, God, please don't let him be dating while we're married.*

And then she giggled.

He looked startled. "What?"

"Nothing. A—" She gasped for breath. "—funny thought."

He looked all concerned. About her.

Sudden tears came into her eyes. "Oh, Brad." She put her arms around his neck and kissed him.

And he kissed her.

Not like a puppy.

She slid her fingers into his hair, encouraging his head toward her, while she parted her lips.

He held her, really held her.

But not for long enough.

Then they were apart, and she didn't know—would never know—if they'd both backed up or only one of them. And it didn't matter. The result was the same. He had his hands on her shoulders, but it was like he wanted to keep a lock on her so she couldn't move in to kiss him again.

Her head dropped. "I'm sorry, Brad. I shouldn't have done that."

With more willpower than he knew he possessed, Brad kept his arms stiff, holding her away.

"No, you shouldn't have."

"I said I was sorry," she said with a bit more snap, which was a hell of a lot better than hanging her head, looking miserable.

"Men get ideas. Especially in their hotel rooms."

She clicked her tongue. "I know that. I'm not a complete idiot." Now she rounded on him, all snap, no head-hanging. "You said you were sorry a week ago that you'd kissed me. On my couch. Like you'd broken a taboo. And other times on my forehead and top of my head and nose—my *nose*—but we're *not* related. And I am *not* a kid."

"No, we're not related and you're not a kid. Not anymore."

"Yet, you treat me like I'm a cross between a halfwit and a permanent innocent. I—"

"I do not. I—"

"I'm not either one—halfwitted or innocent." She lifted her chin. "I'm not a virgin. I've had boyfriends."

"You think I don't know you've had boyfriends? You think I haven't been completely aware of your boyfriends?"

Her defiance evaporated. She blinked. "Why would you be?"

"Why? *Why?* You're asking me why I was aware of your boyfriends? *This* is why."

He took her face between his palms and kissed her. Almost before their lips met, he was sliding his tongue inside her mouth.

Not subtle. But they were way past subtle.

She made a little sound—surprise? How could she be surprised? She couldn't be. Could. Not. Possibly. Be.

His tongue met hers. She hesitated, but she didn't shy away. More like asking *are you sure?* than pulling back.

Was *he* sure? Was she kidding?

What the hell had those people—the pair who raised her—done to her that she didn't have the confidence to know he'd wanted her all this time?

But what about her? Was she sure?

He wrenched his mouth away. "Katie—?"

Now she took his face between her hands. "Yes." And she slid her tongue into his mouth.

Combustion. Instant and total.

He brought one leg forward, between hers, unsettling her balance. She put his arms around his neck to steady herself. Even then one hand fluttered a bit, almost apologetically.

She made that sound. Deeper now.

Speaking of not subtle and of wanting her … He slid one hand down her back, using his forearm to draw her in tighter. Then, slower, in to the small of her back, spreading his hand across the outward curve below. Pressing, tight and firm, bringing her against him. So she couldn't possibly not know.

Oh, yeah, I'm sure.

She shifted, not pulling away exactly, so what was she—? Then she shifted back, her legs apart and he fit even tighter against her. He bent his knees, then straightened, rubbing higher and harder against her, even through their clothing. Their tongues were rubbing against each other in imitation of what their bodies wanted to do.

And if the imitation was this good, the real might kill him.

One of her arms left his neck and reached behind her. He knew that because he was totally tuned in to her body and where it moved.

But apparently he'd disconnected from everything else, because they were suddenly tumbling to the bed, him on top of her, and he hadn't known they were anywhere near it. She must have known. That's why she'd reached back—to cushion the fall. He rolled, bringing her on top so he didn't crush her.

The hem of her dress had come up. She straddled him, so he pressed close and hard against where he most wanted to be.

"Katie? The champagne—?"

"No." Her eyes were wide, but clear and focused directly on him.

"Are you sure about…?"

She slid her knees wider, deepening the contact.

"Yes."

Movies and TV showed lovemaking in lyrical, sweeping strokes. Perfect vignettes of tenderness and passion. Impediments melting away in dissolves that cut out all the moments of awkward fumbling, of clothes crammed into the wrong place, of unfastenings that went awry.

They missed all the fun.

Not that she'd thought it had been fun with those boyfriends she'd told him about. Both of them. The actual sex had been quite nice. Certainly nice enough for her to want more of it in her life … though, she had realized with reluctance at the time, not with them. But the getting ready for it had been uncomfortable physically and emotionally.

Not with Brad.

He approached this the way he approached basketball. With exuberance, joy, regard for the proceedings, and respect for his opponent.

In this case, their clothes.

She sighed against his shoulder as he slid her panties off.

Victory.

But now he was putting on one last item.

Done.

His wonderful hands came back to her. She *mmm*'d with the sensation.

And heard an echo of it from him.

She shifted, hooking a leg over his hip, the rolled to her back, trying to draw him with her.

He stalemated her with them on their sides. "I'm too heavy—"

He bowed over her, putting his mouth over the tip of her breast and drawing.

"Brad." She skimmed her hand lightly over his back. "Brad."

His resistance crumbled. He rolled with her, settling into where she most wanted him.

He slid inside her.

And then he went still.

No, no, no. No stillness.

"Do you feel that?" he asked.

"Oh, yes."

He expelled a breath, part snort, part chuckle, part pained pleasure. "That ... vibration."

She tightened her muscles. "This?"

"Ah. That's ... That's..."

She spread her hands on his butt cheeks, curving her fingers into him, urging him, at the same time she bent her knees, then crossed her ankles over him.

"Katie, Katie. Please. Wait. Slow. Good. For. You."

He was panting. Words. But they made no sense. Nothing made sense except this need.

"Now." That was her voice. That was really her voice.

She raised her head, and kissed his exposed throat, then sucked on it.

"Ahh."

"Now," she repeated. "Move *now*."

She was already moving, rocking.

He moved.

They were together.

"You owe it to yourself to go to Bariavak, Katie."

He'd done a lousy job of keeping his hands off her. Twice. Even now one hand curved over her hip, holding her against him.

Her leg slid between his in micromovements, stirring the sheet that covered them.

Vibration.

That frequency.

It was something in her. It communicated to him like a tuning fork being struck. Amplified ten thousand times.

But he would still look out for her. He would still try to help her to the life she deserved.

"But what about the basketball office?" she asked.

His smile felt forced. "Katie, Katie. Run Ashton's basketball office? Or be princess of Bariavak? Get your priorities straight."

"You said…" It died away.

"Said what?" he nudged.

Her head came up and she met his eyes. "You said you—all of you, the basketball office—couldn't function without me."

He looked away. "Maybe Bariavak can't either."

"It's going to have to. At least I think … I don't know." Her voice had wound down, but now she said quickly, "I'm not sure I even believe in princesses. And to actually run a country…"

"What does your grandfather think of that?"

"I haven't talked to him about much of anything. You know that. I want to be sure before I…"

"Break his heart?"

She was silent.

He shifted around, resting his cheek on the top of her head. "You're going to go, Katie. It's your birthright. It's your family. It's your future."

She reached up, cupped her palm to his cheek. The sheet slid lower. "I'm here now, Brad."

His heart turned over, along with an earthier reaction well south of his heart.

"Yes, you are. Yes, *we* are."

He pushed the sheet down.

"Carolyn? I'm sorry to call so early on a Sunday—"

"Katie? I wish you'd tell my children it's too early to be up and demanding breakfast on a Sunday. But—are you okay?"

Her bags were packed. She had these few minutes to let her friend know what had happened—some of what had happened. "Yes. I—I want to let you know, you and C.J., the DNA test result came in. It, uh, it said I'm…"

"You found your grandfather," the older woman supplied quietly.

"Yes."

"How do you feel about that? All of that?"

"I don't know. I just found out yesterday and…" Images from last night pinwheeled through her mind. "Uh, the other thing I wanted to let you know—I'm going to Bariavak with King Jozef. We leave in a few minutes, so—"

"Did something happen with you and Brad?"

Everything.

Right up until she woke in Brad's arms, knowing that he would protect her from ever having to leave—Ashton or the marriage—if he thought that's what she wanted. Desire stronger than anything she had experienced had flooded through her.

But even as the desire remained, she'd known she couldn't do that to him. To take advantage of him. To let him shelter her.

"What? Why would you think that? He doesn't have anything to do with this."

"Really? How you've felt about him all these years doesn't have anything to do with it?"

"How I…" She dropped her head. "How did you know?"

"I know something about women who close themselves off, Katie, because I was one. I saw that in you and I hoped our friendship might help."

"It has Carolyn. It has. And if I haven't said how grateful I am for your friendship—"

"Oh, honey, there's no need for that. But I'm afraid it hasn't been enough to help you open up to Brad."

She tried a laugh. If a frog tried to laugh, that was the sound it might make.

She'd married a man she'd fallen in love with. And now she'd made love with him and had fallen even deeper.

"Carolyn," she said with calm and reason she didn't know she had left in her, "he's been very supportive and I appreciate that, but he never showed the least interest in me before—"

"You were never in trouble before." The words came so quickly it was as if the other woman had been waiting to say them.

Or perhaps she heard them that way because it's what she'd been fearing. Brad saw her as an underdog he was going to help no matter what.

"You being in trouble is the one thing," Carolyn went on, "that would let Brad get past the stiff-arm you always presented—"

"Stiff-arm? I never—"

"—to him. You did. A stiff-arm that held him safely at a distance. I knew it was because you were scared, but he didn't. He wouldn't push past your defenses when it was solely because he wanted to get closer to you. He'd only do it when he thought it was necessary to protect you. Because he has defenses, too, you know. He—"

A knock came at her hotel room door. "I have to go, Carolyn."

"Will you think about what I've said?"

"Yes. But I'm going and he … It's not possible." Was she telling Carolyn that? Or herself.

"Promise you'll think about it. And you'll stay in touch."

"I promise."

He knew she was gone before he was fully awake. Knew it without reaching across to the emptiness beside him.

He pulled himself up, cramming pillows behind his back.

Of course her clothes were gone, too. Last thing on earth he could imagine was Katie sauntering down the hall to her room without her clothes.

But there was something else.

Something that gave the room an air of dusty desertion.

Or maybe that air of dusty desertion was inside him.

Because he knew—no idea how, but he *knew*—she'd gone. Not just to her room, but out of the hotel. Out of the city. Out of—

He reached around and punched the pillow pressing against his back. Because that had to be where the pain came from.

She'd gone to Bariavak. Where she belonged. Finding her future as a princess.

Out of his life.

CHAPTER THIRTY

Even though she had it memorized, Katie tipped the paper to catch light from the window in the gallery and looked over the detailed schedule issued today by King Jozef's staff for next week's three-day visit by the Ashton University men's basketball team.

Without Brad.

The first time she and C.J. had talked, days after her arrival in Bariavak and the day before the official announcement, he'd told her Brad had withdrawn from the trip.

Though Carolyn was coming, taking Katie's spot, while C.J.'s mother stayed with the kids in Ashton.

The team arrived in eight days. After a welcoming reception, they would play against the Bariavak national team at the university. Saturday would start with morning clinics put on by the coaches for local children at a gym built into the mountain as part of the royal complex. There would be a second game with the national team in the afternoon, followed by a gala for both teams, their families, dignitaries, and other guests. Sunday morning was free. More clinics in the afternoon, this time led by players from Ashton and Bariavak. Then an evening in which each national player took an Ashton player and two youth participants to his home for dinner.

Monday morning, the team would leave.

It hadn't been easy to watch from a distance as King Jozef's staff finalized the plans she'd started from Ashton. But he had tactfully conveyed that she could be seen as intruding.

As reluctant as she was to relinquish involvement, how could she argue when she knew nothing about how things worked here. About how things worked in what was now her life.

Views from the windows still caught her breath, but anyone who became so accustomed to these mountains that they didn't catch their breath at the sight had to be mostly dead. It seemed impossible that any structure could adhere to the abrupt inclines, yet here she was, living in a palace—no, Madame had told her more than once it was a castle—that proved they could.

That was among the aspects she hadn't grown accustomed to. She lived in a castle, with a suite of rooms as her "apartments."

The castle held the highest occupied ground in the capital city, digging its fingernails into the rock sides of the mountain and clinging so ferociously that it was impossible to imagine the mountain without the castle.

One night at dinner, King Jozef had remarked that if the castle were built on flat ground it would be a simple structure. She had laughed, because that was like saying if Neil Armstrong's moon walk had taken place on earth it would have been a simple stroll.

The king had smiled, though she'd heard a tinge of sadness when he said, "That is the first time I have heard you laugh. Your laugh is very much like your mother's."

Comparisons to Princess Sofia were also something she had not adapted to.

And then there'd been the episode with the Magda tiara.

King Jozef had cajoled her into wearing the diamond tiara for a reception with government officials a week after her arrival.

It was dramatic and history-laden—the king's own mother's official portrait showed her wearing it. It also was heavy and awkward. At least it was awkward when she wore it. It hadn't looked awkward on the queen.

She'd nearly lost the damned thing when she bent slightly to pick up the floor-length skirt of her formal dress—thank heavens for Maurice—so she could walk up a stairway.

"Princess Katrina?" a woman stopped before her, waiting patiently for an acknowledgment of her presence.

Katie was even starting to respond when people called her Princess Katrina. Officially she was called Princess Josephine-Augusta. But inside the castle—and in some of the media—she was now known as Princess Katrina. Losing her name was not something she expected to ever become accustomed to.

Elisabeta, the same middle-aged woman here now, had taken her into a private room and applied emergency bobby pins to hold the tiara. The woman hadn't laughed and she'd fixed the problem, so she'd won a spot in Katie's heart. By the end of that evening, though, the bobby pins felt like they'd weighed as much as the tiara.

"Hello, Elisabeta. How are you today?"

"Very well, ma'am. Madame asks that you come to her office."

There was only one Madame in the castle. Perhaps in all of Bariavak.

Madame directed Katie's daily lessons on life as a princess. Katie clung to as much free time as she could, wandering the castle, the grounds, the library, and the town. Between that and an hour daily with the king, she was learning pieces of Bariavak's long, complex history bit by bit.

King Jozef's insistence that she have an escort outside the castle rubbed against her nerves, but she'd acquiesced before the expression in his eyes.

She smiled at the woman. "Will you lead the way, please? I'm not sure I know the most direct route from here and I would not like to keep Madame waiting."

Yes, there was much she didn't know.

What she did know, despite her best efforts to not know it, was an aching soreness under her skin from missing Brad.

She would not think about him. About that last night. About the months before it. She would not.

If there was one thing Bob and Anna Davis had taught her it was how to ignore.

"Good day, Princess Katrina," Madame said. "There is a visitor His Majesty would like you to entertain."

"Me? Alone?"

"Most certainly you. He is awaiting you now in the Brocade Room. You shall have lunch in the ladies' dining room, then entertain him this afternoon. A tour of the castle would be appropriate. The Royal Librarian is prepared to guide you both. Return to the Brocade Room by five o'clock so you can prepare for this evening's small dinner."

Katie's heart sank.

She enjoyed the occasional times when she and King Jozef dined together. Or even when she and Madame had trays here in her office. But the "small" dinners—or lunches, or brunches, or breakfasts— usually included two dozen or more and were a trial.

Not at all like the gatherings in Angelo's back room or when Brad had cooked for her and Andy and—No, she wasn't going to think about that.

"Who is this visitor?"

"Posture." Only after Katie straightened did Madame add, "Your cousin."

"Prince Vatche?" She'd met King Jozef's nephew the first week and hadn't liked him. At all.

He'd been smooth and charming, with smiles and bows abounding, and she hadn't trusted him for a second. She was certain he liked her even less than she liked him.

That hadn't kept him from showing up a lot.

Madame's eyes went frosty, and Katie realized she'd let her feelings about the prince show through.

"Not Prince Vatche. However, if it were—"

"I know. I would be expected to entertain him or anyone with grace and dignity."

Madame folded her hands on the desk. "Yes."

Katie broke the look first. "So who is this cousin?" And why hadn't she heard of him or her before now?

"Prince Karl is a cousin of some distance. You are related through the three-times great-grandfather of King Jozef's mother."

"That's some distance," she said.

C.J. looked up from his desk when his wife walked into his home office and closed the door behind her. Her expression told him immediately that the closed door didn't mean what he'd hoped it might.

"Did you know King Jozef has arranged a meeting of Katie and a prince?" she asked him.

He rubbed his forehead. Unless he'd somehow missed it on ESPN the chances were small he would have. But all he said was, "Where'd you hear that?"

She came close enough for him to pivot his chair and pull her down to his lap. She kissed the top of his head and added, "April Gareaux. She and Hunter just got to Bariavak."

"Then you can stop worrying so much about Katie, because they'll look out for her until we get there next week."

But she showed no sign of worrying less. "They haven't seen her yet. King Jozef sent Katie out with this prince. C.J., is Brad still determined not to go?"

"Yeah."

"Do you think … Could you do anything about that?"

"I can't *order* the guy to take a trip that's supposed to be a perk."

"Why not?"

The Brocade Room was kept dim—couldn't have it become the Faded Brocade Room, Katie supposed—so her first impression was of how he stood.

Easy, but ready to move at any second. It caught at something in her chest. It was an athlete's stance. It made her abruptly and deeply homesick for the players and coaches—she wouldn't think of *him*— she'd so often seen stand that way.

"Hello," she said as she advanced and he turned toward her. Then she saw he wore jeans. *Jeans.* Her homesickness nearly knocked her over. Jeans and a t-shirt and—were those cowboy boots? "Oh, excuse me, I was looking for—"

"Hi, I'm Karl." He strode forward, grasped her limp hand and pumped it. "You must be Katie."

He was as at home in his attire as King Jozef was wearing his crown. And he was genuinely, thoroughly American.

"*You're* Prince Karl?"

Madame would not approve. But he seemed to, judging by his grin.

"Yep. I can see what you're thinking." She was sure he couldn't, since there was nothing as coherent as a thought in her head. "I should have my hair slicked back and a pencil-thin mustache, right?"

Startled, she said, "Why?"

"Ronald Colman. Douglas Fairbanks. Errol Flynn."

"What about them?"

"They're my image of what a prince should look like. Although … I'm not so sure Flynn ever played a prince. Pirate, yes. Prince, no. Either way, we agree I'm not anybody's image of what a prince should look like. Or—"

"I didn't—"

"—sound like. Yep. I'm an American. Born in Wyoming."

"Wyoming? But how … Sorry, it's none of my business."

"Sure it is, since King Jozef is hoping we'll hit it off and get married."

"Married? No. Oh, no. He doesn't—"

"Sure he does. But don't worry, I won't knuckle under unless we decide it suits us. So, you want to hear the Ballad of Prince Karl, a cowboy from Wyoming and a prince of someplace you never heard of?"

Her head spun. But she got out the one word necessary. "Yes."

"Good. I'll grab my hat and we'll get out of here."

"You have a cowboy ha—Oh, wait. We're supposed to have lunch—"

"Got that taken care of. Let's go."

"This is … spectacular. How did you know this was here?"

They were at a pull-off on the road that seemed to rise like a curl of smoke clinging to the mountainside above the castle.

They hadn't talked much on the way up. She hadn't wanted to distract him from driving. Though he seemed totally at ease on the hairpin turns that included nothing but air for an outside shoulder.

From here the horizon presented a jagged edge of magnificence, standing stoically even as distance eroded the peaks from sight. Nearer mountains jutted skyward, the valleys sinking toward the center of the earth beneath wreaths of mist. "Got talking to a guy in the hotel. Turned out we'd been a few places in common. He lined me up with the truck, too. You should see the cracker boxes the rental places tried to pass off as a pickup."

She laughed. "You really are from Wyoming, aren't you?"

He looked across the seat as they both exited the truck, apparently genuinely surprised anyone would doubt what he said. "Yes, ma'am. And I've been longing for a good hamburger and some French fries. My friend at the hotel lined us up with that, too. And this hot box."

He started pulling things from a storage container in the bed of the pickup as he talked. Soon, she bit into a burger.

"Mmmm."

"Good, isn't it?" he asked.

"Almost as good as…"

He looked up. "Almost as good as?"

"A place in Chicago. Supposed to have the best burgers in the city."

"That's saying something. I've had some fine burgers there."

"You spent time in Chicago?"

"Enough to try a few burger spots."

"I'm betting you make time to do that anywhere you go."

"Well, now I know they were right when they said Princess Katie's smart as a whip."

It was good to be called Katie, even with the Princess before it. But how would he know—"Who said that?"

"Hunter Pierce and his wife."

"You know Hunter and April?"

"How do you think I got talked into coming here?" He didn't sound entirely happy.

He was shorter than Brad and broader—more a football player's build than basketball. When sun showed between puffy clouds, she realized his hair wasn't just darker than Brad's blond, but had a fair amount of red to it. He couldn't be called handsome as Brad certainly could be. Though the broad, strong bones of his cheeks, forehead, and jaw were very attractive.

"Not that I can hold April accountable. Hunter was the one. You know they'll be at dinner tonight?"

She stopped with a fry poised before her mouth. "No. I didn't. That's wonderful."

"I suspect it's to make sure I don't go AWOL."

"Is that likely?"

"Possible."

For the first time, she sensed he'd closed a door.

She turned to the view, giving him privacy behind that door. From this vantage, the capital city's setting resembled a flattened bowl with a spout at one end where the Bariavak River exited to the west.

"Different from Wisconsin, isn't it?" he said.

"I *like* Wisconsin. I like Ashton. I like the university. I like my job. I'm so tired of people congratulating me on escaping my little-town life. I *like* little."

"Hey, I didn't mean to step on your tail. I like little, too."

"Sorry." He wasn't the person she was arguing with. And in fairness, King Jozef hadn't said those things. He'd simply assumed she shared his viewpoint. She changed the subject. "I don't understand why the builders who started the palace *castle* " He shot her a look. "—a thousand years ago didn't claim the flatter ground where the city is. It must have been so much easier to build there, especially back then."

"Easier to build, hell of a lot harder to defend." He was surveying the scene below them with concentration. Then his expression eased toward a grin. "Can't imagine our ancestors wasted any concern about the difficulty of building. They weren't the ones toting materiel. They commanded, and it was constructed."

"Our ancestors," she repeated.

"Should have said yours. Mine apparently were flatlanders." He gestured toward the other side of the mountains. "Before we get to that, do you know the difference between a castle and a palace?"

"No. I just know I keep calling this a palace, because I could swear Hunter mentioned one at the very start." She stopped abruptly.

"Probably when he talked about you being kidnapped as a baby from the palace," he supplied. "That's right. You were. And the woman who took you worked there."

He pointed to a large building not far from the university. "That's the palace. Right in the center of town. Made it real easy for the rebels. From what I've read about the rebellion, Hunter's father wanted the royal family to move up the mountain to the castle or even farther away. King Jozef wouldn't hear of it. Afterward, he moved the permanent royal household to Castle Bariavak. Gave the palace to the city to use as a hospital."

She stared down at the building, so peaceful looking now. The distance from the castle wasn't far measured in miles, but what a difference it had meant in King Jozef's life ... and hers.

If she'd been raised here as the heir to the throne ... But she hadn't been.

"...so the quick difference," Karl was saying, "between a palace and a castle is that a palace is built for high living, lots of show, and a castle is built for protection, as a fortress."

"Thank you, Karl. I think I'll keep it straight now. Madame won't have to correct me anymore."

"Don't suppose she wanted to bring it up, seeing what happened there. She's far more tactful than I am."

That lured a smile from Katie. "Madame? Tactful?"

"More than me, I said. And I'll prove it right now by saying I want to hear about you coming here."

"Oh, it's a long story—"

"I know the official story. But since you like your life in Wisconsin why'd you come?"

Odd. No one had asked her that. Everyone had assumed there'd been no decision to make about coming to Bariavak. But there had been. A lot of decisions, in fact. A whole series of them.

"I wanted to know," she said. "I wanted to know me."

Karl nodded as if that made sense.

"So you went straight from the honeymoon into a diplomatic maelstrom? Is this a hint of things to come for your married life with Hunter?"

Leslie's light dryness came through as clearly as the raised brow April saw onscreen. She had placed the video call from a castle guest suite.

"This is a delicate time and no one is better than Hunter—"

Leslie chuckled. "Smooth down your feathers. I wasn't criticizing Hunter. Just checking on *my* chick."

April joined the chuckle, recognizing her overreaction. "I wanted to come. Your chick is fine. Better than fine."

"Ahh. So that means the honeymoon bedroom has been well used and—"

"I am *not* talking to you about our honeymoon or our bedroom. I know you're a cousin but you're too much like my mom to want to discuss *that*. Go talk with Tris and Bette."

"About you and Hunter in the bedroom?"

"Leslie."

"All right, all right. I guess since you didn't say anything about someone listening in or my comments ruining Hunter's career it's safe to talk."

"Yes, but—"

"What's worrying you? If it's not Hunter—"

"It's not. I mean there's nothing worrying me…" Leslie's disbelieving stare made April think advancements in technology were not always good. Without video she might have gotten away with that. A letter would have been even better.

"How's Katie?"

"I haven't seen her yet. She's out with Prince Karl. I told you about him."

"Right. So this is King Jozef's effort at matchmaking?"

"I guess." She chewed on her lip. "It's so … heavy-handed. I had this feeling, and I talked to Carolyn—the professor who's married to Ashton's basketball coach, they're Katie's great friends. Anyway, when I talked to her, I'm afraid she picked up some of my concern. And that was even before we had lunch—Hunter and me and King Jozef and Madame."

"What happened at lunch?"

"I've never heard King Jozef happier."

Leslie made a sound.

"I know, I know," April said. "I should be happy he's happy. And I am, but … He was full of how he's going to direct Katie's life and courtship and her reign over Bariavak—he's got it all mapped out. The more he talked, the more stoic Madame became and when I tried to ask what Katie thought, he brushed it aside."

"Ahh."

"I don't understand it. It's like he's smothering her and he doesn't seem to be aware of it. He was nothing like that with me."

"You're not the granddaughter he feared was dead for many years. Or the heir to his throne."

"No. But … Oh, Leslie, if he keeps on like this, I can't imagine Katie accepting it. And it will break his heart—and hers. I'm so afraid he's going to lose her again. And this time it would be his own doing. I don't know what to say to him."

"Honey, you might not be able to say anything. As much as you care about him, he is a king, and that might be what comes first."

CHAPTER THIRTY-ONE

While Karl fueled her with chocolate chip cookies, Katie poured out her disjointed thoughts and feelings about her upbringing, about Anna and Bob Davis, about how the magazine article on April and King Jozef had led to the items in the attic, about her talks with Hunter and April, Carolyn and C.J.

Everything except Brad. And certainly nothing about the wedding at the Ashton Courthouse.

When she told Karl about calling King Jozef to say she would come to Bariavak for an unspecified time, she talked about her grandfather's joy. She didn't mention she had just left Brad's bed.

Still, for the first time, she shared the emotional and sensory overload of these past weeks—an unknown language, vertical landscape, staring eyes trying not to stare, people she'd never known having expectations of who she was.

She'd been so careful talking to her friends at home, not wanting them to worry. In her one conversation with April, she been even more careful—the woman had finished her honeymoon for heaven's sake.

Finally, she wound down to "I can't believe I've told you all this. We just met."

"Maybe that explains it. Besides, we're related."

She smiled. "Of course. I'm sure you won't tell—"

"No," he interrupted her firmly. "I won't, Cousin."

"Thank you," she said quietly. Then she rallied. "Okay, cowboy. Time for the Ballad of Prince Karl."

He grinned ruefully. "I did promise that, didn't I? Okay, here goes.

Better get comfortable." He handed her another chocolate chip cookie.

"First, tell me—are you a soldier?"

He raised one eyebrow—the way King Jozef and she could do. "How'd you come to that?"

"AWOL, materiel, terrain being easier to defend, and … *something*. We are related after all."

"Yeah. I was a soldier. But that has nothing to do with the Ballad of Prince Karl. So there's this place next to Bariavak called Gelicia." He bit into his cookie. "It doesn't have mountains around it like Bariavak, which means the land's better, but the defenses aren't. And it sits where a bunch of countries past and present come together, so it's been claimed, won, lost, given away, and transferred by treaty enough times to give anybody a headache. For about five minutes in the 1800s it was independent and somebody had the bright idea to put this guy named Grunnard on the throne. That was Grunnard the first, last, and everything.

"When he died, his two older sons started fighting over the throne. It got nasty. One was killed and his family fled the country."

"Your ancestors?"

"Nope. So that left Felix as king. Only the fighting had weakened the already flimsy army, and the next country that came sweeping through knocked him right off the throne and abolished the Royal House of Grunnard."

"And his descendants moved to Wyoming."

"Nope. You're jumping ahead, Princess Katie. Got to learn to let a story unfold in its own time." She chuckled, but he didn't seem to hear. "Felix didn't have any descendants. His dead brother did, though, and that line led on down to a guy named Prince Stefan Carlos, who was maybe ten years older than me."

"He's another possible candidate as heir, right? So he's your cousin?"

"Cousin by a thread. And, yeah, he *was* a candidate," he said sourly. "But now we go back to Grunnard, because he had a third son. Youngest of the ones that survived childhood—I'm telling you, I saw that family tree and not many reached that point. Anyway, this son was a real rebel. Always in trouble. But the icing on the cake was when he'd tried to overthrow Grunnard."

"He tried to kill his own father to become king himself?"

He grinned. "Nah. Tried to push Grunnard off the throne and make the country a republic. When he failed, Grunnard banished him. He first came here to Bariavak, stayed with a prince who'd known him from childhood. But, strange as it might seem, his king-dumping ways made the king here nervous, so he shooed him out. That's when the third son changed his name and moved to the United States, ending up in Wyoming Territory. Got married, had kids. They got married, had kids. And so on, until you come to me, the oldest son of the oldest son, of the oldest son, right on back to that third son."

"What an amazing heritage."

"I never knew about it. There was some family story that old Harvey—that's the name the third son picked—had a title back in Europe, but to tell the truth, his credibility wasn't the best. I suspect everyone thought it was a tall tale.

"And, hell, even if we had known about his title, the place doesn't exist anymore as a separate country. So who'd think it mattered? And then this distant cousin I'd never met, never heard of gets himself killed and—*bam* my life gets turned upside down. You know how that is."

She nodded with feeling.

"Yeah, I bet you do," he said with surprising gentleness. The gentleness was gone from his next words. "One day you're a cowboy with a little spread of your own, home from the wars at last. Course you still get together with some of your old unit. So you're at a weekend gathering, catching up, and telling tales. Then somebody knocks on your hotel room door in Sherman, Wyoming damned early, too, and it had been a full night with a fair amount of lubrication to keep the reminiscing going strong—and this somebody tells you you're a prince.

"I thought I must've been a hell of a lot drunker the night before than I'd thought I was. If Hunter hadn't been there with the guy from

Bariavak, I never would've believed him. They wanted me to throw my life over all because of an as—uh, jerk."

"Who was the jerk?"

"Stefan Carlos. Apparently he ran around with the beautiful people being a professional prince. And died in a stupid jet-ski collision."

She smiled. "Stupid? Because jet-skiing isn't as risky as being a cowboy or, um, war?"

"It was the way he did it. Jackass was killed in a road-rage incident on a jet-ski. From what I've read he instigated it, he accelerated it, and he had no right to expect any other outcome. Never once thought of what he was doing to anybody else," he finished glumly.

She patted his arm. "It's a dirty job, being prince, but somebody's got to do it."

"It gets worse. According to some experts I'm not even Prince of Gelicia, because it's a title of pretence. How do you like that? Prince of pretence. Prince of a country that doesn't exist, and taking the leavings of some guy named Stefan Carlos who was a bully on a jet-ski—I told them to forget it."

"How'd that go?"

He shook his head. "Hunter Pierce doesn't give up."

"I know."

They exchanged commiserating looks before Karl picked up his tale. "So, he says come meet somebody in Washington. Turns out it's King Jozef. He starts telling me the family history and showing me photographs and paintings, and darned if one doesn't look like my sister. Turns out that was the king's mother as a girl, who was related somehow or another to Grunnard. And then King Jozef says it was his ancestor that my great-grandfather stayed with in Bariavak. They'd been boys together and there was this bond..."

"He's persuasive, isn't he?"

"Very." It wasn't a compliment. "And he's going to be unhappy if I don't get you back for this dinner."

"Where is Katie?"

"Hello to you, too, Andy," Brad muttered into the phone.

He propped the soles of his bare feet against the edge of his coffee table. His grandmother hated feet on her furniture. And his were particularly bad right now since he'd weeded Katie's yard today after mowing and edging.

How was that for a pathetic act of rebellion? Doing something his grandmother couldn't see to furniture that wasn't hers.

"Never mind that. Where's Katie?"

"You know where she is. I suspect you've known from the start, probably from Carolyn or C.J. For sure you know where she is now, because I can hear the TV in the background reporting what she's doing in Bariavak."

He happened to have the same show on, which he'd muted before answering the phone.

"She's all alone in that foreign country and now there's this prince after her. How could you leave her to these foreigners?"

"He's an American. And she's with her grandfather." Plus, apparently this prince was some kind of relative, though not the king's nephew.

"He's a *prince*—that's not American. And you sent her off—"

"She went. I didn't send her."

"Well, you better apologize for whatever you did that sent her off that way—" He'd be damned if he apologized for loving her. "—when you see her on the team's trip over there, and you better hope it's not too late with this prince—"

"I'm not going. I've got recruiting assignments," he lied.

That didn't stop his grandmother for more than a quarter of a second. "Well, when are you going after her?"

In a way, he preferred this to the careful conversations he'd endured with people around Ashton these past weeks. In another way, he didn't.

"I'm not."

"Bradford Alan Spencer—"

Do you Bradford Alan Spencer take Katharine Mary Davis…

"Don't make this a big deal, Andy. We worked together and—"

"Go ahead, lie to me. Tell me she was just a girl you work with when I know she wasn't. But—."

"Andy—"

"I know that girl loves you. Gave herself away when I pretended to be criticizing your being a coach. You should have heard her. Oh, yes, she loves you. And you love her. So go ahead and lie to me, but don't you lie to yourself."

King Jozef had used most of their dinner together to instruct her on Bariavak's diplomatic history with Turkey. She had to leave soon, so she was almost out of time, and she needed to get this on the record.

"Grandfather," she said quickly, before he could start on Italy. "I've learned enough in these weeks about your methods to recognize you're pushing Karl and me together. You must stop."

"You don't care for Prince Karl? But you seem to have such pleasure in each other's company. I believe you go to a play tonight as his guest, is that not so?"

"That doesn't mean we're headed for a wedding, the way that awful gossip website said. And now TV is picking it up."

"When you are queen, you will understand such trivialities—"

"No."

"Now, do not be squeamish. It is natural I will die and you will ascend to the throne."

"No."

"Katrina—"

"I am Katie. When you die, I will still be Katie. But I don't believe I will ever be queen." She hadn't meant to get into this. Not yet. But perhaps this needed to be said even more than the hands-off warning about her and Karl.

"You are my granddaughter—"

"Yes, I am. And I hope you will remain my grandfather."

"Of course. Nothing can change that. As nothing can change that you are destined to become Queen Josephine-Augusta."

"Grandfather, we cannot remake the past. We cannot try to capture what might have been. Princess Josephine-Augusta would have been raised here, living and absorbing the history, the rites, the role."

"You have learned a great deal already. In no time you will—"

"I don't want to, Grandfather. I don't … I won't be a queen."

He stood and stared out the window, hands behind him. "What shall I do? What shall my poor Bariavak do? I am undone."

She held her tongue, watching.

He looked over his shoulder. "You say nothing?"

"I've seen you use that maneuver two other times since I came here, and it did not turn out well for your verbal opponents."

He glared for a slice of a second, then roared out a laugh. "I have taught you too well."

"You are a wonderful teacher."

His laughter faded into a sigh. "Or you have learned too well. But still you think to leave me with an abyss before the future of Bariavak."

"I don't believe that. What did you plan before you fo—Before we found each other?" As she shifted her sentence, he reached a hand to her, and she joined him to sit together on the window seat. "I won't believe you hadn't made meticulous plans to provide for Bariavak's future."

"An extremity that is unavoidable must be faced. But to accept an extremity when the natural remedy—"

"I can't imagine being Bariavak's queen."

"It is this American who plays games who pushes you toward this unnatural decision."

She smiled, trying to mask stinging in her eyes. "No. You and Brad are of one mind about my royal future."

"Are we?"

"Don't get that expectant look. It won't do you any good. Not anymore than your efforts to hire Hunter have done."

"Stubborn Americans. I am beset by them."

"Karl's not cooperating, either, huh?" she said with no sympathy.

"I do not despair of him," he said with great dignity. "Nor of you. You shall have a great deal of time to prepare to become queen. I am very healthy now."

"Even if I were willing to be queen, you wouldn't like the result. I don't mean the methods, and certainly not the violence—"

"All preamble. Now if you please, the *but* and then the meat of the dish."

"But," she said obligingly, "I am not unsympathetic to the ideals of the rebellion."

He stiffened. "Those animals. Those murderers. Those—"

"Not all of them. As I said, I don't agree with the methods—how could I? But I have read what they were seeking and I believe if I had been an adult then, I would have agreed with their goals. As Prince Leopold and Princess Sofia did. As—"

"And look what those animals did to them!"

"You say Bariavak must come first—the people and the country you serve so diligently. But in this one area your grief overwhelms all else. I do not believe that is the legacy Sofia and Leopold would—"

"Your *mother*. Your *father*."

"I call them Sofia and Leopold in this discussion to separate from the emotion of that connection."

"You say I do not? That emotion colors what I do?"

She raised one eyebrow, not needing to confirm with words.

"You will not abdicate a thousand years of—Enter!"

The door opened to Hunter, April, and Madame.

"We don't want to interrupt," April said. "But you said you'd like us to keep you company while Katie and Karl go to the play."

"Of course, of course. We lost track of time, talking of when Katie becomes queen. Perhaps with a consort."

"Grandfather—" Katie started with exasperation.

"Go, go now, you and Karl to your play. Hunter and April and Madame shall be my company."

Katie kissed him on the cheek before departing, but April had seen something in her expression.

When the king brought the conversation around to his plans for the future—a future with Katie and Karl married and prepared to rule—she said, "Sir, it might not be the best strategy to push Katie so hard."

"Bah. I have a great deal of experience at strategy," he said.

"Not with Katie."

"She is my granddaughter." Clearly that settled the matter to him.

April glanced at Madame, but the older woman did not look up. However, she received a level look from Hunter she had no trouble interpreting. She did not say any more.

King Jozef smiled at Katie. "Where do you go now?"

At last it was Friday. *The* Friday. "To the airport. The Ashton team arrives soon."

"No." His smile was gone.

"It's not too early. The plane lands in less than an hour. I can't wait to see Carolyn and C.J. and all of them. I'll help them get settled in the hotel, then—"

"I do not permit you to go."

She stilled. "You do not permit me to?"

He gave a slight, impatient gesture. "You are young and unaccustomed to what is expected of you. I am instructing you."

"It's expected of me that I not be there to greet friends who are arriving in this country?"

"You will greet them in an appropriate manner at an appropriate time. It is important that the people of Bariavak see you in the proper way. Not among the bustle of everyday people at the airport."

"Sir—"

"I ask this of you."

A shaft of sunlight cut across his desk, catching his hands, showing the raised veins, the battering of age.

"Yes, Grandfather."

She regretted her acquiescence.

Regretted it as hours went by that she could have been spending with her friends while waiting for the late afternoon reception.

Regretted it when word came from the king that she was to wear the Magda tiara. She understood its import to him, but that other time she'd worn it she'd felt like she had a bowling ball on her head, not to mention the near-disaster. The young woman who had brought the word—and the tiara—was only a messenger, so she couldn't even argue.

Regretted it when she arrived at the assigned anteroom to find Prince Karl there, looking unhappy in a suit with an official sash across his chest.

"Command performance," he muttered as the king came in precisely one minute before the appointed time.

Regretted it when King Jozef did not meet her eyes, but only nodded to the man by the door.

Regretted it when the man threw open the double doors, revealing a precise semicircle of Bariavakian officials at ramrod attention. The man began intoning King Jozef's name and titles as her grandfather walked out, straight-backed and regal.

"Your Highness," urged Elisabeta.

Katie started after her grandfather automatically, sensing Karl behind her.

April and Hunter were at the near end of the semicircle of officials. They both turned toward her. April smiled warmly. Hunter winked.

Her spirits lifted.

This wasn't the way she wanted to greet her Ashton friends, but after the formality her grandfather insisted on, they would have the rest of the weekend. She started to turn toward them, smiling to show that this—

Brad.

His face above her.

His hands on her.

His mouth drawing on her.

It was memories making her think he was here. Because he'd refused to come. Didn't want to see her…

Brad.

He was real.

He was here.

Inside her.

Moving with her.

She stutter-stepped.

Karl's hand under her elbow steadied her.

Brad's expression darkened. He looked away from her, toward the king, who had begun to speak with formal, precise words. Misery burned in her chest as she kept her gaze on the expanse of floor that isolated the Ashton contingent.

She couldn't meet their eyes. Not C.J. or Carolyn or any of the others. Certainly not Brad. She felt herself drawing in, shrinking, the disappearing trick of her youth.

The king finished his remarks. The man who'd announced them gestured to the Ashton group to form a line to be formally received.

C.J. muttered something that brought Katie's head up.

He took a stride forward, Carolyn caught his elbow, halting him for an instant. Then Katie saw Carolyn's hold on his elbow change as she urged him forward. C.J.'s long strides reached her before anyone could object and he wrapped her in a hug.

She hugged back, fighting tears. Carolyn was there now, too. One hand stroking up and down her back. In another minute, Katie turned into her hug, asking how the flight was, saying how glad she was to see her, babbling.

Over Carolyn's shoulder she saw Karl step forward, bridging the gap with his hand extended to shake with assistant coach Martin Brewster.

Katie also stepped forward, now hugging Maura, then players, Tony Corston, more players. Hunter and April joined the group.

King Jozef remained where he was.

C.J. and Carolyn introduced the others one by one to the king, but after those formal words, each one returned to the swirling group in the middle of the floor, talking and laughing.

On the far side of the swirl and outside of it stood Brad Spencer. As straight and solitary and separate as the King of Bariavak.

For a flash their eyes met. Katie felt herself lean toward him.

Then he turned and strode out of the room.

CHAPTER THIRTY-TWO

"Ah, if you please, I shall steal Princess Josephine-Augusta away."

King Jozef's hand under her elbow turned her away from Brewster and toward Karl.

She supposed it was time to let the team get to the bus or they wouldn't have time to warm up properly before the game.

The king gestured Karl closer.

"We have now a dinner arranged with these officials," he said, not looking at her. "You will attend with Prince Karl. It is important that you both meet these people and beneficial it should occur on such a basis."

"I cannot, sir. You know I am attending this evening's basketball game and—"

"A basketball game," he said with exquisite inflection. Not quite dismissive enough to be insulting.

"Yes. A basketball game that will feature the Bariavak national team and will be attended by many citizens. I will not disappoint them by breaking this commitment nor any of my commitments for the duration of the Ashton team's stay. It would be an insult to your staff who worked so hard on this event and a poor representation of Bariavak."

A flicker crossed his eyes but his expression didn't change and from the way he smoothly switched to urging Prince Karl to accompany her—"you young people," he called them no one who wasn't in the direct line of that flicker could have known how displeased he was.

She wasn't too pleased herself.

"Impromptu" her ass.

Halfway down the corridor leading to the parking court, Karl asked from behind her, "Are you going to slow up so I can keep up without needing a horse?"

She spun around. "Were you part of that ambush?"

"Me?" He was unbuttoning the collar of his shirt. His tie and the sash trailed out of one jacket pocket. "No way."

"Then why are you acting as King Jozef's watchdog?"

"From my angle it was a choice of hanging out with stuffed shirts all night or going to a basketball game. No contest."

She let out a breath. But she wasn't ready to acquit him completely. "What do you think of what happened in there?"

"I think King Jozef made a power play, complete with careful staging, to stake his—and Bariavak's claim—to you. And he did a damned good job of it.

"Not only the set-up, which spoke volumes. But also that speech. He intimated he appreciated they'd been willing to come to Bariavak when that seemed the only way to get you to come. But now you were here, where you belong. So they weren't really necessary, which meant he's not beholden to them, and yet he was gracious enough to welcome them anyway. As long as they didn't interfere."

"He didn't—"

"Nope. Never said it directly. But everybody knew that's what he was saying. If it hadn't been for C.J. Draper invading no-man's-land, that's how it would have stayed, too."

"So sending you along with me was a fall-back position for him when I refused to stay for dinner?"

"Guess so." He grinned. "He has no idea my momma's side of the family tree's chock full of rebels."

"One minute," Katie said to the driver who held the car door for her. Karl was opening his own door on the far side of the vehicle and tossing in the abused sash and tie.

She started toward where Ashton's players were loading onto a bus to take them to this evening's game.

Brad had already boarded. There was surely cause and effect in action here, but she had no interest in unraveling whether he'd boarded because he'd seen her or whether she felt comfortable enough to approach the group because he'd already boarded.

"His Majesty would not like—"

Without turning, she raised her hand and the driver fell silent.

"C.J.," Katie called to him.

He passed through players, managers, interns, and others lining up for the bus, one arm curved around Carolyn to buffer.

"There's something I should tell you," she said when they were close enough not to be overheard. "The facilities here are not going to be what you're used to."

"Figured that. No worries."

"You might not say that when you see the castle gym you'll be using for the youth clinics. They've cleaned, but it's small and old and with all this rock…"

Prince Karl came up behind her. "If you can imagine where the Count of Monte Cristo would've played hoops in prison, you'll start to get the idea."

C.J. grinned. "It sounds a lot like the Ashton gym when I started coaching there. Can't hurt to make us all appreciate what we have at home. Say, Katie, would you mind taking Carolyn with you in that Princess-mobile? She wants to talk to you. Privately."

"Mr. Subtle," Carolyn murmured.

"That'll work great," Karl said immediately, "because I was hoping to go on the team bus."

"You're a good man, Prince," C.J. said, clapping him on the back as a means of steering him toward the bus. "A glutton for punishment, but a good man."

Chuckling, Carolyn took Katie's arm and they walked toward the car and the anxious driver. "Do you mind?" she asked.

"Of course not. In fact, I want you to know, that reception was not—"

"Oh, we know. Don't worry."

Once they were settled in the car, with the privacy barrier raised, Carolyn picked up. "But I do hope grabbing you this way didn't intrude on time you wanted to spend with Prince Karl."

"No. Not at all. I mean, he's nice. Very nice. But—"

"And attractive."

"Yes, attractive but—"

"And a prince."

"A prince of pretence, according to him," she said with a smile.

Carolyn added mildly, "And your grandfather's choice."

Katie did her best to sound as calm as her friend. "King Jozef knows Karl and I have just met."

"Does King Jozef also know about you and Brad?"

"There's nothing to—"

"Of course. That scene just now was a meeting between a couple of pals."

"There was no scene. We didn't say a word to each other."

"Precisely." Carolyn looked almost smug.

"It was a surprise. A shock. You told me Brad wasn't coming."

"He wasn't. Not until the last minute."

"You could have told me—"

"We weren't sure we'd get him on the plane—or off it once it landed in Bariavak. So you can say you were surprised, but he knew he'd be seeing you today. And yet..." Carolyn gave her a searching look. "But what I actually meant when I asked if King Jozef knows about you and Brad was, uh, what the two of you did before we all met for that lovely dinner in Angelo's back room with Frank and Thomas and Ellis."

Katie stared. "*You* know—?"

Carolyn nodded. "Suspected initially. Then had it confirmed—oh, not by any of your co-conspirators. But some things are public record, you know."

Of course. How on earth had neither she nor Brad thought of—

"C.J. knows?"

"Uh-huh."

"Anybody else?"

She didn't answer directly. "Did you know Hunter's partner came through Ashton the day after you left for Washington?"

"Why would—?" The passport. She'd been relieved Hunter delivered it unopened, but he might not have needed to open it to know of her new last name. "Do you think anyone else knows?"

"Hunter made background checks before we were all cleared to come. He's very thorough. After he'd been to see her I had a call from Andy."

"*Andy?*" That would be as bad as King Jozef knowing. "Oh, no. She'll hate me."

"Why on earth would she hate you?"

"For the same reasons you should hate me. For taking advantage of Brad. For getting him to—when he didn't … He's never—I knew that. But we were friends and now—he wouldn't even look at me. And I'm—" She swallowed hard. "—pitiful."

"You are *not* pitiful," Carolyn said with absolute conviction. "You have never been pitiful when you had every right to be and you certainly aren't now."

"What could be more pitiful than pining after a man who wasn't interested in you—pining for years? There's no point in pretending otherwise to you now, Carolyn. Years."

"I know. But, Katie—"

"You *know?* Oh, God, of course you know. Everybody probably knows."

"So what if they do. Now, let me get my question in: Have you ever wondered why Brad hasn't left Ashton?"

"What?" She felt like she had whiplash from the abrupt turn in the conversation. "You mean why he hasn't gone after a head coaching job?"

"No, I mean he hasn't *taken* a head coaching job. He's had offers. He's turned them down. Because of you."

"*Me?* No way on earth. Have you heard what I said? Pining. Unrequited—"

"I'd wondered. Then the way he reacted when Hunter showed up, I was sure. Oh, I'm not saying he was jealous, exactly."

"Of course he wasn't jealous," she said with scorn. "Me. Unrequited pining for him, remember? Pitiful. Dreaming with no hope of ever having it come true."

"He wasn't jealous because Hunter was so clearly not interested in you—"

Katie snorted.

"—or any other woman except April. As for dreaming with no hope of ever having it come true … you *are* married."

"Gallantry. Pity. Genor—"

"Has it been consummated?"

"—osity. And that's even more pitiful than all the rest—" A corner of her mind recognized a kind of cleansing in saying this out loud. "—taking advantage of his generosity and kindness and pity—yes, pity—to lure him into marriage. And then—"

"Lure? From what I heard it was Brad—"

"—binding him to it, because he's an honorable man, by throwing myself at him in his hotel room."

"Oh?"

Carolyn's syllable stopped Katie. Because it was all wrong.

It should have held censure, disappointment, dread because Carolyn and C.J. loved Brad.

Instead, it was bright, interested, even … *delighted?*

"It was despicable," Katie said firmly.

"That good, huh?" Carolyn said with a chuckle. "So it *was* consummated."

Katie felt heat surge up her throat. *Oh, yes. That good and better.*

"Looks like we're here," Carolyn said cheerfully. But then she turned to Katie, taking both her hands in hers. "Listen to me, Katie. You and Brad have to talk—really talk. And since you left him—especially the way you left him and when—you must be the one to go to him."

The driver opened the door.

Carolyn said in a low, urgent voice, "Go see him, talk to him."

According to the schedule, the clinic the next morning should have been over.

From her years working in the basketball office, Katie thought she had timed it perfectly so Brad—always last out of the gym and therefore the last one showered and dressed—would be about to leave. And he'd be alone.

Instead, as she edged into the gym so she could see around the bleachers without being seen, she realized he was still teaching a group of kids about middle school age.

A young man she'd noticed at last night's game dogged Brad, calling out translations of whatever he said like a distorted echo.

T-shirts clung to their chests from exertion. Only Brad's chest looked nothing like the kids'.

Her breath came faster. She wasn't sure if it was from watching him so utterly focused on these kids or … from just watching him.

The kids formed two lines at half-court, about ten feet apart. Brad bounce-passed to the closer player. That player dribbled twice then passed to the first player in the other line, who'd also advanced. Player 2 dribbled twice and passed back. They continued that way to the basket, where Player 1 threw up what might have been meant as a layup.

Brad clapped. "That's the way to do it. Good, good." He bounce-passed a new ball to the next player and the scenario repeated, including the miss at the end. Again earning Brad's praise.

The third pair was trouble. Katie saw that from their body language even before the first one received the ball. He dribbled four times instead of two and it took Brad's "Pass it! Pass it!" to get him to give up the ball. Player 2 began dribbling toward the basket. At the third dribble, as Brad called "Pass it!", Player 1 dove toward Player 2. Player 2 hugged the ball to his chest and raced toward the basket.

Player 1 chased. But Player 2 was too fast.

Apparently he was also deaf, because he paid no heed to Brad's shouts, to the translator, or to the whistle Brad blew with determination. Player 2 pulled up and shot. As the ball slid into the basket, Player 1 tackled him and other players swarmed around chattering loudly. Player 2 popped up, chanting something gloatingly. It had to be the Bariavakian version of "Nyah, nyah, nyah, nah-nyah-nyah."

Brad was going to have to shout to be heard over them.

Instead, he stood still and silent.

A few of the kids looked at him. Then more. The noise level lowered, until the only sound was Player 2 chanting.

Player 1 snapped something, which had the tenor of "Shut up."

One of the other players picked up the loose ball and handed it to Brad, who acknowledged the delivery with a small nod. Every player now focused on him.

Holding the basketball, he crouched down before the two players, with the others fanned out behind them. She couldn't hear what he said and didn't understand the few words she picked up from the translator. But she could see the tender way he turned the basketball in his hands.

She remembered him cooking. Thinking about those hands being so skilled with a basketball, in a kitchen.

Now she could think only of his hands on her. And their skills there.

Stop.

Stop remembering.

Stop feeling.

"Princess Josephine-Augusta."

One voice—the translator, she thought—said her name, then a murmur picked it up.

She'd been so intent on watching Brad that she'd strayed from the shadow of the bleachers, and she'd been spotted.

Kids turned, gaping, then rushed over to her, "Princezha Katrina! Princezha Katrina!"

They hopped and bobbed, waving their arms, calling out things she couldn't understand. She tried to shake hands as fast as they came at her. Left, right, whatever she could reach. The translator hurried up, "So happy. Great pleasure. Most wonderful." She didn't know if he was translating or they were his words.

With his reluctance so clear to her, Brad came last.

"I apologize for interrupting," she said to him.

"Princesses don't have to apologize." He seemed to regret the harshness and added more easily, "You seem to be the hit of the session."

"But you were doing so well with them—"

"We're way over time. Okay, that's enough. Pick up all the balls," he ordered, and the kids appeared to understand the tone without needing translation. "Then hit the showers."

The translator fumbled a few words, then barked one she thought meant *wash*.

Over the kids' heads, Brad's eyes met hers for an instant. Almost he smiled.

Almost.

The kids and translator loped toward the exit, still calling out. She waved after them.

Then it was only her and Brad and the echo of the young voices.

"I have to supervise these rug rats." He jerked his head in the direction they'd gone. "See you later—"

"I'll wait."

"Is that an order?"

"It's a … I'll wait here."

He glanced toward her, not making eye contact. "Suit yourself." Then he jogged after the youngsters.

CHAPTER THIRTY-THREE

The practiced phrases fled her mind when he strode toward her in khakis and a white shirt.

He still wasn't looking at her.

If he couldn't even look at her … Oh, God, Carolyn was wrong. Completely and totally wrong…

Into a silence that had gone on too long he said gruffly, "You're the one who called this meeting."

"Don't you think we should talk?"

He shrugged. The kids had missed a basketball. He stretched a leg and caught it with his toe, drawing it close.

"Don't you *want* to talk?"

"What about?"

"About…" She swiped her upturned hand in the air between them.

"You left." For a fragment of a second she thought he was going to add the word *me*. How different those words would have felt with that addition. "To find your future. What would I have to say?"

"I didn't leave…" She stopped. Of course she'd left. She'd meant leaving hadn't been her goal. Not entirely. "You gave me so much. You were so generous, so willing to protect me. You were right, I needed to find out … To get to know…" She hated she was stumbling through this. "To find out what my life would be like here."

"Yeah, I gave you so much," he said dryly. "Married in a court-house. Reception at Angelo's. What every girl dreams about."

"That's what … *that's* what was bothering you at April and Hunter's wedding?"

"Wasn't it bothering you?"

"No."

"The hell it wasn't. The fancy wedding dress. The flowers and music. The reception with all your friends and family."

"I don't have—I didn't have family. And you said you liked my dress."

"I do like it. But women don't want their wedding dress to be one they can wear again two weeks later. God, no wonder you're nuts for all this fancy stuff." He looked her over without the survey ever reaching her face. "Looks like your life here suits you fine."

She was starting to get irked. "If you think I've changed beyond—"

"Not changed. Realized."

"—clothes and—Realized what?"

"Who you are. Who you really are."

"The DNA result doesn't change—"

"It's not DNA. It's *you*. Not who the people who raised you tried to make you think you were. It's not only about being a princess, either. It started before that. You realizing." He was stumbling too. Was that good? Or bad? "Walt and Heath."

"What?"

"That's when I first saw it. With Walt and Heath. You realizing. You starting not to hide anymore. It wasn't like their attention was water for a dying plant or anything. More like your *handling* the attention started bringing you to life. Sort of blooming." His mouth twisted. "Fancy for a basketball jock, huh? You never looked like that when I flirted with you."

"*You*?" She was stunned. "You *never* flirted with me. Ever. You—"

Now he looked at her. Glared at her. "The hell I didn't."

"—were always my friend."

"The hell I was. Well, I was, I guess. But I didn't want to be. But you were a kid. And—"

"I was *not* a kid. What I was—"

"—I'd've deserved to be horsewhipped if I'd gone after you."

"—was ordinary. Completely, thoroughly ordinary. Not like the women you dated at all."

"Dated? *Dated?* I've practically been a monk, working so hard to keep my hands off you."

"Oh, yeah, wracked with lust for wanting me and—"

"Damn, I almost forgot."

He grasped her hand. For a crazy instant she thought he was going to pull her to him…

She felt the silk against her palm before her eyes caught up.

"I got this out of your attic. Thought you should have it. Maybe give it to your grandfather."

"Brad."

He scooped up the basketball. "It's good we had this talk. Wrapped things up. Finished things. Of course there'll be legal stuff. Send a lawyer or a diplomat or something and I'll sign whatever needs signing. But what's important is now we both know. Now we can both move on. Forget…"

He pivoted, and in one motion slammed the ball against the floor in the direction of the carrier, the sound of the impact echoing from the stone walls.

"You were a kid," he repeated in a harsh, low voice, not looking at her. "And now you're a princess. Good-bye, Katie."

She would have given a lot to skip the afternoon's game. But she had promised to be there.

King Jozef and Madame might talk about royal duty, but it was no different than her job at Ashton. People counted on her, so she would do what she'd said she'd do.

Brad was impossible not to see. But there was no need to talk or make eye contact. He made it easy by never looking her way.

Besides, as she'd told Carolyn, she'd gone through years of pining after him. With all that practice, she could pull this off.

At halftime, she saw April and Carolyn talking earnestly and caught both of them glancing at her … then carefully not looking at her. But neither said anything then or after the game at courtside amid a casual whirl of introductions and greetings among players, coaches, officials, and family members.

She eased toward the edge of the group. How many times had she left such events at Ashton unnoticed? Too many to count. This was a skill she could count on. This was something she knew how to do—

Carolyn slid a hand under her arm as she had yesterday. This time it occurred to Katie the gesture made it hard to get away.

"I'm getting a ride with you again," her friend said. "Don't argue and don't frown. Your driver will tackle me if you keep glaring at me."

She pasted on a smile, but said. "I don't want to be rude, but—"

"Good. Here we go."

In the car, Carolyn wasted no time. "I take it this morning's conversation with Brad didn't go well."

"It was fine. He's simply not interested."

"Simply not—? What did he say—no, don't tell me. It doesn't matter what he said. He's an idiot. A tall, good-looking, big-hearted—and, according to his grandmother, brooding—idiot. And—"

"He is not—"

"—so are you."

"—an idiot. Me?"

"Yes. For listening to him. Words. I love the English language, but sometimes I swear words get in the way. So forget whatever Brad said. Look at what he's done."

"Nothing bad, not really bad."

Carolyn laughed. "I was thinking of things he's done *for* you."

"Oh. You mean the ... courthouse."

She raised her brows. "Is that how you're referring to it? Well, yes, it's certainly impossible to miss that the man arranged to marry you so you would be sure to have a passport to come home to him."

"That's not—"

"But look at all the other things, Katie. He's always been protective of you."

"That's because he thought I was a kid. He's that way to everyone. Like the interns."

"Oh, Katie, really? You know with men like C.J. and Brad you have to look a little deeper. It's not that they won't be romantic, it's that their idea of romantic and ours might not be the same. Did I ever tell you about the brown things C.J. gives me?"

"It's your favorite color."

She chuckled. "No, it isn't. But I like what C.J. gives me that's brown, because it has significance between us. Yes, I see that skeptical look, but it's true. When he started giving me brown things I thought it was to annoy me. He'd given me grief about being monochrome— hair, eyes, wardrobe, life. Then he started speculating on exactly what color brown my hair was and he gave me things to try to match it. A teddy bear and ice cream, things like that." Her smile softened and her eyes brightened. "The first time he said he thought he'd matched it was with the velvet box of an engagement ring."

"Oh."

Carolyn nodded. "Face it, our guys are not the kind for a dozen roses."

"But I don't think Brad has—I mean other than the courthouse, and of course I could never thank him enough. But—"

"Going on red alert when Hunter showed up. Making sure you were okay afterward. Taking you to Chicago to get you more comfortable with—well, not with this, because I don't know how anything could prepare you for this, but still, more confident. Introducing you to his grandmother."

"Oh, that wasn't—"

"Yes, it was," Carolyn interrupted firmly. "Making sure he was with you when you met April and her extended family, and then the king so—"

"But that wouldn't have happened if he hadn't ambushed me."

"Exactly. C.J. and I would have sat back and let you avoid the whole situation. Brad has so much faith that you can handle anything that he pushes you where you wouldn't go yourself."

"I don't know about that."

Carolyn smiled again. "One word: Trees."

Click. The sensation was so strong Katie thought for sure it had been audible.

Carolyn nodded. "That's right. He cleared away the vegetation to let the sun in and to let the world truly see you. Same thing with the DNA and this trip to Bariavak. In a way, it's the most unselfish kind of—"

"What do you mean with this trip to Bariavak?"

"You know, it's a good sign you're asking questions instead of arguing. Who do you think pushed C.J. into changing the team's itinerary? Who lobbied the NCAA and the administration to get approval?"

"But … why?"

"He didn't know then that the DNA test would come through so quickly or so definitely. He wanted to be sure you had a chance to explore the possibilities, to see Bariavak, to spend time here. But when the DNA said you are who you are, and then media speculation started about you and Prince Karl, he said he wasn't coming. He didn't want to cramp your new style."

"Idiot."

Carolyn chuckled. "Oh, yes. Also stubborn. Andy tried and I tried, but the only thing that finally worked was C.J. making it an order from Coach that he come on this trip, and sticking to it."

"I need to think."

Carolyn leaned forward, resting her hand atop Katie's. "Think less, feel more, Katie. It's the greatest lesson I've learned from C.J."

Madame was waiting for them when the car pulled into the castle's courtyard.

"This can't be good," Katie muttered.

Madame gestured imperiously for the driver to remain behind the wheel. She held the door herself as Carolyn exited.

"Remain in the vehicle," she ordered Katie, then pinned Carolyn with a stare. "The princess has an appointment. Excuse us."

Carolyn turned back to her. "Katie, do you want me to—"

Madame slid in and shut the door, raising one hand to the driver, who smoothly pulled away.

"I don't have any appointments on the schedule until—"

"There is a woman I take you to meet."

"The gala tonight. I have to get ready." *And to find glue to hold myself together.* She wondered where they kept glue in the castle. "Another time—"

"Now. We shall return in time. It is short way. Visit will not be long. She is sick. Very sick. She dies soon."

"The woman you want me to meet is *dying?*"

"More I wish her to meet you. The woman you knew as Anna Davis was her sister."

CHAPTER THIRTY-FOUR

Madame began what sounded like a long introduction. Katie caught a few words then was irretrievably lost.

She gave up listening and looked, seeing the resemblance immediately to Anna Davis. Yet there were many differences.

For all the pain of illness evident in the woman's face there was also a contentment Anna Davis had shown in only the briefest of moments.

Katie suspected this woman's contentment came from the people clustered around her in the modest room. Two daughters, she thought, And the man in the corner had to be a son. The rest, grandchildren, other relatives.

All the time she'd been growing up so solitary, she'd had all this family. Cousins of one sort or another—No. What was she thinking? They weren't family. Because these people would have been her cousins only if she hadn't been—

"—Princess Josephine-Augusta, Her Royal Highness of Bariavak," Madame concluded. Then, more prosaically she added, "Martila speaks enough English. Do not worry."

"I'm honored to be in your home," Katie said in the English version of the traditional Bariavak greeting Madame had taught her.

She extended her hand to shake.

To her embarrassment, the woman took her hand in both of hers and lowered her head to kiss it briefly.

"Such honor, such honor," she said over and over.

Madame said something to her sharply in their native language.

Martila gave Madame a defiant look and gathered herself together.

She was in control when she squeezed Katie's hand, then released it. "I think of this much over all the years. To see at last, the princess my youngest sister steals."

"But it was only revealed last month."

"Bah. I know. We know." She gestured around the circle. "We know her. We know *him*. The princess is taken. She is gone. He is gone. We know. Her greatest strength is greatest fault. It undoes her." She added a word in her native language.

"I don't—" Katie looked to Madame.

"Loyalty," she translated.

"She is hired before even you are born. So proud to work in the Palace. So exalted, she is. Yes. I imagine that is why he chases after her. Takes her heart, steals her mind." She looked around at the others and spoke two words—Davogner Bordanic, the name Bob Davis had been born with, Katie realized. The others frowned. "We do not like him. Not from the first moment he steps from the street into this house and our eyes take him in. My mother tries to tell Annika. Tries to warn her.

"But she is a girl, as girls are. So sure their mothers know nothing." She focused on the youngest of the women in the semicircle, who pursed her lips and glowered.

Turning back to Katie, she went on, "Ah, it is a time of crazy. The unrest bubbling, bubbling. Annika giddy with her new job and that man. And then the fighting starts, and everywhere is madness. The prince is killed and Annika cries and cries and cries for the sorrow of the princess and for the child never knows its father. And worse the fighting gets. Worse and worse. And Annika is coming home less and less. With the princess, she says, but she is seen here and there, not good places. Always with that one.

"And then the princess has her baby. A new princess. And there is hope. The fighting is so close done ... Then she is gone. Gone. The princess baby, yes. And also our Annika. Gone, gone, gone. And we know. With shame and horror, we know. She takes our princess's baby. She does it for that one. She is gone with him. But where? Where?

"She is not bought for money or his beliefs. He convinces her she loves him, and she will not release that. But she leaves you? No. Never, never. So she goes. Always. Everywhere. And is sure you live as long as she lives.

"We know that. We do not know if he kills you both or her alone. Or if all die. We do not know until you are found." She spread her hands. Then let them drop. "You are found, and we know our Annika is dead. Dead these years. Dead so far away."

One of the daughters began to cry, rocking in her chair.

"Bah. She is dead to us long, long. When she takes you. When our princess dies of grief, then she is dead in the ground to us."

"She raised me," Katie said quietly.

A sound came then, as if everyone had sighed at once.

"She kept … some things. They helped me piece together my history." She reached in her pocket and touched the silk material.

"Yes, she is like such." The woman's gaze dropped to her hands. "Her life…? She hungers?"

"No. We always had enough to eat. A house. Clothes. I went to school."

"She is happy?"

Katie had thought about this. "No, I don't think she was. After Bob died, I think she was … content."

The other woman slowly nodded. "She has fear of him."

"Yes. But … I also think she was frightened *for* him, too." Flashes of memories kaleidescoped in her head. "And for me. After he died, I think she was prepared to accept whatever came."

The rest of the woman's face remained fierce, but a sheen covered her eyes.

Katie met those eyes. "She worked very hard to help me receive an education. I will always be grateful to her for that."

A slight smile touched the woman's lips for the first time. "She has pride of you."

Katie felt the muscles of her face ease. "Yes, I think she did."

They were quiet on the return trip until the car stopped at the entry nearest Katie's quarters.

"I don't know what to think," she said.

"You are not meant to. Not now. In time."

"Maybe." She turned to the older woman. "Whatever I come to think … thank you. Thank you for taking me there to meet her."

"It was for her. It was better to do for her than go to her funeral."

Katie laid her hand on Madame's. "Of course. Still, thank you."

"You go now. Gala begins soon."

Impulsively, Katie leaned over and lightly kissed her on the cheek. Madame jolted.

But as Katie exited the car, she could swear she'd caught a glimmer of pleasure in the woman's eyes.

"You're not ready."

Brad turned away from the hotel room door he'd opened to C.J. and Carolyn, all dressed up for the gala at the palace.

"Thought you'd be gone by now," he muttered.

"We were. When we realized you weren't there, we came back to get you."

He retreated into the room and resumed his seat on the bed, stuffing the pillow back behind his head to cushion it from the ornate carvings on the headboard.

They both followed him in.

"You think you're not coming?" C.J. asked.

"I know I'm not."

"I've never known you to not go after something you wanted, Spence. Hardheaded as all get-out about not knowing what was good for you, yeah, but something you wanted, you'd fight and work for all day and all night. I saw that in you from the beginning."

"And recognized a kindred soul," Carolyn said softly.

C.J. turned to her, and the look they exchanged made Brad want to pump his fist and drive that fist into a wall. Or maybe into the headboard. It would hurt like hell, but then he'd have a smooth place for his head.

"The professor's right, of course," C.J. said, swinging back to face him. "I recognized a kindred soul. That's why I don't understand you now, Brad. You not going after Katie. When you—Or am I wrong? Have I misread this? Is it because you don't want her?"

He didn't intend to answer. But the man had been his coach, his boss, his mentor, and his friend for too time. "You're not wrong."

He saw Katie's eyes again. The way they'd looked when they'd made love. If he hadn't reminded himself how many ways this was impossible…

"Then what the hell's the matter with you? Go tell her how you feel and kick that prince's butt. Do what you do best—go after what you want."

"What you're missing, C.J.," Carolyn said, "is that what he wants is no longer the most important thing in the world to Brad. What Katie wants is."

The professor was right, of course.

CHAPTER THIRTY-FIVE

Katie paused with Karl at the middle of an arched bridge beautifully lit for the enjoyment of those wandering the grounds.

They'd finished with the reception line—no sign of Brad—and slipped away for a break from the social duties. If only she could take off the tiara. But she'd never get it back on securely. "This bridge is so perfect. *Everything* is so perfect. It's like none of this is real."

"It sure isn't Wyoming," Karl said. "Or some other dusty places I've been."

"Want to talk about that?"

"Wyoming? Sure."

"The other places."

"No."

Yet she had a feeling the seemingly easy-going man beside her might need to talk about those other dusty places. To somebody. "Let's see what the bridge looks like from down there."

"By the stream? What about your dress?"

"I'll be careful, and there's a path, see?"

They went a half-dozen yards on the single-file path to a small clearing that provided a private spot for viewing the bridge, complete with bench. Every convenience.

She turned to her companion. "Karl, those other dusty places…?"

"Shouldn't be brought up in surroundings as beautiful as this. Or with someone as beautiful as you."

Prince Karl leaned toward her. She knew what was coming. She liked this man. Admired him. Trusted him. Okay and she didn't entirely dislike the idea that he might want to kiss her, but … *Brad.*

Always.

Brad.

Sweeping across her mind, through her heart, into her veins. She wanted Brad. His touch. His love. His kiss. Would she ever stop wanting that? Did she *want* to stop? Could Carolyn be right? And if she was, how could she ever get Brad to—.

Karl's lips touched hers.

Oh, God, she'd waffled her way right past the point where she could have prevented this.

There was a moment … like a question on both their lips, flavoring both of their mouths while they held their breaths and waited for the answer…

Then simultaneous sighs escaped their mouths. Kurt muttered a word, a curse from the tone of it. He brushed her hair back, giving her a rueful smile. "Nothing? You felt nothing?"

She smiled back. "As much as you felt."

He sighed again. "It would have resolved so many issues."

"I know." She sat on the bench positioned for an ideal view of the bridge. "King Jozef would have—"

"Been ecstatic." He sat beside her, adding dryly, "I think your friend, the assistant basketball coach, however, would not have been."

"Brad? He wouldn't care. As far as he's concerned I'm Princess Josephine-Augusta, and he's done with me."

"Katie, you're a marvel in a lot of ways. But not in this. That guy? He'd care."

Brad watched C.J. look at Carolyn, then turn back to him, searching, assessing his face for the accuracy of her words.

"You think Katie doesn't want you? Are you nuts? Have you been blind all these years? The first time she saw you, it was like someone turned on the light inside her. And the more buttoned-up and professional she is, the more it leaks around the edges."

Carolyn chuckled. "My poetic husband."

The corners of his eyes crinkled, but C.J. didn't relent in his eyes-pinning-to-the-wall routine. "That's why I waved you off, Brad. She was—"

"Just a kid."

"Yeah, and you weren't. But that was years ago. You think I'd have sent her to Chicago with you if I'd still thought she couldn't handle you? And these past months is been pretty damned clear you'd gotten into that light-turned-on-inside-of-you mode, too. Yet, here you sit instead of going after her. Why"

"You know the fairy tale stories with princesses in them?"

"What has that got to do with—?"

"Give him time, C.J.," Carolyn said. "What about fairy tale stories with princesses in them, Brad?"

C.J. sat on the edge of the other bed, leaning forward with his elbows on his knees, like he often did when he was taking in something difficult or complex. But this wasn't that complex.

"They have a princess who's been locked up, or put into a coma, or sent off to the woods with dwarves. One way or another, she's been denied what's hers by right. Forced to live a different life from what she should be living. That's what happened with Katie." His mouth quirked a little. "Only in Katie's case, she was sent off to Ashton's athletic department and surrounded by basketball players. And—Carolyn?"

She waved a hand, a gesture that said the tears in her eyes didn't matter and he should keep on.

"Well, that was about it. Katie was in exile before. Now she's where she was always meant to be. She has the life that's rightfully hers." He dug his hands into his pockets. "All I could offer her is a return to exile."

C.J. leaned across from the other bed and clapped a hand on his shin. "I see what you're saying, Brad. That's tough. Damn."

Carolyn threw up her hands. "Oh, for heavens' sake." She jerked Brad's suit coat from the back of a chair and threw it at him. "Then you still don't know Katie. Either one of you. Andy said you were brooding and I—"

"Andy?"

"—stuck up for you and said you needed to sort some things out. But now—Quit sitting there gaping at me. Get up right now, Bradford Spencer, get changed, and go find Katie. *Talk* to her. Tell her how you feel. Find out what she really wants. Not what you *think* she wants. Because if you don't, I will get Andrea Colecchi Spencer on the next plane over here to kick your butt."

"We should be getting back," Karl said.

Katie sighed as she gazed at the little arched bridge again.

Poor man. She'd rambled so disjointedly—about Brad, the king, the visit today to Annika's sister, and Brad again—he couldn't possibly make sense of it. Yet, she felt better.

She sighed again.

It was a blissfully romantic spot. And Karl was such a wonderful person.

"I'm comfortable with you." Her words sounded like a complaint, and in a way it was—against the fates or Cupid or whatever lunatic was in charge of this heart stuff. "It feels like I've known you forever."

"Yep. Same to you. Maybe because we're the only two around who know what it feels like to be pitched into this stuff. Trouble is, we're so comfortable because there's not a shred of heat between us. It's like you're my sister." He considered that as he guided her. "Only we never fought about you taking too long in the bathroom."

They were laughing as they stepped back onto the path where it rose to cross the little bridge … and looked up to find Brad at the crest of the bridge, looming over them.

"Brad."

She was aware of Karl looking toward her and thought she sensed amusement, but her focus was on Brad.

"Evening, Coach Spencer," Karl said easily.

Brad gave a curt nod, then said, "I'd like to talk to Katie. Alone."

"Sure thing," Karl said. "If that's what Katie wants."

She blinked, abruptly recognizing the subtext. "Oh, yes, that's fine. Thank you, Karl."

He squeezed her elbow before releasing it. "See you later, then."

He reached the crest in two strides. For a breath it seemed Brad might—but, no, he turned and let Karl pass, continuing the motion to come down to where she stood.

"What were you doing?" he asked.

"Walking with Prince Karl. I wanted to see the bridge from down beside the stream and he kindly escorted me. It's amazing how well everything is maintained and the lighting—"

"You kissed him."

It was no question, and that made her look up at him.

He swiped the side of his thumb beyond the corner of her mouth and displayed a smudge he'd come away with. "Lipstick."

"Oh." She put the tips of two fingers to the tingle where he'd touched. Then a thought occurred. "Oh, dear. Karl might have lipstick—"

She'd automatically started after the prince, but Brad grasped her arm above the elbow. "He'll have to deal with that emergency on his own. I want to talk to you. I need to talk to you."

"Is something wrong?"

"No," he said with unconvincing grimness. He guided her off the path, back to the spot where she'd stood with Karl. He dropped his hand and drove it through his hair. "Are you and that prince, I don't know, engaged or something?"

"Of course not." How could she be when she was married to him? Only technically and only because he was looking out for her, of course, but still that was one heck of a technicality. True, she'd kissed another man. But that was because she and Brad weren't really married. Well, they were, but—Her head throbbed, not because of the tiara this time.

"Because if you are and he's what you want—"

"No."

"Okay, then. I have something to say. Should've when you came to the gym yesterday, I guess. But after the way you left and then seeing you here … But they think—not that I'm blaming them."

Her breathing stopped. She thought her heart stopped for a moment, too. Was he going to say he truly cared about her? That he wanted—

"There's no way in hell this can work."

The crash of her hastily erected dreams deafened her. She could see he was still talking but it took long, painful moments before words started coming through.

"…no getting around you're Princess Josephine-Augusta and nothing's going to change that. And that's good. You've found your grandfather and who you are. You deserve every good bit of being a princess. Nobody's going to take that away from you. Nobody. It's the last thing I'd want to do. The very last thing."

He looked up to the sky, expelled a breath, sucked in a longer one, then tipped his head down.

"I had that all thought out. Almost from the beginning. Maybe it was seeing you with the king at the Monroes' house that first day, but I knew down in my bones—And then after you left, I thought it through again. Looked at it cold and rational, and it was all clear."

Brooding. She heard the word in her head like a chorus of Andy and Carolyn's voices.

"The trouble is when I look at you."

Her heart clenched tight inside her, then released with a joyous leap.

He brushed the back of his fingers across her cheek. And the leap became acrobatic.

"Because when I look at you, I see my Katie. My Katie Davis."

The clench in her chest was different this time. An instinctive reaction she didn't understand.

"Yours. But—" She was shaking her head, trying to make the jumble come together.

"You are Katie Davis. You are *my* Katie Davis. Do you understand?"

"I am not anybody's Katie Davis. That's—I—"

"The hell you're not." He grasped her shoulders and tugged her to him sharply. He brought his mouth down on hers.

It wasn't like the other times. Oh, there'd been other kisses between them that also were demanding and hot. But those had seemed only to come when he forgot himself, was caught unaware.

Not this time. He intended this.

That thought as much as the kiss sucked the oxygen out of her brain, leaving no room for thoughts. Or doubts. Only for the sensation of Brad kissing Katie. This was *him* and *her*. It startled her. It rattled her.

And then the demand of the kiss became such a rush of heated giving that her knees buckled.

His hold kept her up, but her head dropped back under the physical press of his kiss—and the desire. His and hers.

She held onto his shoulders. His arms around her waist pulled her flush against him, the contact announcing the changes in his body. Instinctively, she arched, pressing deeply against him. It dropped her head back even more. His tongue was in her mouth. She was meeting it.

A meeting so sweet and hot that she abruptly felt completely lightheaded. Spinning and sailing.

Lightheaded … Like a weight had been removed … A weight … Gone. Oh, my God, oh, my God…

Horrified, she reached back with one hand. Hair. Only hair.

She used both hands, feeling. Nothing. Gone. Oh, my God, oh, my God … It was gone.

"Katie—?"

She spun around, trying to reach toward the ground behind where she'd been standing. His arms still held her around her waist, leaving her like a folded over rag doll. If a folded over rag doll was desperately trying to explore the ground with hands that were a good foot above it.

"What're you doing? Katie—"

"The tiara. The tiara. Five centuries. Tradition. Magda. My great-grandmother," she gabbled.

"That crown thing?"

"*Tiara.* Let me get down. I have to find it."

"Your dress—The stream—"

"Oh, *God!*" What if it had fallen in the stream? She bundled the fabric of the dress to her, preparing to wade.

"You stay still. I'll find it."

"But your suit—"

She was interrupted by the sound of footsteps on the bridge. Then a light flashed over her, before quickly and discreetly moving aside.

Two things happened simultaneously.

A deep, official voice said, "Princess?"

And Brad called out, "Got it!"

The deep, official voice had the final say. "King Jozef requires your attendance."

CHAPTER THIRTY-SIX

The searchers had suggested Brad wasn't wanted. He'd ignored them, speaking only to her when he said, "You're not going alone."

King Jozef was less oblique when Katie and Brad, joined by Madame who apparently had also been summoned, entered his study. "Leave," he commanded Brad immediately.

"Not until Katie wants me to."

Without looking at her, King Jozef said, "Tell him."

"No." Now he looked at her. "I—" She swallowed, not from nerves about King Jozef's reaction, but Brad's. "—want him to stay."

The king's eyes' narrowed, his jaw clamped. But he dropped the subject.

When he next spoke, with cold precision she had not heard from him before, she decided he'd dropped the issue of Brad's status because he would not be distracted from the main cause of his anger.

"It has come to my attention that you visited a private home this afternoon without security."

"Yes," she said.

"You have been told to have security at all times. You are never—*never*—" He slammed his palm on the desk. Katie jerked. Brad took a half step forward. Without breaking eye-contact with her grandfather she lifted a hand and Brad stilled "—to go to that house or to see those people. For any reason. That is a command."

"I have—"

Madame spoke over her. "I took Princess Katie there."

He whirled toward the woman. "*You* took her there. You did this?"

"I did."

"I wanted to go," Katie said.

He didn't even look at her, bearing down on Madame. "You who also lost so much to those people—no, those animals."

"Martila's family were never rebels. You know they did no wrong. They deserved to know of Annika's fate. And Katie deserved to meet them, to know more of the woman and man who—"

"Them? Know more of *them?*"

"Yes." Katie stepped forward. "And there is no use shouting at Madame. It was my choice. I wanted to understand better. To see—"

"That is irrelevant. Madame knows better than to—"

"It's entirely relevant," Brad interrupted. "Katie wanted to go, so she goes. That's the end of it."

"End of it? End of it? It is not. I am—"

"The king. I know. We all know. Hard to miss." Bull's-eye. The way the king's swelling wrath deflated was the giveaway. But Brad wasn't done. "The head of the royal family. But you cannot force that kind of life down Katie's throat. I won't let you."

"Pah. You?" The king's rage had ebbed, but cold anger remained. "You know nothing of this. You have no standing in this discussion."

"The hell I don't. I care about Katie and—"

"She is my granddaughter."

"She is my wife."

With that word, the universe seemed to go frozen and silent. Yet with a thrumming certainty rising that the stillness and silence was sure to be broken—

"*What?*" King Jozef rounded on Brad. Undiminished, despite being so much shorter. "You lie."

"I am not in the habit of lying." That cool dignity brought sharp tears to her eyes. "Katie and I are married."

"She cannot be. To marry you is—" He made an abrupt, jerking motion. "—not possible."

"She did."

The king turned to her. "You did this? You did this to me? To throw yourself away?"

"That isn't fair—"

Brad stepped beside her. "She couldn't trust you."

"Brad, that's—"

"You are insubordinate, young man. I will not allow this—"

"I can't be insubordinate because I'm not your subordinate or your—"

Katie tried. "Both of you. Stop."

They talked over her and each other.

"A member of the royal family cannot marry—"

"—subject. And neither is Katie."

"—without my approval. It is not allowed."

"Allowed," Katie repeated. Her voice was so soft it shouldn't have been heard, but the gusts from the two men had abruptly ended, and her words came through perfectly. "Brad, Madame, will you please leave my grandfather and me alone."

"Katie."

"Thank you, Brad. I must handle this." And now in this instant, she saw what Carolyn had been saying about how many times he had protected her. She smiled slightly at him. "This time I have to cut down the trees myself."

She saw his understanding half a second before he gave a slow nod. He walked to the door and held it for Madame, glancing back to give her another nod. Encouragement.

She took the small silk square from her pocket and extended it to King Jozef. "This was in the attic of my house in Ashton."

He looked into her eyes for a long moment before shifting to the fabric. He stroked a finger over it lightly. "Sofia. She embroidered … before your birth."

"Annika kept it, hidden away. I found it in my attic."

"Why did you not show this to me before? This proves—you did not need the DNA. You *knew* as well as I did. You will explain yourself," he commanded. "You have known you are Princess Josephine-Augusta. You could not have made this marriage."

"I did. *We* did. And I am very grateful to Brad. I was in a precarious position and he provided me a solution."

"Precarious? How precarious?"

"I had realized that if … since I was smuggled into the United States and I wasn't the child of a citizen that I was, in fact, there illegally. I was not a citizen."

He flicked that away. "You are a Bariavakian."

"I had no legal standing in the country that has been my home."

"I would not forbid you to visit."

"I do not want to be prevented from returning to Ashton."

His chin sank, but she thought it was in contemplation, rather than defeat. "He said you did not trust me."

"I didn't know you," she said carefully.

He looked at her. "You trust me now." This sounded of command.

"I think as my grandfather you love me, at least who you think I could be. As the king—You said you would not forbid me to visit. But you think you *could* forbid me and you think you have the right to limit me to visits. You think you have the right to decide my future. I don't accept that."

"Instead, you will let this … this basketball player decide it?"

"He is a coach, as you know. But, no, I will decide my future."

"Your future is to marry Karl."

"No. Even if I weren't already married to Brad—"

"I am your king! You are not allowed to marry without my permission."

"Then it's a good thing I already did it. I showed you this now, Grandfather, so you understand I married Brad knowing I was born a princess."

"It shall be annulled."

"It's been consummated."

Brad was aware of another presence in the gym the next morning, but didn't look around as he drove down the empty court. If he let his

body express his emotions, he'd deliver a punishing, thunderous dunk. But letting emotions run the bus wasn't the way to get anywhere. Andy had tried to pound that into the malleable material of his youth. Coach and Carolyn had honed it in college.

It was Coach here now, watching. Brad completed his drive to the basket, laying up the ball with restraint, even tenderness.

Or maybe that was with exhaustion, since he'd been at this for hours.

He'd been up late, talking with C.J. and Carolyn. Then he'd been up even later, hoping he'd hear from Katie. The way she'd kissed him by the stream ... But maybe he'd misread that. When she'd asked him to leave and what she'd said about clearing her own trees, he'd thought ... But then why hadn't she called or come?

"Spence," C.J. called from the entryway where Katie had stood a day ago. "Someone's waiting for you."

He knew from C.J.'s voice it wasn't Katie, so he didn't hurry wrapping a towel around his sweaty neck, putting the final ball into the old-fashioned wooden basketball cart, picking up the cell phone he'd had out ... just in case.

As Brad approached he saw C.J. looking at the court almost mistily.

Using a dose of offense as a defense against C.J.'s pity, Brad asked, "What's with you? See a ghost."

C.J. grinned. "More like a vision. Carolyn and I once had an interesting discussion on a court not too different from this one. Your visitor's in the office."

Brad swung open the office door, checked slightly when he recognized the King of Bariavak as the man standing in the tiny office, then pulled the door closed behind him and kept his voice remarkably even. "Your Majesty."

King Jozef nodded absently. He also frowned, but that appeared to be for his surroundings. "This facility is not of the standard of your Ashton University."

Brad started to breathe again. The king wasn't here to tell him

Katie wanted nothing to do with him. His brain said she'd never have handled it that way, but his lungs were just getting the message. "No it's not."

"Is that a result of the difference between a university and a program for young people?"

"Mostly it's the result of indifference—the indifference here to whether kids get to play basketball or not."

"Bariavak does not have the resources to devote to developing NBA players."

"How about the resources to let kids have some fun? Because this program sucks."

They glared at each other.

"I will give this program resources," King Jozef said. "You will leave the Princess Josephine-Augusta alone."

"You think I'd *trade* her?"

"It is separate. I will provide resources for this program. That is done, complete." He gestured to one side. Then he brought his open hands back in front of his heart. "And here is my granddaughter's future. Her potential. Without you. So you will not see her or talk to her from this day forward."

"No."

"I demand it."

"You can't. Only Katie can. She can tell me to get lost, but not you. And if you force Katie to say it when she doesn't mean it, I'll know."

"You have no right—"

"I have the best right there is. I love Katie. I loved her before Princess Josephine-Augusta came on the scene. I didn't know it, because I was an idiot—I have that on good authority." The phone call had come at midnight Chicago time … shortly after Carolyn and C.J. left him. "I love her now. And I expect to always love her."

"She is my granddaughter. My family. My only family. I love her as you cannot."

"Do you? Do you love Katie? As a person? As your granddaughter? Or only as your restored princess?" He let the moment stretch before he added, "Your Majesty."

The king came out of the gymnasium, his bodyguards falling in behind him.

April exchanged a look with Hunter as he got out of the backseat of the car where they had been sitting and held the door for King Jozef. Hunter closed the car door and got into the front seat beside the driver—on the other side of the privacy barrier.

The king looked straight ahead. "You are the only other person who knows me as a grandfather, at least an ersatz grandfather."

"I told Katie you'd practiced with me. But you treated me solely as a granddaughter. Was that because you knew from the start I wasn't the princess?" Concentration drew her brows down. "I also told her what you'd shared with Hunter about regretting not focusing earlier on life, love, and family."

They rode in silence some minutes before he spoke. "Perhaps the hardest thing in being a king is you must command people to tell you what you do not want to hear. Or else become ever weaker from not hearing those things." He faced her. "What more would you say to me, April?"

"Are you focusing on life, love, and family with Katie?" she asked immediately."

"She is a princess. In a great sense her family is all of Bariavak. That cannot be denied. Or changed."

"It *can* be changed," April said quietly. "Katie can change it. She can renounce the title and all that goes with it."

Outrage flared, then sank as he said, "Including me?"

"Are you making it a package deal?" When he didn't answer, she added gently. "Which is more important to you, a princess or a granddaughter?"

King Jozef of Bariavak shifted his position on the side of the bed that had been his daughter's.

Since recovering from surgery at the beginning of the year he felt much stronger. Alas, the surgery had done nothing to ease the aches in his bones. Or his heart.

He knew who had entered before he heard sound or caught the change in the currents of air.

Without turning to face her, he said, "He would not pledge to leave her alone."

A click of her tongue scoffed that anyone would have been so unwise as to have expected—or hoped—otherwise.

"The princess royal of Bariavak, married to a coach of basketball—no! I will not have it."

He rose and strode to the window. Between his hands he felt the silk of the embroidered square his granddaughter had given him last night.

Behind him, Therese made a sound. He would not have stood for it if the sound had held pity. But this held exasperation.

On second consideration, pity might have been better.

Silence followed, and after moments of it stretched out, he acknowledged even exasperation would have been preferable.

"She is breaking my heart," he said.

Again the click of her tongue. "You are breaking hers, as your father did yours."

His head snapped up. And then he could not look away from her, away from the truth of their past.

"As you did to Sofia," she added softly. "Sofia was enough your daughter, Jozef, to rebel, to push and prod and madden you. But in the end, she needed your love too much to stay away, and she married, Leopold, as you required."

"She loved him. He was a good husband to her."

"Only she knew if either or both of those statements were true. But I will tell you this, your Katie does not depend on your approval or your love as Sofia did. She will not make trouble for you as Sofia did.

She does not need to. Because she can leave here. She can leave you."

"I am her only family."

"She does not see family as you do, as ties of blood. Consider that what she thought were ties of blood held little love or attachment. Why should she value them now? She has, however, another life, another country—indeed, a family, she does value."

"And so?"

She came to him. They sat on the settee under the windows, both her hands in his.

She released a long breath. "And so you cannot win her as a granddaughter by making the same mistakes you made with her mother."

He looked at their intertwined hands, at the heavy ring he wore, at the precious silk square.

He rose and picked up the phone from the bedside table. "Inform the princess that I would like to see her in Princess Sofia's suite. Immediately."

CHAPTER THIRTY-SEVEN

After another round of solo shooting drills, Brad took a long, mostly lukewarm shower—the hot water was long gone. Another issue with this facility. Not that it was his problem.

He had enough other ones. With each minute that passed without hearing from Katie…

After dressing, he came out of the dinky locker room and found her standing with her arms crossed and her chin set belligerently. Apparently it was his day for disputes with the royal family of Bariavak.

He'd known where he was with the king. This was shakier ground.

"Katie," he said neutrally.

She shattered neutrality. "I've had a really rough couple of days, Bradford Spencer. Not all of that's your fault, but a lot of it is. Starting with seeing you so unexpectedly and you saying absolutely nothing to me. Some of it was because of a woman who's dying, though Madame was right about that. And almost losing that damned tiara last night. Then almost no sleep last night because I was thinking."

"About?"

"You. Me. Trees. Tiaras. The past. The future. Of course when I say a lot of it's your fault, you're probably tied with my grandfather, but any way you look at it, it's been—" She waved a hand. "So, I'm past being polite. I'm not making demands of you or saying you feel this way, but you'll just have to accept it, Brad. I'm in love with you."

"You—"

"In case you couldn't tell from the way I kissed you—"

"I kissed you."

"—last night. We kissed each other." Her crossed arms dropped to her sides and her voice went soft. "We kissed each other. Oh, Brad…"

He squeezed his eyes shut a moment, then opened them with resolution. "Your grandfather's right, Katie. You're a princess. I'm not a prince."

"I don't want you to be."

"How the hell could it work? You'd come to games I'm coaching? Sit in the bleachers? Come to tournaments?"

"Yes."

"No." He shook his head. "When you were Katie Davis—"

"No." Her vehemence cut across his words. "You're wrong. Completely wrong. When you said last night about my being your Katie Davis, I felt something—but it wasn't until a little while ago I realized—It was like you said, Brad. I haven't changed. I've *realized*. One of the things I've realized is this never could have worked when I was Katie Davis."

"You're saying you never cared about me when you were Katie Davis?"

"I was *crazy* for you when I was Katie Davis. That was never the issue. I would have gone on worshipping you, but I couldn't have let you love me."

"Why the hell not?"

"Because I never felt … *real*. I didn't know what was wrong, but I knew something was. There were too many lies and pain in my being Katie Davis. All my life I sensed it. That's what I was trying to put into words last night by the stream. I'm not *anybody*'s Katie Davis, including yours, because I'm not that person anymore."

"No. You're Princess Josephine-Augusta."

She was shaking her head again. "No. I'm not her, either, not completely. I once told Carolyn that I wasn't a very good Katie Davis, so how could I possibly be a good Josephine-Augusta. I don't feel that way now. Katie Davis and Princess Josephine-Augusta are parts of *me*. I'm at peace with that. I've learned that here—it's why I had to come. But neither one is all of me. For the first time in my life, I know who I truly am, Brad. I am Katie Spencer."

He opened his mouth. No words came out.

She stood taller. "Even if you want an annulment, I'll keep that name. It's who I am now."

"No annulment."

"If you're going to be technical, a divorce then."

"Katie—"

"Do you want a divorce, Brad?"

"No, damn it. But—"

"Good, then it's all settled."

"Katie, nothing's settled—"

"Yes it is. My grandfather told me you said only I could tell you to get lost and I don't—"

"He told you that?"

"—want that, so it's settled. No annulment, no divorce. I'm Katie Spencer. I love you and you…" For the first time she faltered.

He wrapped his arms around her. "And I love you more than anything. My Katie."

They hadn't spent all the time kissing. They'd done *some* talking.

But they were kissing again when C.J. and Carolyn came around the corner.

"It's about time," C.J. said.

Katie jumped away from the wall. Brad put his arm around her and held her close to his side.

"Yeah, I suppose it is," he said. "And you can be the first to congratulate us and—Carolyn? You're crying *again*?"

"When was she crying before?" Katie asked.

C.J. put an arm around his wife. "When we were trying to get this stubborn ass of yours to go to the gala last night."

"But why?" Katie asked. Both men shrugged that it was beyond them. "Why were you crying, Carolyn?"

"I was scared. Scared not only that this wouldn't work out for the two of you, when I so wanted it to, but also that it might take the heart out of Brad completely. And then, when he was telling us about you being a fairy tale princess, but instead of being Snow White in the woods with dwarves, she was exiled to the Ashton athletic department offices with a bevy of basketball players—"

"You said that?" Katie looked up at Brad.

He shrugged. "She makes it sound more literary than it was."

"He did say it. But more important, he smiled, just a little. And I was so relieved. That's why I cried then. Because I had hope that even if his heart was broken he'd still be Brad."

"Now, *you're* crying?" Brad demanded of Katie.

"Oh, Brad." She put her arms around his neck.

He kissed her but before he could do a proper job of it there was another interruption.

"Oh!" It was April. With Hunter right behind her. "Does this mean—"

"Yes," Brad and Katie said together.

"That's wonderful."

After handshakes and hugs, C.J. added, "What's also wonderful is we can all stop pretending we don't know they're already married."

"Oh. Right," April said in a very different tone. "We were sent to find you. King Jozef wants to see you both. I gather he knows about you being married?"

Katie put a hand on her arm. "It's okay. At least I think…"

Brad tightened his hold around her waist. "It's going to be fine. But we need to run something past you on the way, C.J."

King Jozef looked only at Katie as the six of them—she and Brad, April and Hunter, and Carolyn and C.J. crossed the room to where he and Madame sat by a trio of windows.

She released a long breath, then said, "Grandfather, Brad and I love each other. There will be no annulment or divorce. Our future is together."

King Jozef turned from her to scowl up at Brad. "You think you will take the Princess Josephine-Augusta away from Bariavak?"

"No," he said evenly. "I think Katie and I will go wherever the two of us decide is best for us."

Katie broke the tense silence. "And what we have decided is best for us is to stay here for a few more weeks, then return to Ashton in time to prepare for the upcoming season, since he will coach basketball and I will work for C.J."

"Out of the question. I cannot protect you there. You will—"

"Protecting her's up to me," Brad said.

"I don't need protecting in Ashton," Katie said at the same time, then added, "And if I did, I'd take care of it myself. But I don't."

"As Princess Royal—"

"But I won't be. I'll just be me. Besides, you are the king, for heaven's sake, out in the public all the time and you have hardly anyone with you. I know how you slip away from your security detail."

King Jozef turned his glare on Hunter, who looked back impassively, but said, "She would still be on our radar."

Katie set that aside to be dealt with later and said gently to the king, "It was a long time ago, Grandfather."

"It was yesterday. You are only a child. You do not understand—"

A sound best spelled "Agggh" emanated from Madame, checking King Jozef's words.

Katie took advantage of the opening. "However, Brad has an idea, one I don't completely approve of because he should accept one of the head coaching positions he's been offered—"

"Katie."

King Jozef's gaze shot to Brad at that quiet word.

"Okay," Katie conceded. "So, instead of advancing his career as he so easily could and because he says he truly prefers this, Brad has proposed he become a part time basketball coach at Ashton, a proposal C.J. has said he'll accept if that's the only way to keep Brad on the staff and if—and I quote—the damned idiot won't take a head spot. But—" She had to pull in air after that spate of words. "—that only works if there's something that would make good use of his talents the rest of the year. And where that opportunity was located would determine where we spend, say, several months a year."

The king watched her closely, shot another look at Brad, then came back to her. But he said nothing.

"Katie, just tell him—"

Never taking her gaze from her grandfather, she said to Brad, "We agreed I would do this."

Again the silence stretched.

Brad made a sound of exasperation and walked to the window, hitched a hip on the stone sill and crossed his arms over his chest. "It's a damned good thing I tricked her into marrying me, or I can see the stubborn Bariavak blood would have kept her saying no for decades."

More silence.

Madame slowly stood. "Jozef."

His gaze flickered but did not leave Katie.

"Jozef," Madame repeated. This time his gaze went to her. "You are not a stupid man. But if you make this mistake with your granddaughter as you made with your daughter, I will stab you in the heart to save you the pain of dying from it breaking. Say the words. Now."

King Jozef looked at Brad. Then at Katie. Finally back to Madame.

"Basketball for youth," he said to her.

Katie jumped in, "A series of camps. Which you will officially open each summer. And you will begin the transition—"

Brad reached across to take her hand and squeeze, but she went on.

"—toward democracy, I hope."

Brad and Madame groaned simultaneously.

King Jozef drew in a swelling breath. "Democracy? End the royal family of Bariavak? Throw out centuries of tradition? Basketball camp, yes, this I permit—for the children. But this—this you talk of—"

"Later," Madame said. "You will talk of it *later*. But what has been decided has been decided. For your love of your granddaughter."

Slowly, King Jozef of Bariavak lowered his head in a solemn nod.

"Grandfather." Katie hugged him with one arm because Brad still held her other hand. "This is best. You'll see—"

Brad tugged on her hand. "Not now. Give him time to adjust."

And then Carolyn and C.J. were shepherding them away.

"C'mon, you two," C.J. said, turning Katie and Brad toward the door. "Let's get out of here with our victory before the opposing team talks the ref into pushing this thing to overtime."

April and Hunter each held a door open for them as they left, then followed them out.

EPILOGUE

Seven weeks later
Ashton, Wisconsin

"He's going to be okay, you know." Brad leaned back against the closed door of his bedroom—their bedroom, at least for tonight as they sorted out what they would do with her house and his apartment now that they were back in Ashton. "So no need for that frown."

They'd left Bariavak and King Jozef, and it hadn't been easy on his Katie.

"I know. Eventually. I do know that. But that's not why I was frowning. Brad, this is important. You have to know I won't hold you to what you said about not taking a head coaching job. I won't take advantage of you—of your weakness."

"Weakness? You mean my weakness for you? Hate to tell you, Katie, but you've been taking advantage of that one since the day you walked in the office."

"Your grandmother told me. You have a weakness for underdogs. You have all your life and—"

"Yeah, yeah. And how she used that to get me to go to Ashton instead of the party school. That's her tale, anyway."

"You *know?*"

"Sure. I've always known. Let her think it was her underselling Ashton that got me here, but it was a combination of thinking Ashton could pay off big if the program caught hold and being in awe of Coach."

"Oh." She absorbed that for a breath then rallied, "But that doesn't change that you *do* have a weakness for underdogs. I've seen it with the team. And with the kids. And … and of course that's why you married me." She looked up at him through her lashes.

"Yeah, right. That's why." He advanced on her.

"And why, in Bariavak—because who was more of an underdog than me? One woman, trying to stand up again a king and—You're laughing? You're *laughing at me?*"

"Hell, yes, I'm laughing at you, Josephine-Augusta—my Katie." He kissed the top of her head. "If you were any less of an underdog with your grandfather, with Bariavak, and most of all with me, we'd all be puddles at your feet." He kissed her nose. "My princess."

"Don't…"

But he was wrapping his arms around her waist, drawing her tight into his body and her protest evaporated in the heat.

"Katie Spencer."

She arched into him. "Yes."

A very satisfying time later, he stroked her bare shoulder, then kissed a mark his mouth had made earlier. "Uh, Katie?"

"Hmm."

"I have a question."

"Yes?"

"You remember you said that when you were Katie Davis you worshipped me?"

"Yes."

"So, all that grief you gave me? That was worshipping? Does that mean it's going to be worse from now on?"

"Much, much worse."

"Okay. I can live with that. As long as you don't love me the way Madame loves the king—whew! Stabbing him in the heart to save his heart from breaking."

"I know. Don't worry, I could never be as fierce as that. I'm a nice Midwestern girl."

"Yeah, right. Nice Midwestern girl who's about been the death of me."

She ran a hand down his chest … and lower. "You don't feel dead to me."

"Maybe not quite yet. But before we test that theory, I want you to promise to do something for me. Maybe when we finally take a honeymoon."

"What?"

"Wear that tiara like you did at the gala."

"I won't wear a crown. And that dress—"

"Not a crown. And definitely not the dress. Just the tiara." He looked down at her, watching a smile come into her eyes. "So I can kiss you right out from under it again."

Thank you for reading Katie and Brad's story!

King Jozef is reunited with his long-lost granddaughter, but the winds of political change threaten to buffet his mountain kingdom. In *The Forgotten Prince*, Book 7 of The Wedding Series, Jozef has an ally, and possible heir, in U.S. Army veteran and Wyoming rancher Karl Wethers. Karl has a plan, if he can pull it off. But complicating that plan is Harmon Reed, a former Army brat who broke Karl's heart after a youthful summer fling. Now, the slim hope of a second chance at love becomes entwined in a royal scheme.

We meet young ranch hand Karl in *Not a Family Man*, the prequel to *The Forgotten Prince* and the story of Wyoming ranch foreman Tucker Gates and Jenny Peters, the city-bred new owner of the Double Bar X.

The Forgotten Prince
Not a Family Man (prequel to The Forgotten Prince)

April, Hunter, Jozef, Madame and friends ask if you'll help spread the word about them and The Wedding Series. You have the power to do that in two quick ways:

Recommend the book and the series to your friends and/or the whole wide world on social media. Shouting from rooftops is particularly appreciated.

Review the book. Take a few minutes to write an honest review and it can make a huge difference. As you likely know, it's the single best way for your fellow readers to find books they'll enjoy, too.

To me—as an author and a reader—the goal is always to find a good author-reader match. By sharing your reading experience through recommendations and reviews, you become a vital matchmaker. ☺

For news about upcoming books, as well as other titles and news, join Patricia McLinn's Readers List and receive her twice-monthly free newsletter.
www.patriciamclinn.com/readers-list

And for you Wedding Series readers, I have a special incentive. If you join my readers list at www.patriciamclinn.com/lp-su-tsk, you'll receive an exclusive offer to download a free short story. ***The Soldier's Kiss,*** a prequel to ***The Forgotten Prince,*** introduces Harmon Reed, the heroine of ***The Forgotten Prince,*** and shares how her father, Lt. Col. Brooks Reed, discovers his true love, artist Ann-Elise Jerakenko … with help from a cat.

The Wedding Series

Prelude to a Wedding

She's all work and no play. He's an expert at fun. Their romance could be the biggest game of all.

Wedding Party

As one couple ties the knot, the best man hopes to find love with the bridesmaid.

Grady's Wedding

Marriage can be catching. Will the last bachelor take the leap?

The Runaway Bride

Escaping a bridal disaster in Illinois, her life takes a wild, wild turn in the West.

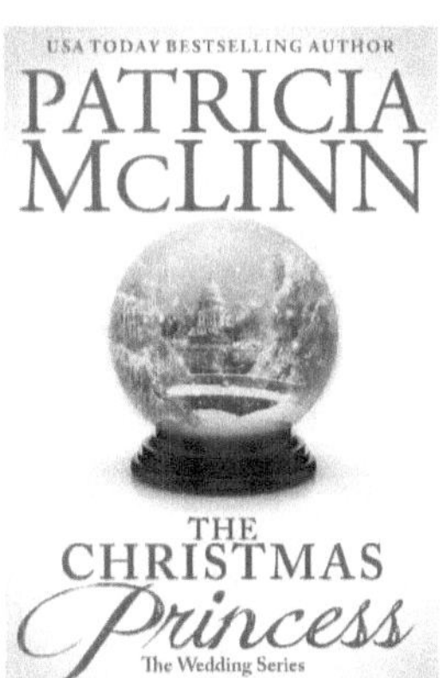

The Christmas Princess

A princess for a few weeks … a prince for a lifetime.

Hoops (prequel to The Surprise Princess)

Can the coach and the professor play on the same team?

Not a Family Man (prequel to The Forgotten Prince)

City girl Jenny, the ranch's attractive new owner, spells trouble for foreman Tucker.

The Forgotten Prince

Karl and Harmon have a history, but a royal matchmaker helps them rewrite it.

Praise for The Wedding Series

"A wonderful series that will make you laugh and cry. Each page is filled with love that will eventually come to the people who so need it. A must read!"—*5-star review*

"McLinn is an expert at revealing the layers enveloping her characters. With each reveal, sometimes exquisitely subtle, we are pulled in deeper to be active participants in the emotionally charged, yet heart-melting romance."—*USA Today*

"Love this series … so many twists and turns that take you all over the world!"—*5-star review*

"Fun and serious all at the same time. Love how the friends intertwine and add new along the way. It was refreshing to read the different stories and having them all come together. Really enjoyed this series!"—*5-star review*

"Perfect. The characters were multi-dimensional and played off each other in warm, thoughtful, loving ways. Each couple faced a different situation and overcame their obstacles together and with the insightful comments of their friends. … Heart-warming."—*5-star review*

"Full of warmth, understanding of human nature, and great characters. They are connected, following the lives of college friends, and by the time you are finished, you feel as if you are a part of their extended circle. A dash of sex here, but not to the point that it overshadows the well thought out storylines. Definitely a feel good experience."—*5-star review*

Also by Patricia McLinn

Marry Me Series

Wedding of the Century

The Unexpected Wedding Guest

A Most Unlikely Wedding

Baby Blues and Wedding Bells

Seasons in a Small Town series

What Are Friends For? (Spring)

The Right Brother (Summer)

Falling for Her (Autumn)

Warm Front (Winter)

Wyoming Wildflowers Series

A Place Called Home Series

Bardville, Wyoming Series

Explore a complete list of all Patricia's books

patriciamclinn.com/patricias-books

Or get a printable booklist

patriciamclinn.com/patricias-books/printable-booklist

Patricia's eBookstore (buy digital books online directly from Patricia)

patriciamclinn.com/patricias-books/ebookstore

About the Author

USA Today bestselling author Patricia McLinn spent more than 20 years as an editor at The Washington Post after stints as a sports writer (Rockford, Ill.) and assistant sports editor (Charlotte, N.C.). She received BA and MSJ degrees from Northwestern University.

McLinn is the author of more than 50 published novels, which are cited by readers and reviewers for wit and vivid characterization. Her books include mysteries, romantic suspense, contemporary romance, historical romance and women's fiction. They have topped bestseller lists and won numerous awards.

She has spoken about writing from Melbourne, Australia, to Washington, D.C., including being a guest speaker at the Smithsonian Institution.

Now living in northern Kentucky, McLinn loves to hear from readers through her website, Facebook and Twitter.

Visit with Patricia:

Website: patriciamclinn.com

Facebook: facebook.com/PatriciaMcLinn

Twitter: @PatriciaMcLinn

Pinterest: pinterest.com/patriciamclinn

Instagram: instagram.com/patriciamclinnauthor